I0742529

THE ORB, THE LINK & THE LIBRARY

PART 2

AVALANCHE CLOCKS

//

D.M. Rosewood

Published by *Ingenious Works*®, LLC

This is a work of fiction. With the exception of the names of real cities, all names, characters, places, and incidents are products of the author's imagination or are used fictitiously and are not real. Any resemblance to actual events, locations, organizations, artificial intelligence beings, or persons, living or dead, is entirely coincidental.

Published in the United States of America by

Ingenious Works°, LLC
12587 Fair Lakes Circle, Suite 315
Fairfax, VA 22033
www.IngeniousWorks.org

D.M.Rosewood
www.DMRosewood.com

ISBN 978-1-7321314-2-2 *eBook*
ISBN 978-1-7321314-3-9 *Paperback*

This book is dedicated to the dreamers of this world—
those who read this story and dream, then turn their dreams into reality.

CHANGE The act of making or becoming different. Such a simple concept, and yet we stress over it, resist it and sometimes even fight it. In the pages that follow, change will come to those the story consumes. Not the kind of change we are used to, but the outcome will be the same. We will be different, but the question is, will we master change and thrive, or embrace it and discover love? Each must choose his or her own path and decide.

ACKNOWLEDGEMENTS First, I thank you, my readers, especially those who reached the end of the middle, Part 2, and can't wait to pick up Part 3 in early 2019. I hope you enjoy reading my work as much as I enjoyed writing it.

For the extraordinary spaceflight company who flew my manuscripts into space, thank you for your confidence and your willingness to try something new and exciting. My hope is that this will bring a new generation into the space-age and stimulate their interest and passion in this great adventure with space.

I thank the great writers of Science Fiction, especially those who started it all and some of my favorites—Isaac Asimov, Arthur C. Clarke, Ray Bradbury, H. G. Wells and Jules Verne and so many more. Inspiration is a very important part of life and it comes from the words people share, the stories they tell and the tales they spin. Thank you.

I thank my family, especially my wife, for her patience and her editorial mind in correcting the thousands of words, sentences and paragraphs I wrote. And to my son and daughter for the experiences I had with them that continue to shape my journey. Thank you to my grandson, Luke, as I write this story and who at the age of nine, suggests creative twists in my plot, characters and settings.

Thanks to Megan Young, who served as the outstanding Creative Director & Art Director for the interior and cover design of this second book in the series, and to Chase Stone who served as the artist for the cover illustration. Extraordinary job.

I want to thank all the people I have known, the places I've been, the experiences I've had, and the adventures I've gone on. They all created ideas, built my imagination, shaped characters, settings and plots that can be found between the lines, the words and the letters in my writing.

And, I continue to thank space; for its existence, for the pull it has on the minds of creative explorers and adventurers and for the extraordinary setting it provides for all our futures — those who write about it and those who go there.

PROLOGUE In Part 1 of *The Orb, the Link and the Library*, Anna and Bryan, close friends since childhood, enjoy the final weeks of summer at a special hideaway known by Anna as her Rock House. This shallow cave in a rock quarry had become her 'sanctuary', an escape from all the parts of life she didn't like. During a visit there one Saturday, they discover a strange artifact that became dislodged from a piece of petrified wood during a minor earthquake, an object that soon becomes known as the Orb.

Anna and Bryan engage with the mysterious object through the frightening process of absorption and begin to develop telepathic abilities with the Orb and between themselves. Anna learns she has been chosen for a quest by the alien race that placed the Orb on Earth. The Orb tells Anna she must go with him to Sanctuary, the location of a more powerful alien being located near Sedona, Arizona. There she will learn more about her quest.

Bryan's fear of this object leads to NASA learning of their discovery. While preparing to leave with the Orb to find Sanctuary, NASA arrives, taking them and the Orb into protective custody to investigate the potential of radiation poisoning—a ruse to learn what they know about this mysterious and extraordinary extra-terrestrial artifact.

With the help of the Orb, Anna and Bryan manage to escape from the NASA facility and continue their efforts to find Sanctuary. Bryan is recaptured as Anna manages to reach Sedona where she finds and engages with the Link, the far more powerful artificial intelligence placed on Earth by an alien race known as the Visitors. Anna learns her quest is to save mankind from its own annihilation.

While planning a means to help Bryan escape from NASA, Anna is recaptured, and they are returned to the facility where they were previously being held. She soon discovers she is pregnant, but not by the means she believes and not by the means that NASA believes is true.

With the help of the Visitors, Anna and Bryan manage to escape from NASA once again. She gives birth to a baby girl, Athena, who is fully human in appearance but possesses the extraordinary mental abilities of the Visitors. The three of them and Carol, a collaborator from NASA who sympathizes with their situation, travel to a home near Sedona to hide from NASA and the Visitors.

THE ORB, THE LINK & THE LIBRARY
PART 2 AVALANCHE CLOCKS

CHAPTER 32

SEDONA AND THE VILLAGE OF OAK CREEK

///

Anna woke as the Gilmores' SUV pulled through the gated entrance of a beautiful lodge-style home made of natural gray stone and rustic timbers. The windows were set deep in the stone with a thin maroon-crimson-colored trim. It was striking. The house was set in a beautifully manicured landscape amongst a smattering of pinion oak and alligator juniper trees. This was Shirley Blackman's residence in the Village of Oak Creek.

Anna stepped out of the car carrying Athena and heard the trickling of water from a fountain as it flowed over sandstone rocks into a small pond near the front entrance. There was a patch of green grass surrounded by three juniper trees with a beautifully carved wooden bench positioned near the edge of the grass next to the pond. The sound of the trickling flow of water over the rocks was soothing. Anna could smell the deep aroma of the juniper trees. It reminded her of home. She looked down at the fish swimming in the pond as the afternoon sun sparkled against the multicolored scales of koi. They had variegated patterns of deep red, black and white patches. "Aren't they beautiful, Athena?"

"Yes, Mom. They're brilliant, but only in their color. They can't speak and they only express instincts of survival. They're hungry and think you are here to feed them."

Anna looked down and shook her head, bewildered at how her daughter knew this. The front door opened, and a gray-haired woman greeted them with a warm smile.

"Welcome. I see you are admiring our koi fish. This is one of my favorite places to sit at sunset. It's so . . . comforting," Shirley said as she walked out and stood next to Anna. "You must be Anna. It is so wonderful to have you here. And this must be . . ."

"Athena . . . This is my daughter, Athena. She is just a week old," Anna said.

Athena squinted up at their host with an ever so subtle smile and then squirmed to look over her mother's arm to watch the fish. Anna looked at Shirley as they stood in this beautiful setting. She had long gray hair pulled back into a ponytail and rustic dark skin, no doubt from years spent in the Arizona sun of the high desert. Her right ear had three beautiful pierced earrings along the edge and a triquetra pendent hung from her neck. She wasn't much taller than Anna and wore a light blue-green blouse, long khaki pants, and striking red hiking shoes.

"This is my assistant, Phyllis," Shirley said as she turned to introduce her. "She lives here with me and, well, does just about everything I can't do. My eyes aren't what they used to be, so she sometimes even serves as my sight. But I can still see beautiful things," she said as she looked down at Athena and ran her hand across the top of her head. She drew a breath and pulled her hand back as a large smile grew on Athena's face. "Your daughter seems to have a touch of the Sedona vortexes," she said as she turned, raising her eyebrows and looking at Anna. "You all must be thirsty. Won't you come inside? We'll finish our introductions there." She placed her arm around Anna's shoulder and they walked through a massive arched door to the interior of her home.

Shirley was a warm and friendly person and, except for her assistant, lived alone in her home in the Village, as the town was known by its residents.

Anna settled in the guest room that would be her and Athena's residence for the foreseeable future. She pulled the drapes open and drew a sudden breath. There in the distance, perfectly framed by the window, was Bell Rock, the place where a miraculous event had created her daughter. She stood for a moment holding Athena. Familiar scenes flew into her mind; the images of the Visitors world as they raced toward her in the tunnel; the overwhelming sounds, smells and sensations before she was absorbed by the Link; and the strange visit to Pearl Harbor . . . and those other worlds. She could feel her heart begin to race.

Bell Rock was one of the most beautiful of the Sedona Red Rock buttes, rising to almost five thousand feet. Like its name suggested, it was carved into the shape of a bell by wind, rain and the seas of the Permian period over 270 million years ago, with sandstone ridges that lapped over each other like giant mushrooms. As the late afternoon sun cast shadows around the peak, it created a beautiful and striking image against the reddening of the wispy clouds in the backdrop of the western sky.

"Do you see that, darling?" Anna asked, as she watched her daughter stare out the window. "That's where you were . . . conceived, the home of Phronesis, the Link. Every time I think of her I have this beautiful vision of the elf Galadriel from *The Lord of the Rings* story."

"Galadriel, what a beautiful lady, Mom. I'd like to meet Phronesis someday."

I wasn't sure how I felt about that, as I recalled the challenging time I experienced when I first entered the cave on the upper reaches of the mountain, now more than five months ago.

"Anna, come have some lunch," Shirley said as she walked into the bedroom. "Oh, you've discovered my husband's favorite view. Bell Rock was always our favorite butte here in Sedona. We'll have to find time to hike there."

"Perhaps we will," Anna said as she stared at the beautiful mountain.

After lunch, Shirley and her assistant gave them a tour of the rest of the home, followed by a brief walk on a local hiking trail where they saw a grouping of petroglyphs carved in stone.

"Come feel the drawings," Shirley said as her assistant guided her over to the large stone surface and she ran her hand across the rough surface of drawings chiseled into the rock. "These were created by early Native Americans or possibly early *Homo sapiens* who migrated to this area. Archeologists aren't really sure."

That evening after dinner, they sat in the living room with a warm inviting fire crackling in front of them. Fred, Shirley's brother, and his wife, Glenda, whom Anna had stayed with on her first visit to Sedona when she discovered Sanctuary and the Link, sat on the couch of the living room next to Carol and Bryan. Shirley sat on one side of Anna, facing the fireplace. Anna rocked Athena slowly in a dark redwood rocking chair that seemed to rock almost by itself on the beautiful hardwood floor. Bryan was fidgeting, looking out toward the window every few moments.

Anna looked at him. "What's the matter?" she asked.

"Nothing. Just keeping an eye out for Dr. Tyson. We need to be diligent. No telling when he might find us."

"Don't be silly. He won't find us here," Anna said as she frowned and turned back to look at Athena.

"Are you going to play for us, Shirley?" Fred asked his sister.

"Well, I haven't played for a while, but I think Athena might enjoy Pachelbel. Phyllis, would you bring my violin?"

Phyllis was perhaps ten years younger than Shirley, maybe in her early sixties. She had brown hair and wore it back in a bun. She was about the same height as Shirley but thinner. Anna actually thought she might be a runner. She had an interesting gate, almost a run, or a very fast walk.

After removing her violin from its case and checking the tuning of the strings by ear, Shirley began to play Pachelbel's Canon in D Major. Anna was holding Athena, who appeared to be sleeping as they sat slowly rocking in front of the fireplace. Athena's eyes opened within a few seconds of the violin bow gliding gracefully across the four strings of the instrument. Anna turned so Athena could watch Shirley play. Her large black eyes sparkled from the reflections of the fireplace flames that seemed to be dancing in synchrony with the musical notes.

Shirley looked over at Athena and their eyes met. Her music continued. Anna sensed that it was one of the most extraordinary performances of the piece that Shirley had ever played — full of musical balance and proportion and harmonic fullness.

Harmonic fullness? Sometimes I surprised myself in using the knowledge Phronesis was giving me.

Shirley's playing was so rich and full that it sounded as if there were two violins playing with her. Soothing colors surrounded Anna as she became absorbed by this beautiful piece of music. Shirley's eyes never parted from Athena. When she finished, everyone clapped.

"That was beautiful, Shirley," Fred said after the clapping died down.

"Thank you. Thank you. I haven't played that piece in a long time. I . . . can't get over how it seemed to flow from my strings," she said as she stared at her instrument. "I have to credit this violin. It is a Ceruti made in Cremona, Italy, centuries ago."

"It was beautiful, Shirley, simply beautiful," Carol said.

"You were extraordinary, Shirley," Athena said telepathically.

"Thank you," Shirley said, searching quickly with her eyes to see who had complimented her in the strange-sounding voice. As her eyes reached Athena, they paused, staring at this beautiful child. Athena broke a soft delicate hint of a smile as she stared back. She was wrapped in a fluffy blue blanket with the same wispy hair inherited from her mother, falling over her ears down to her neck. Wrapped in the blanket, Shirley couldn't tell her head was larger than the proportions of the rest of her body, other than her hands. They were beautiful gaunt hands with long thin fingers that seemed to say, "Come here, I want you to hold me."

"It's been a busy day. I think I'll put Athena to bed," Anna said.

"Oh yes, Anna. I wasn't being much of a host. Let me walk you back to make sure you have everything," Shirley said as she handed her violin to Phyllis.

The guest bedroom areas were in a wing of the house to the north, down a long, wide hall filled with original paintings. They seemed to come alive when Shirley turned on the soft art lights above them. Anna stopped to look at the painting of Bell Rock. Athena turned to look, reaching out to point at the upper reaches of this beautiful mountain. An image of the Link suddenly jumped into Anna's mind. She smiled as she turned to look at Athena and whispered. "So you know where Sanctuary is."

Athena and Anna were staying in one of the rooms facing toward the northwest. It was dark out, but she could still feel the heat the sun had left on the closed drapes before it set. Three table lamps produced a soft warm glow against the rich rosewood-paneled walls.

"This was my husband's favorite guest room. He loved sitting here working on his consulting business," Shirley said as she seemed in a daze.

"Shirley, thanks for opening your home to us."

"I'm glad you're able to stay here, Anna. In the brief time you have been here, I have fallen in love with having you as my guests. You are welcome to stay as long as you like."

Anna listened to her thoughts. Shirley loved having children and young adults back in her home. It took her back to a time when Shirley's children were Anna's age and also when they were older, and the grandchildren would come and play.

"I know Mr. Gilmore . . . or . . . your brother, has talked to you about this, but you know NASA will be looking for us and will do anything to get us back."

"Anna, my husband worked for the CIA for over thirty years. The government engaged his services to conduct activities that were illegal in the countries where he was assigned. Our government doesn't frighten me. Besides, I'm too old to worry about the consequences of making good choices in life. Having you all here, well . . . in a way it's bringing me back to life."

"Thank you. Bryan, Athena, and I feel so relaxed here already. And the music you played this evening . . . I've never heard anything that beautiful."

"Why, thank you, Anna." As Shirley walked to the door she turned. "I would recommend you and Athena avoid contact with my neighbors or the local population. Best if they didn't know that you are with us."

"Yes, of course. Good night, Shirley."

She turned to leave.

"Good night, Shirley."

Shirley turned with the sound in her head of a second voice—the same one that congratulated her in the living room.

"Good night." She squinted with eyes that could barely see and then turned slowly away.

Anna lay in bed with Athena snuggling next to her rather than putting her in the crib used by Shirley's grandchildren. It would be easier to nurse her when she was hungry. She still couldn't believe she had a baby girl in her arms and that she was hers. Her thoughts moved from excitement to panic. How could she be the mother of this child? She was so precious, so vulnerable. Would she be able to protect—

"Mom, if there is one thing I'm not, it's vulnerable. We will be fine," Athena said in her head.

She pulled her closer. "I hope so, darling, I really hope so."

She left one of the small lights on in the room, so she could see her daughter's face whenever her eyes opened. She could see herself in Athena's beautiful face. She reached over to the side table to a bag of things she carried with her from home and pulled out her billfold. She flipped open the small section of pictures of her family and leafed through them, stopping at a picture of a young baby. She whispered as Athena slept. "Look at this, you little pumpkin. You look just like me when I was a little older." After looking at it for a moment she flipped to the next photograph. It was a picture of her parents, Kat and her. Anna yearned to have her parents here to see their grandchild, although she knew her mother would look at this situation very differently—accusing, blaming and ridiculing her—another great disappointment, in her mother's mind. She felt bad about the vision she had created in her mother's mind when she visited Anna in her room at the SOC. She had written them a letter that Fred and Glenda would mail from Phoenix to let them know she was all right. She rolled over on her back and listened to Athena breathe, smiled, and fell asleep.

It was a Friday afternoon when the intercom on Shirley's front gate announced a visitor.

"Hello, can I help you?" Phyllis asked over the intercom.

"Yes. I'm looking for Anastasia."

Bryan stood suddenly as his face went blank and he looked up at Phyllis.

"There's no one here by that name. This is the Blackman residence," Phyllis said.

"I was assured by her father, Mr. Broulette, that I could find her here."

"One moment, please."

"I'll go get her," Bryan said as he ran down the hall, meeting Anna walking briskly toward him carrying Athena.

"There's someone at the gate asking for you. He says your father told him you would be here," Bryan said.

"Yes, yes, don't let him in," she said as she handed Athena to Bryan. "Watch her for a minute, Bryan? I'll go see who it is."

"Don't you want me to go with you?"

"No, I'll be fine, just take care of Athena."

Bryan peeked out the front window through the slats of the wooden blinds of the dining room while holding Athena away from the window. There was a lone figure standing outside the front gate. Anna walked out the back door and around the side of the house and stood looking from the corner of the house through the shrubs at the man standing at the gate. She didn't recognize him. She reached out to his mind. He was very nervous and agitated. His mind was flitting from one thing to another, bringing his attention back to the front door every few seconds. He was frightened and timid. There were feelings of hesitation and uncertainty. He had his hand in his jacket pocket. He was grasping something and thinking, "I shouldn't do this. What am I doing? How can I shoot someone I don't even know?" Then she saw it; the image of putting a gun in his pocket; images of *her* face from different angles; then an image where she was walking . . . all coming from the mind of someone she didn't know and had never met.

She couldn't just walk up to him. No telling what he might do in the nervous state he was in. If she could distract him somehow. The thought of Abigail and her mental abilities leapt into her mind. She closed her eyes and began to create a feeling of fear, fear of something terribly evil, terribly dangerous, something unknown but desiring to rip her apart limb from limb. She could see her arm being wrenched from her body and blood spewing everywhere as she screamed. Everything around her had turned red as she built this emotional feeling making it more vivid and stronger until it began to overwhelm her. She could feel it right next to her, smell it in the air, taste its vile presence, and hear its wretched breathing. Then she placed it in darkness, so dark she couldn't see her hand in front of her face. Holy shit, this was really working. She was scared to death.

She moved her mind into the mind of the visitor and unleashed the feelings she'd created, holding them there while she backed slowly out of his head. Her world brightened, while his turned to blackness.

The man jerked, looking in one direction and then another as darkness consumed him. He backed up, trying to escape the fear that was growing in his mind. He pulled his hand from his pocket holding the gun, waving it in front of him, his hand shaking as he swirled around. He crouched down, trying to hide.

His eyes grew large and darted back and forth, straining to see the unknown danger in his pitch-black world. He backed further, pulling himself into as small a space as possible, crouching down, his lips quivering, his body shaking. Suddenly, he stood, turned and ran full speed into the fence along the narrow drive at Shirley's entrance. It knocked him to the ground and the gun flew from his grip. He began feeling the ground around him, searching for his gun in the darkness.

Anna couldn't believe how well this was working. She was smiling at what she had done, until she saw his gun lying on the ground. She walked quietly up to the gate and released the magnetic latch. As the gate swung open wide enough to walk through, the hinges squeaked, and the man stopped moving. He was looking in the direction of the sound as he lay shaking, hiding in a darkness that only existed in his mind. Anna walked over and picked up the gun.

"I'm holding your gun and pointing it at you."

He lurched upward, turned to run away from her voice, tripped over a low hedge, and fell face down onto a large prickly pear cactus. He shrieked.

She winced, watching him trying to extract himself from the cactus plant. "If you ever come back here . . . you will *never* leave," Anna warned him with a booming voice in his head.

He crawled along the side of the road with one arm extended in front of him like a blind man, while trying to remove the cactus thorns from his face. She reentered the man's mind, returning some of his sight but leaving a remnant of the terror she had given him. He began running as fast as he could down the road toward town, never turning to look back.

"Who was it?" Bryan asked as Anna entered the back door.

"A stranger who didn't belong here. He won't be coming back."

"He began acting very strange. What did you do to him?" Bryan asked.

"I frightened him . . . a lot," Anna said as she took Athena in her arms and walked back toward the bedroom, thinking about those who had sent the stranger—the Visitors. She would need to be better prepared next time. After her experience during Athena's birth, she should have known they would keep trying to reach her—to threaten her or to kill her. She placed Athena in her crib and stood for a moment as she pulled the gun from underneath her shirt and stared at it.

"That's a remarkably ineffective weapon compared to your mind, Mom."

She looked over at Athena as she thought how she had used her emotions to protect her daughter . . . *the Arionis*, the Orb had said . . . *a specially gifted being with a capacity for extraordinary emotional power*. She put the gun on the top shelf of the closet and closed the door.

CHAPTER 33

THE VISITORS' HISTORY

///

Months passed as Athena approached her six-month birthday. So far, there hadn't been any more threats from the Visitors and no sign of Dr. Tyson, although they continued to be extra careful about their visibility in the community. Bryan, Carol, Athena, and Anna had settled into a routine at Shirley's house, with Fred and Glenda visiting regularly. Their days were spent thinking about her quest and what they could do about the potential end to the human race. It seemed so impossible. Anna cherished the distraction of caring for Athena and interacting with her, using that as an excuse for not finding a way to move forward on her task so vaguely outlined by the Link. They read about the continued expansion of war overseas in the local newspaper and about the increasing number of regional pandemics. They had no idea if these would balloon into the beginning of mankind's doom.

"Fred, you're being careful to make sure you're not being followed by anyone, aren't you?" Shirley asked one morning after he and Glenda arrived after the short drive from Sedona.

"Yes, sister. For the umpteenth time, I'm being careful."

"Just want to be sure. When Carl was alive, he never took his eyes off the rearview mirror."

Bryan and Carol had all but forgotten about the threat of the Visitors, but not Dr. Tyson. Bryan was forever looking out the windows, closing the drapes and turning away from passing cars when they would go for hikes on trails that crossed the local streets. Anna spent as much time as she could in front of the pond in Shirley's yard with Athena lying on the grass. This was one of her few relaxing pleasures when she tried to push the thoughts of her quest and what their adversaries might be doing out of her mind. While there, Bryan couldn't stop thinking they were being watched. He had borrowed a pair of binoculars from Shirley and would walk the perimeter of the yard like a prison guard while Anna was outside with Athena, looking off into the distance for someone hiding in the shrubs or in a parked car down the road.

"See anyone spooky yet, Bryan?" Anna called over to him sarcastically.

"Not yet, but we can't be too careful. Did you notice that white SUV two doors down? I don't remember it there yesterday," Bryan said as he stared into the binoculars and adjusted the focus.

"Yes. A suspicious baby boy in a carrier was put in the back seat by Karen, Shirley's neighbor. Do you think he might be working for Dr. Tyson?"

Bryan pulled the binoculars away from his eyes and smirked.

One morning, Carol, Athena, and Anna decided to go for a walk along the trail to the east of Shirley's home. It was early morning and the air was cold and unseasonably humid as fog rose from the creek bed and flowed like a stream of molasses into the surrounding trees. Athena was sleeping in a front carrying pack that Carol was wearing.

"Why do you think the Visitors are monitoring Earth?" Carol asked.

"They came to observe and record our history. They want to learn about every planet that has intelligent life and they are watching over two thousand planets. Can you believe it, two thousand planets with intelligent life! They say they don't ever want to interfere in the evolution of the planets they observe, but that's ridiculous. As if not interfering *isn't* interfering. And look what happened to me.

"They were here long before the first humans evolved and have been observing us ever since. The Visitors Council, one of their ruling bodies, have all sorts of penalties for disobeying their noninterference rules." She stopped walking and squeezed Carol's arm. "They showed me what it would be like if they took my memories. It's worse than any death you could imagine."

"Took your memories? How do they do that?" Carol asked. "I couldn't believe they could talk to me in my mind when they wanted me to help you escape from the SOC. Are they already here on Earth? And if they have a strict rule of noninterference, how could they allow you and Bryan to be changed and you to become pregnant?"

Anna shook her head. "They're not here, exactly. They use some advanced form of communication that reaches our minds and they seem to be capable of relaying that to and from their world almost instantly. They manipulate the matrix of what we call 'Dark Matter' and 'Dark Energy.' It uses something like *spooky action at a distance* that Einstein wrote about. Way too complex for me to figure out. As for their interference, I think that was unexpected, an accident. But even so, it's still interference."

Or, maybe it was planned by someone, I thought, someone who disagreed with the Visitors' rules of noninterference. But why would they have done that to me? Then again, why would they have done what they did to Abigail? Even if the damage they did to her brain was an accident, what about her child? Did all this have anything to do with my mission to save the Visitors' society that the Orb had mentioned—the Arionis thing? That was something that wasn't in the vast knowledge available to the Link.

"Hard to believe a society that advanced would make such a mistake," Carol said. "Are you certain they don't have some other motive? Maybe even to invade Earth?"

"I think you've seen too many science fiction movies, Carol," Anna laughed. "I seem to know they mean no harm, at least harm from their actions. Harm from their *inaction* . . . well, that's another story. They would let our stupidity lead us to killing each other. And they wouldn't interfere." *But Carol was right. As advanced as they were, how could they make all these mistakes – first our absorption by the Orb, planned, but not allowed? Then absorption by the Link, then my pregnancy, and all that had happened to Abigail. All too much to be accidental.*

They hiked further down the trail as she thought about Abigail's question of why she should trust the Visitors.

"Do you understand what they did to give you and Bryan your telepathic abilities? It still seems incredible that by touching you they could change how you communicate, how you acquire knowledge, and then there's your pregnancy. I mean I still can't believe we are using telepathy even though I know we are." Carol stopped to adjust the carrying pack and to peek at Athena.

"We made contact with the Orb, and . . . he changed us through absorption. There was a glitch, maybe a software bug." *Or maybe someone modified the Orb and instructed him to change us.* "Anyway, somehow, it happened." *It didn't just happen. They chose me. Why? I still didn't understand, and these special skills—I didn't understand them either, but I didn't want to share all that with Carol.*

"After the Orb absorbed me—surrounded Bryan and me with whatever it was made of—it had this amazing ability to modify our brain structures and the way they function. Then the Orb made changes to our brain cells and our DNA. As the new cells began to replicate and dominate, our ability to communicate using telepathy grew. It seems to have affected me more strongly than Bryan. Then I found the Link. I guess she thought I was a Visitor since I had some of their abilities conveyed by the Orb, especially telepathy. And then she absorbed me. I was modified even more by her, and—somehow my egg was changed, and it began to reproduce and now I have Athena. It's all very bizarre as I think about it . . . but, pretty cool in other ways, don't you think?" she said as she looked down at Athena sleeping quietly in front of Carol.

Carol stopped midstride, staring at her. "And they chose to initiate your pregnancy?"

"I don't think so. Like the absorption, the pregnancy was an accident. They had no idea it could happen. They were quite disturbed that this occurred." *At least I thought they were. But something in my mind suggested there was more to this—not an accident, a plan.* Carol began walking again.

"Athena carries their DNA. She'll have extraordinary abilities far beyond mine." Anna stopped and stepped closer to Carol and held her arm as she looked at Athena sleeping in the carrier. "Carol, we have to protect Athena. Nothing must ever happen to her." Anna squeezed Carol's arm tighter. "She's very important to the future of our world and vital to the Visitors' world. I can feel it."

"I'll do everything I can to protect her, Anna. But how do you know she's so important?"

Vital to the Visitors' world . . . where had that thought come from? Sometimes my words didn't seem to be my own. How could Athena have anything to do with the problems the Orb had told me about on the Visitors' world?

The fog had thickened around them as she walked next to Carol on the trail. She could no longer see the trees to their left; then the dirt trail began to reform into a sidewalk. She pulled on Carol's arm and stopped abruptly. Carol was standing next to her, but not seeming to notice anything different. Buildings grew out of the mist on either side of them, replacing the trees. They were huge—like they were suddenly on Xynthanthium. She drew a sudden breath as she noticed someone in the distance walking toward them on another walkway. It was a Visitor. Then two more appeared, walking with the first. Just ahead, the walkway she and Carol were on intersected with the walkway the Visitors were on. She started walking slowly toward the Visitors, walking closer to Carol and with her hand holding Athena's hand as she slept. Anna was breathing faster as she gripped Athena's hand tighter. They came together at the intersection that led into a beautiful park. They stopped as the Visitors kept walking toward them. They stopped in front of them as Anna looked at them.

Anna looked at Carol. She had stopped walking but didn't notice the Visitors standing right in front of them. She was stroking Athena's head and running her fingers through her hair.

"Do you see this, Carol?" she whispered, staring at the three Visitors. They looked familiar to her.

"I am . . . Segam, Anastasia. This is Aliana and Fliona."

They each nodded their heads.

"I remember you. We met at the Visitors' Council meeting." She could feel her heart pounding faster.

"We're sorry to interrupt you, but we thought it best to discourage you from sharing your knowledge of the Visitors and our world with Carol. If the Visitors Council knew you were doing that, the consequences would not be to your liking."

Anna was suddenly startled by a huge multicolored translucent sphere expanding in size behind the Visitors in the park. She jerked backward, grabbing Carol's arm thinking that the sphere, which looked like a giant soap bubble, might grow to engulf them.

"Don't let it frighten you, Anastasia. That is just an artistic expression of one of our artists here on Xynthanthium," Fliona said. "Do you find it pleasing?"

"It grew so fast . . . but . . . it's beautiful." She couldn't take her eyes off the sphere. It had grown to the size of a large fireworks explosion, maybe 150 feet across only far more fascinating. It was like the aurora borealis in the shape of a ball. The colors on its surface shifted and morphed into different shapes. It just floated there in front of them.

"You understand, Anastasia, that it is not just you who might be punished," Segam said, looking over at Athena.

She gripped Athena's hand even tighter and her memory of her experience in front of the Visitors Council and the demonstration of the taking of her memories was suddenly vivid, as if put there for her to experience again.

The giant sphere in front of her filled with beautiful colors turned suddenly gray and a face grew on its surface, as if the sphere had become a human head, only — the face was lifeless. *What my mind imagined this person's face might look like without its memories.* As she watched, the giant sphere began to look more and more like — Athena. Anna gasped and moved her hand to cover her mouth, staring up at her daughter's image. Then the image slowly came to life as the colors returned, and a beautiful smile formed. Anna drew another breath, glancing over to see Athena still sleeping in Carol's arms. She turned back to the three visitors.

"I understand. But, why am I — "

"It's going to be all right, Mom." Athena's voice boomed from the face in the sphere. Her lips on this giant face moved as if she were talking out loud while smiling down at them. The three Visitors turned to look up. They turned back to look at Anna, their faces emotionless, but she felt a sense of astonishment from them. Segam turned to look down at Athena. The three Visitors slowly faded into the trees as the park in front of her began to disappear in the fog. Athena's face in this giant sphere continued to smile as it slowly dissolved, and the sun shone through the trees where the sphere had been. Anna stepped back and tripped over a rock on the trail and stumbled.

"Are you okay, Anna?" Carol asked as she reached quickly to grab Anna's arm. "What did you mean when you said she was vital to the Visitors' world?"

"Oh . . . I'm not sure how I . . ." She looked over at Carol who was acting like nothing out of the ordinary had happened. Anna looked around them for any sign that the Visitors had actually been there. It was as if Carol had been asleep for the last few minutes.

"If something happens to me," Anna began anew as she glanced around. "I . . . need you and Bryan to watch over Athena, to protect her and to raise her as your child. Would you do that for me, Carol? Will you promise me you'll do that?" She grabbed Carol's arm.

"Yes. But nothing's going to happen to you, Anna."

"I hope not," she said as she stared into the trees. "But you have to protect her, hide her if necessary. Under no circumstances is the government to find her and take her. They would turn her into a lab specimen." She pulled very close to Carol's face and her mind spoke in a whisper. "You will need to hide her really well. *Hide her so that even the Visitors can't find her,* at least until she is ready." Anna gritted out the last few words through her clenched teeth.

"Okay, okay," she said, wincing from Anna's grip. "I understand. I know what it's like to have your child taken from you," she continued as she put her arms around Athena.

'At least until she is ready?' Ready for what, I thought. It seemed at times, like someone else was in my head speaking for me.

They walked on for another quarter of a mile. Carol appeared to be in a daze as she looked down at Anna's daughter.

"I'm going to protect you, little one. Your mom and I will always be here for you." Carol raised her head to look ahead at the trail and Anna heard the questions that lingered in Carol's mind. "Are these Visitors really harmless? Do they have other motives? Has Anna been duped into believing their intentions are peaceful? Penalties for disobedience — how are those inflicted?"

"I'll tell you more about the Visitors sometime, Carol, but not now," she said as she looked around again. "It's important you know, so if something happens to me, you'll have some understanding of them." Then without a hint, Athena began speaking telepathically to Carol.

"The Visitors evolved as a very peaceful culture, Aunt Carol. The competitive instincts, similar to what human beings exhibit, were lost through the evolution of their culture and their direct genetic manipulation many millions of years ago. They grew to focus on learning and bettering the lives of every member of their society."

As Carol listened, she and Anna began to see visions of people working together in concert. Anna could feel their desire to help one another, as if she were one of them.

"There was no hierarchical caste system or survival of the fittest culture. They were a benevolent society. As on Earth, members of the Visitors' society had different functions to perform, and all those functions were considered equally valuable. It was like a doctor's role being equal to that of a repairman. Both necessary, neither more or less important. The purpose of their government was to ensure all the essential functions were performed. The only hierarchy was that related to intelligence and creativity. Those with less of these were given tasks with less intellectual challenge. There was an enormous use of artificial intelligence and robotics to perform menial tasks."

Carol and Anna began seeing visions of vast factories, all operated with robotic beings. Unlike autonomous robots envisioned on Earth, looking all alike and very similar to a human, these robots were all different shapes and sizes, seeming to have been designed specifically for the tasks they performed. Some small enough to crawl inside a device to help construct it and then remain inside and become part of the mechanism that made it work.

Anna thought about the comment Segam had made a few moments ago in the park about not telling Carol about the Visitors.

"Athena, I don't think—"

"It's okay, Mom. Aunt Carol needs to hear this. As a result, their society had no competition, drive for survival, or motivation for one Visitor to be better than any other. They functioned a lot like academic institutions here on Earth. Learning and improving their knowledge and understanding of the universe was what mattered most. Ownership of physical and tangible goods was meaningless. Knowledge discovery and knowledge creation was a huge part of their entire society. In the early stages of their development, selfishness had been removed from their genetic makeup by direct intervention, in parallel with the evolution of their cultural norms. Their society was perfect, peaceful, and caring."

Anna and Carol felt this amazing feeling of peace and tranquility as they continued to watch the scenes Athena was creating in their minds. They began to feel just like a part of this society as they walked among the people of Xynthanthium. Anna looked down at her daughter, who appeared to be sleeping soundly.

I wasn't sure if what Athena had just conveyed was entirely true. There was something lingering in the back of my mind that told me this wasn't the whole story about the Visitors' world. But where had Athena learned all this and why was she telling Carol right after the Visitors had warned me not to?

"They have traveled the universe for hundreds of millions of years," Athena continued, ". . . exploring planets, asteroids and worlds within their galaxy and in many others, including our own. This is one of their society's most important activities—exploring, observing and learning from the many cultures of the universe. They have developed a means to travel from galaxy to galaxy faster than you could ever imagine. Even with this ability, there are vast regions of the universe that remain unexplored.

"They understand the makeup of the universe and of matter and energy far beyond any human's comprehension. But they struggle with the less tangible aspects of human culture — your capacity for love, your constantly changing emotional engagement and your insatiable lust for power. They lost a capacity for emotion, or the desire for it, as they adopted a singular focus for their society — to remove conflict, desire, and coveting — and to focus on learning. They view emotions and the desire for things as dangerous."

I found this thought strange, considering that the Orb said I had been chosen for my ability to "sense the feelings and emotions of others."

"We need to move your society in this direction, Aunt Carol, if for no other reason than to preserve human survival. The current path you are on will lead to your extinction and the Visitors will just watch this happen. They won't help you. They won't stop it. Their rules of engagement prohibit them from interfering."

Much that Athena was telling Carol was new to me. Maybe I needed to pose more questions to the Link. I couldn't help but notice how Athena spoke of "you" and "your" when talking about Earth's culture. She didn't view it as her own.

"I know things aren't perfect here on Earth, but we will naturally correct, we always have," Carol said. "We've been through war, famine and pandemics, and we survived."

"No, Aunt Carol, believe me, you won't. Earth is on a path to destruction, the same path every other culture the Visitors have studied is on, thousands of them. And you are not far from the end. There is a point from which you cannot return — what is best described as 'Avalanche Time.' You are precariously close to that. If you don't change your direction, and quickly, there will be no stopping your progress toward the end of life as you know it.

"On most planets, this happens within the microcultures of the societies that exist there. As this process of cultural evolution — growth, thriving, stagnation, and death — progresses, these individual cultures that grow as subcultures are absorbed by larger ones and eventually the forces that infected these elements of society infect the entire population. This evolution and merging of cultures, combined with the development of weapons of mass destruction and your greed and desire to control, are the main factors that are moving Earth to its Avalanche Time. It can also be the result of an unchecked pandemic or exhausting a vital resource, like food or water or energy."

Anna and Carol began seeing images from large cities on worlds with very different beings, all fighting and struggling for survival over food, water, and energy. It was frightening. It was awful, and it was just like Anna had seen when she was absorbed by the Link. The image of the young child who died of starvation right in front of the child's parents sprang into her mind, just as she had remembered it from her visit to Sanctuary over a year ago. As an unfriendly death consumed this young innocent child, the ashes from her decaying body fell to the sheet where she lay and blew into the air in front of her.

"Societies do not survive when one or more of these events occur on a large scale. They destroy themselves, and in some cases, the very world they occupy. The Visitors won't let that happen — the destruction of the worlds these species occupy. These societies represent a deadly virus that must be eradicated."

That last message from Athena jarred me. "They must be eradicated?" What did that mean? That sounded like more than interference. I could sense Carol's mind was overwhelmed with what Athena had created and shared — images of dying worlds, and then our world dying. Her words were one thing, but the visions of our world's near-term path to destruction, now drawn so vividly and real for Carol, made it all absolute. And why would the Visitors want to save the world that this species occupied? What would they do with it?

Carol stood staring at Anna. Tears filled her eyes. She was grasping Athena tightly as she winced from the horrible visions of devastation and death. "This can't be true."

"We can make the necessary changes, Aunt Carol. We must. This is what Mom was chosen for. And between the three of us and Bryan, we have the knowledge to do it. Nothing will stand in our way, not Dr. Tyson and not the Visitors. We have little time, but we *will* fix this."

I stood there, wondering where my six-month-old daughter had found these words. My mind continued to fight with itself in the vacuum between belief and disbelief. I felt trapped there, bouncing from optimism to uncertainty, from excitement to fear. How could we do this, how could we stop Armageddon?

"Aunt Carol. Mom will need your help to solve this problem."

Anna watched Carol's thoughts as if the future of their world were in fast-forward — filled with devastation and death. Carol's mind became flooded with images from a strange world, surrounded by throngs of aliens of every conceivable character, as if the peoples of the universe had gathered to meet on Earth. Carol could no longer see the trail ahead or the trees around her. She fell forward to the ground. Anna reached down to help her up.

"You okay?" Anna asked.

"I think so. I became disoriented and must have fallen. Are you okay, little one?"

"I'm fine, Aunt Carol. Sorry. I was trying to show you the future."

Carol froze, stunned and not speaking for a moment. *"Sorry. I was trying to show you the future? Is that what she said?"*

"Sometimes I can't imagine it myself," Anna said as she watched her daughter smile up at Carol.

"Don't you think we should try working with the government to stop all this? They — "

"No! Never, Carol," Anna said loudly. They would take this away from me — I mean Athena, take Athena from me. I'll never let them do that. I can handle this. I just need you to take care of Athena if something happens. Okay?" Anna was yelling at Carol now.

"Okay, okay." Carol pulled Athena closer to her.

I could see it in her mind. Carol thought it was better to let the government deal with an alien species and the future of our planet. But the Visitors selected me for this. The government would just screw it up like everything else. There was no way I would let them take this from me. I can do this. I will do this.

Anna reached over to take Athena in her arms. "I'll carry her the rest of the way home."

CHAPTER 34

ATHENA'S INFLUENCE

//

They arrived back at Shirley's house, and Anna took Athena into her bedroom. Carol followed her.

"Athena looks like she's grown noticeably from only a week ago," Carol said, trying to ease the tension between them.

"She has," Anna said.

"Is this normal?"

"Normal for her, at least the alien part of her."

Carol glanced over at Anna as she stared out the window of the bedroom at Bell Rock.

"What's normal?" Carol asked.

"She's growing at twice the rate of a normal child her age."

"How's that possible?"

"It's her genetic makeup. She's different. Haven't you noticed how much she eats? Instead of doubling her mature cells every day, she does that in half the time, depending on cell type of course. That eventually tapers off, but she'll be fully developed before she turns five. She will be much shorter than a grown adult, but her intelligence—well, I don't even want to try and guess. She'll be like a giant in comparison if we measured her intelligence by her height.

"Her brain functions will be much more advanced. She will reach her full mental potential before she turns one. In a few weeks, she will be far smarter than the most intelligent human on Earth."

In many ways, she already was, I thought. Phronesis had shared with me Athena's phenomenal mental growth rate. It was difficult to imagine what she would do with her intellect. Her words shared right after her birth gave me chills. Would she become the ruler of Earth?

Carol began trembling. "I'm thinking about the fall on the trail. I held the most intelligent human on Earth and I almost dropped her. I shouldn't even be handling her." She placed Athena in her crib and backed away in a daze of uncertainty. "Maybe from now on, you should carry her."

"Aunt Carol, you can carry me. We'll be all right." Athena's face grew a large smile.

"She has your smile," Carol said as she reached back down and picked Athena up.

"Do you think so?" Anna asked as she walked over. "Have you ever seen anything so beautiful?"

"No, I haven't," Carol said. She is the most beautiful creature in the world. I didn't mean to say — "

"It's okay, Carol. I know what you meant."

They returned to the kitchen.

"Hello, you two, or should I say three? How was your walk?" Shirley asked.

"Oh, it's beautiful out there, Shirley. Anna and I had a great hike. The fog was just burning off. The air was fresh and cool, and the sun just came up over the mountain. The hiking trails are great. I can see why you like it here so much."

Yes, and you can meet aliens along the trail who threaten you, I thought.

"It looks like it's going to be a beautiful day. I'll bet you're all hungry. Pull up a chair. We're having waffles with strawberries," Shirley said.

"I love strawberries, and I'm famished," Bryan said as he rounded the corner into the eating area adjacent to the kitchen.

"How did you sleep, Bryan?" Shirley asked.

"Pretty well. I thought I heard someone outside my bedroom around 2:00 a.m. I got up to check all the doors. It turned out to be the wind." He hurried over and took Athena's hand and leaned over to Anna. "What did you mean about meeting aliens on the trail?"

"I'll tell you later," Anna said.

"Hopefully the food today will be even better than the bed you slept in," Shirley said.

"It will. I could eat a horse. Well, maybe not a horse, but definitely a waffle."

Athena smiled and held Bryan's finger.

Bryan spent much of his free time with Athena. He liked her a great deal, and in time, treated her as if she were his daughter. After all, she didn't have a real father and he felt she needed one. He learned amazing things about her second home on Xynthanthium, the home of her other family—how long it had existed, what it was like there, how the *other half* of her lived. She would take his mind there and walk with him on the streets of Xynthanthium, see the beautiful artistry of their culture and learn of their way of life. Bryan fell in love with these trips, and with each visit he fell more in love with Athena. And he shared his own childhood with her, what it had been like growing up with Anna, his best friend, and the one he was so passionately in love with now.

I still saw Bryan as my best friend, but there was something growing between us after these many months, something that neither of us could explain. I didn't want to be away from him for very long and my desire to touch and hold him had grown.

Bryan shared with Athena the trips to the Rock House he and her mother had taken so often, and their first encounter with the Orb following the earthquake. This was the beauty of telepathy: Anna could hear every conversation they had, there were no secrets, just the sharing of their thoughts and feelings.

Living in Athena's mind, sharing her experiences and feelings, and learning of Athena's world was something Bryan could hardly imagine, let alone understand.

"It's difficult to describe; it's amazing—no, it's extraordinary . . . no, thrilling; that's it, thrilling," he finally decided. It was like going to their favorite theme park, but each visit was like discovering something completely new and exciting.

How all this knowledge came to Athena was beyond me. I couldn't believe the Visitors were communicating this to her. But they had to be or somehow it was a part of her DNA, that which Phronesis had given her during the time I was absorbed by her. Could Athena's DNA contain all this knowledge? She was born with the knowledge of language, why not the Visitors' history? It seemed too hard to believe, but how else could this happen?

"This is partially how she has learned, Anna," the Link said, as Anna jerked at the sound of a voice in her head. She had not heard from Phronesis in some time.

"Athena also receives much of her knowledge directly from the Library. They are very close."

"She mentioned right after her birth that she viewed the Library as her father," Anna said.

"Yes. That is closer to the truth in the context of your culture. He is teaching her."

"I was worried about Athena sharing so much information about the Visitors' history with Carol, after the warning Segam gave me while we were hiking."

"Yes. You should not share that with anyone and do not allow that memory to surface in your mind when you communicate with the Visitors Council. You would be endangering Carol's life."

I hadn't looked at it quite that way. I was more concerned about all that my daughter shared with Carol. I wasn't sure why Athena chose to do that. It made me a bit jealous. Maybe it was a reaction to my asking Carol to take care of Athena if anything ever happened to me. Then after Carol had suggested contacting the government, I thought I had made a mistake. Maybe she wasn't a good choice to care for Athena if something happened to me. Maybe Bryan was the better choice. But he wouldn't have a motherly instinct, and he was just a little older than me . . . not prepared to care for an infant child — even if she was becoming the most intelligent being on the planet.

///////////////////

It was now October and winter was arriving in the Village. Anna, Bryan and Carol struggled with making any real progress in determining what might kill mankind and what they could do to stop it. There was the challenge of doing the impossible, coupled with their desire to engage with Athena, discover new things she was capable of manipulating in their world, and marvel over her encyclopedic knowledge of the universe.

At the age of nine months, Athena continued to grow much faster than normal. She was taller than a child twice her age, almost thirty-two inches, but remained gaunt. Her black eyes were mesmerizing, but it was her mind that baffled those closest to her. Her extended family, Bryan and Carol, experienced an enormous attraction to her. They wanted to be around her as many of their waking hours as possible. There was something about being in her presence that made them feel more alive and invigorated, smarter and capable of doing almost anything.

Carol was still trying to understand what was happening when she was around Athena. One morning, she walked into the kitchen, where Anna was reading.

"Anna, take a look at this," Carol said.

"Sure."

"I made these two lists about dealing with Dr. Tyson if we learned he was close to discovering our whereabouts – the things we talked about yesterday."

Carol put a group of writing tablet papers on the table.

"This list on the left I developed here in the kitchen while Athena was eating her lunch." She put the list with three sheets of paper full of actions in front of Anna.

"This second list I made a few hours later while I was sitting on the deck and Athena was taking a nap." She placed one sheet of paper on the table with a list of items written on it.

"Look at the differences between these two. I tried my hardest to do a good job on both when I was working on them. The one I wrote here in the kitchen next to Athena is four times longer, more detailed and much more insightful. It's filled with options, ordered by most likely to succeed and with much more attention to trade-offs, and factors related to the likelihood of escaping Dr. Tyson's grasp. The other list . . . is brief, not detailed and with limited ideas or any imagination on how to prevent him from capturing us. It's amazing. Oh, and my feelings about success in escaping Dr. Tyson's grasp were so positive in the presence of Athena, but while on the deck I was afraid it wouldn't work. I was filled with uncertainty and worried about us being captured and taken away."

"You know what happened, don't you?" Anna asked as she walked to the sink. "Athena was listening to your thoughts and entered your mind to work on it with you. She has an uncanny ability to do that without you even sensing she's in your head. The Visitors are masters of this."

"That's amazing. It makes me want to be with her every waking hour, only she seems to need a lot less sleep than I do."

One afternoon, Shirley brought out a variety of manipulation toys for Athena to play with. Carol was watching her play with an imbalanced ball that would roll in a wobbly way and eventually come to rest with its center of gravity settling to the point closest to the floor. Athena was rolling the ball a few feet in front of her while sitting on the floor. After the ball settled to a stop she reached out with her right hand toward the ball, the one containing her black birthmark. Her birthmark looked strangely similar to the mark Anna developed after the shrapnel injured her hand in Pearl Harbor. As Athena reached out, the ball magically rolled to her hand. Carol sat with her mouth open as she leaned closer to Athena to see what was happening. She watched again as Athena rolled the ball forward and moved her hand toward the right of the ball's path. The ball mysteriously moved to the right as it executed its wobbly path forward, eventually curving around and returning to Athena's right hand. Her next toss led to the ball rolling in a circle around her as if she had an invisible string attached to it. Then, after the ball came to rest in front of her, it mysteriously started up again without Athena touching it and rolled smoothly around her in the opposite direction. It was as if the ball had gone into orbit around her. After that, Athena smiled and began clapping, then hitting the floor with both hands, bobbing up and down on her bottom.

"Have you been watching what she's doing?"

"She isn't doing it all."

"What do you mean?"

"She has given the ball intelligence."

"Intelligence? How do you give a ball intelligence?" Carol asked with a chuckle.

"I don't. She does," Anna said as she nodded toward her daughter.

"But . . . how could she create the ability to sense the need to move and put that into a ball made of rubber?"

"It's called enhanced molecular restructuring, Aunt Carol. All the kids on my home planet do it. Some of it's what *you* might call 'dumb intelligence.' After modifying the microstructure of the organic molecules — the synthetic polymers the ball is made of — and incorporating some secret sauce . . ." Athena stuck her tongue out and wiggled it at Carol. ". . . the object is trained to go in a circle, but that's all it knows. I designed it to use the friction between itself and the floor to supply the centripetal force, so it wouldn't change the radius of curvature as it moved. The one that works the best . . .", as Athena reached over and picked up a tiny yellow ball, "is this one. It's called a *su...per* ball. It has polybutadiene, silica and zinc oxide in it. It has much better tangential compliance than other balls. That makes it work a lot better." Athena threw the ball down hard on the floor and it bounced high, hit the ceiling and rebounded off the wall, landing right in Athena's hand as it rested in her lap.

Carol turned to look at Anna as her jaw dropped and shook her head.

As the weeks and months passed, Athena astonished Carol well beyond her ability to control a rubber ball. One afternoon while putting Athena down for her nap, Carol placed her hands on the edge of the crib where Athena lay. As Anna listened to her mind, Carol felt sleepy and entered a dream state — only the dreams weren't her dreams; they seemed to be stories about people she didn't know, about their motivations, aspirations and desires. It was like she had turned on a TV show that she was becoming a part of. The imagery was as vivid and alive as if the scene was right in front of her. At one point she said something, either out loud or within her dream, Anna wasn't sure which, and the people turned to her and began conversing. Carol couldn't tell if this was reality or a dream. Frightened by what had happened, she turned in the dream and began to step back, detaching her hands from the edge of the crib, causing the scene of the bedroom to return. It was as if the crib had been alive with memories.

"Incredible," she said as she looked down at Athena, who smiled back at her.

On Saturday, Carol was feeding Athena some yogurt with a cute bright orange spoon and a Disney character on the handle. As she dipped the spoon into the yogurt and moved it toward Athena's mouth, she thought she could feel the spoon turn cold. She felt the spoon after pulling it from Athena's mouth, and it was freezing. So much so that the yogurt was beginning to freeze on the surface of the spoon.

"She really likes her yogurt cold," Anna said.

"How much of the house has she changed?" Carol asked.

"Everything she's touched."

"Wow. Is she changing us when she touches us?"

"She doesn't need to touch us to do that, Carol."

"Oh, my God. If she can do this at less than a year, what will she be capable of at four years?"

"I can hardly wait to find out," Anna said as she walked over to run her fingers through her daughter's hair.

Being in the house with Athena and watching her grow intellectually and in skill was nothing like watching a normal human growing in maturity. Every moment with her was filled with amazement. As soon as Carol thought she had seen everything, something new and extraordinary occurred. Like the Tuesday afternoon in Shirley's living room . . .

Athena had crawled over to a bookshelf and pulled herself up to observe an electronic picture frame that had a variety of Shirley's family digital photographs on it. The pictures changed every few seconds. Athena reached out and held the edge of the frame in her left hand while holding the bookshelf to steady herself. Moments later the screen filled with a photograph from a strange world with strange exotic plants and people that looked like the Visitors. Then the picture frame changed perspective and began to display what looked like a motion picture. There were images of a large blue-green sun hanging over a huge city with strange tall buildings that looked like huge rectangular steel structures extending into the clouds above them. Athena pointed to the upper corner of the display and the camera appeared to pan upward. There were four moons in the sky—at least they looked like moons—smaller than Earth's moon. It was as if a camera had been filming a scene on this simple electronic picture frame. That is, until Athena moved her finger downward and the camera encountered a Visitor standing on a balcony overlooking the city. The alien turned to look at the camera.

"Anna," Carol called in a loud whisper, waving at her frantically to come over close to her.

They stood watching the scene on the electronic picture frame from behind Athena.

Athena was watching the Visitor as she pulled the frame closer to her. The Visitor in the scene walked toward the picture frame, staring into it, as if he could somehow see Athena through the device.

"There's something familiar about him." Carol walked closer. "Of course, his arms and legs are like Athena's, other than their gray color."

"That's a Visitor," Anna said.

Carol took a step back. "A Visitor? You mean—the aliens we—"

"Yes. That's what they look like."

Athena, while still holding the picture frame and leaning against the bookshelf, drew it even closer to her and placed her frail right hand on the face of the picture frame screen, at which point the alien in the scene stepped back and placed his left hand on the screen from the opposite side so that their fingers were aligned. It was as if they were on opposite sides of a windowpane, but from opposite sides of the universe. The screen faded and returned to showing Shirley's family photos as Athena withdrew her hand and pushed the frame back away from her.

Carol heard Anna let out a breath from behind her. She turned to look.

"Did you *see* that?"

"Yes," Anna said as she bit her lower lip and stood still with her arms crossed in front of her.

"Holy shit," Carol said as she turned back toward Athena "I'm sorry. I shouldn't have used that word."

"That's okay, Aunt Carol. I won't use that expression. Dirty shit is more appropriate."

Carol and Anna broke out in laughter.

"How did that happen?" Carol asked in a more serious tone as she stood watching Anna stare at the picture frame.

"I don't really know, but I'm worried the Visitors now know where we are. Do they know where we are, Athena?"

"Yes, Mom. Sorry. But they've known for some time. Since before the stranger came to the front gate."

Anna could taste the blood from biting her lip.

CHAPTER 35

CHALLENGES

///

That evening Anna lay quietly on the couch in Shirley's study and dosed off. Phronesis opened a mental window into the conference room where Anna had met the Visitors Council and learned about neurological inhibition.

"Anna, the Visitors Council is meeting to discuss the unprecedented situation on Earth. Except for Segam, Fliona, and Aliana, the remaining members of the Visitors Council know little about Athena other than her origin and the fact that she is living and growing," Phronesis said. "Our quantum processors have modeled all the possibilities and shaped these into the most likely outcomes for our daughter. They have created a simulation of a variety of models of Human-Visitor avatars and have been exploring what each may be capable of doing. What they don't know and what no computer could predict is how Human-like or how Visitor-like she is. They aren't sure if there are capabilities she has, or will develop, that are enhanced beyond their own minds' ability to comprehend or beyond their own willingness to believe.

"Beyond Segam, Fliona and Aliana, who are your champions — although that may not always be obvious — Chairman Petrarch along with the least experienced member of the Council, Darmon, and two supporters of the Chairman, Vilach and Kelong, are present in the conference room. None of these four are your friends. Listen carefully."

The meeting began.

"She has a knack for guessing correctly," Segam said.

"How do we know it is a 'knack'?" Vilach asked.

"More importantly, how do we know it is guessing?" Darmon asked.

"She could not have known how to convert the device into a viewer.

How could she have known that? That knowledge does not reside in the Link." Chairman Petrarch frowned as the scene of Athena manipulating the picture player kept replaying over and over in their minds in the conference room on Xynthanthium.

"The probability of Athena being able to reach through the Link's portal to the Library is assessed at 0.013%. It could not have happened. Some minds have a tendency to fabricate knowledge in the absence of it," Fliona said as she glanced around the table at the other members.

"If we believe she could reach through the Link to the Library, then she may know more than we," Kelong said as he turned to the Chairman. "Perhaps we should have her neutralized." He looked across the table at Segam.

"She could not have done that. We would have been informed following the protocols of the Library," Aliana said.

"Shall we move on? Physiologically she cannot have that capacity. You saw her appearance. Her 'brain,' as they call it, is far too small and human neurological architectures outside the brain are nonexistent. Her neurological density is one-one-hundredth of ours," Segam said.

"Suppose the genetic changes initiated by the Link resulted in a new form of neurological microstructure. The density of her 'brain' matter could be substantially higher. The very structure of connectivity may be different. We have never experienced cross-species generation like this. Our models and simulations do not take this possibility into account," Vilach said in a serious tone.

"Why are we considering such remote possibilities? We should concentrate on the more likely outcomes. When you translate the lower density of her neurological tissue into intelligence, it is over a thousand times less effective," Fliona said, while looking at the Chairman.

"We have evidence that Athena's capabilities may be far greater than our models predict. If our observations are correct, then using our models will lead us to false conclusions and we will be ignoring one of the most dangerous threats to our very purpose that we have ever dealt with – the creation of a being whose abilities we vastly underestimated and one that could potentially penetrate the Library. The seriousness of such a conclusion is so great, I believe we must make this our first priority to confirm," the Chairman said as he looked back at Fliona.

"Are we in agreement? We must confirm Athena's abilities. If they are as we suspect, we must inhibit her. The mother, Anastasia, knows most of her capabilities. We must engage with her and learn of Athena," Kelong said, seeming to sit taller in his chair.

"If necessary, how will we inhibit? Clearly her mother will not support our objective," Darmon said.

"We will have to engage another of their species," Kelong jumped in to keep the momentum of his suggestion moving.

"We must return to reality. We are violating critical Directives with any such suggestion. Are such actions any better or worse than what actions Athena may or may not have taken? We have an opportunity to observe a new life form, one that has never existed before. To consider its destruction is not justified, especially when presented by junior members of the Council," Segam said as he glanced first at Kelong and then to Darmon.

"We can only operate on probabilities. To do otherwise could lead to unpredictable outcomes," Aliana said.

"We have already agreed to ignore the probabilities of our models. Such inconsistencies are disturbing," Fliona added.

"We will question Anastasia to discover what we can about Athena and then deal with our next steps. We must be cautious not to let our speculation enter the realm of a story, one with false and improbable conclusions. Nor should we narrow our interpretations to so few possibilities that we fail to recognize the true threat before us," the Chairman said in conclusion.

The seven members of the Visitors Council adjourned as they each mentally returned to their residences.

Anna sat up suddenly in a stupor with her heart pounding from what seemed a nightmare. She looked around the room and saw the familiar surroundings of Shirley's study.

"Why are you showing me these meetings? They're going after my daughter," she said as she sat leaning over with her head in her hands while trying to recover from observing the meeting of the Visitors Council.

"It is important for you to observe the Council, understand their motivations and plans. You must be prepared, Anna. Learn who your enemies are and your friends. You remember your teachings from one of your earlier dreams. Be very careful if you are brought before the Council. . . or you may never return," Phronesis said.

"What do you mean, 'never return'? I only see them in my dreams."

"You don't understand, Anna. Your dreams are becoming your reality. Imagine if you entered a dream and could never return from it."

That thought had never occurred to me as I sat staring across the room. Couldn't return from a dream? How could that ever happen?

"Your mind and brain are changing. This is why you are able to see visions of Xynthanthium, to visit there and to see the Council. Soon you will not be able to tell the difference between your physical world here on Earth and your mental world on Xynthanthium, other than your inability to physically interact when in the Visitors world, but even that difference will diminish in time. Remember when you entered Bryan's mind and participated in his soccer game while dreaming? You entered the game and kicked the ball. Do you remember how vivid that was? You couldn't tell the difference between that and your real world. The Visitors can trap you in their world. And if they do, your body here on Earth will atrophy and die. You must never let them trap you there. I will teach you ways to bring your mind back to Earth."

Great. Now something else to worry about . . . being trapped in a dream. As if I didn't have enough to be apprehensive about, trying to protect my daughter. But I needed to use my abilities and these engagements to keep ahead of the Visitors. Being surprised by them is what will get us killed. And maybe, just maybe, I can learn from them how to overcome the looming death of Earth's dominant species . . . my species.

/////////////////////

In the passing months, Anna watched Athena's impact on Carol's view of the world and to some degree, Bryan's and hers. Wherever she went, everything Carol saw, whatever she touched, the ground she walked on, the air she breathed, the trees, rocks, the water that flowed in the stream in Shirley's garden area - they all had a new appearance of something living, something to be cared for. Carol didn't think much about inanimate objects—that is, until Athena had engaged with them, and suddenly they had a character of life in them, and Carol begin treating them different.

Athena hadn't stopped at inanimate objects; she was influencing the social, emotional, and intellectual elements of human relationships with these same abilities. She began formulating a philosophy for those she touched, one grounded in collaboration and compromise, focused on giving more than taking, sharing more than coveting, a win-win world, or as she called it, a 'non-zero-sum game,' one to be communicated within her circle, the radius of which was growing and would eventually encompass the entire globe, she hoped. Anna was more skeptical.

CHAPTER 36
THE DAWNING

///

It was midsummer a year later and Athena, now a little over eighteen months, was sitting at the kitchen table having a snack of yogurt. It was a month earlier that she had started speaking aloud with her human voice.

They hadn't heard or seen anything from or about Dr. Tyson or NASA looking for them, which was worrisome in itself, and so far, no further intervention by the Visitors taking any action against them. But Anna was certain they were watching, waiting, and scheming, as Bryan still stared out the window with his binoculars, looking for signs of someone lurking in the neighborhood. Perhaps the Visitors were satisfied they weren't a threat to them—that they wouldn't violate the Visitor's coveted noninterference directive. Anna didn't believe that for a minute.

"It's time to start, Mom," Athena said as she took a bite of her yogurt.

"Start what, honey?"

"We need to stop all the things that will cause the human population to die. We only have a short time left."

Bryan and I had spent the last year working on this problem. There were so many possibilities and even with the Link's knowledge we made little progress in finding ways to mitigate them. We had a list of possible causes and how they could be dealt with, but it meant approaching the government, and that was too risky, if they believed us at all, which was unlikely.

There were so many distractions—the time I needed to spend caring for Athena, keeping a watchful eye out for NASA and Dr. Tyson, spending quiet time with Bryan, and there was that ever-looming question of our potential actions violating the Visitors cardinal rule of noninterference and what they might do if they thought we had.

I thought, in many ways, this kept me from moving forward. I still remembered the Council meetings and discussions to take aggressive actions against us. Nothing had happened, so maybe the one called Segam had convinced them to leave us alone.

"I have a plan."

"You've been planning already, Athena?" Carol asked.

"Yep," Athena said between bites of lemon yogurt her Aunt Carol was feeding her.

"And how are you going to solve this huge problem, my little genius?" Carol asked as she tickled Athena under her chin.

"Well, we'll start with one doll in our dollhouse and fix it, Aunt Carol. Then we'll get a lot more dolls and fix them," Athena said, smiling and giggling from her Aunt's tickles.

"So how do dolls and dollhouses help us?"

"Well, think of it this way. Earth is our dollhouse; now imagine one doll becomes two and then four and before long six billion. Now as the dolls start filling the dollhouse, they bump into each other; they start taking each other's stuff; one of the dolls is jealous that another doll has a larger bedroom; several of the dolls get together and decide to push that doll out of her room and take it from her. Then the dolls who are in the kitchen and doing the cooking decide to keep all the food for themselves; the ones who are growing the food in the garden decide not to give it to the dolls in the kitchen because they're not sharing. One day, one of the dolls decides to start a fire in the dollhouse fireplace and the air is so filled with smoke that everyone must leave. Of course, the doll that started the fire says she just wanted to stay warm. Another doll builds a vacuum and it works great, until one day she decides the carpet is the wrong color, so she sucks it all up and throws it away. Then one of the dolls gets sick and instead of staying in bed, she plays with the other dolls and they all get sick. Do you see how this is working?"

"Yes," Carol laughed. "But I don't understand how this helps us discover what is going to kill everyone in the dollhouse."

"Oh, that's easy. We go back to the first things that caused the dolls to stop working together, sharing and helping each other, and fix that."

"Ha. Actually, that's a great plan, but how do we fix six billion dolls now?" Carol asked.

"Oh, that's the most important part. We do it one at a time. We fix one and get them to pass the fix on to two, then four, and eventually six billion. Do you know how long it would take us to count by a factor of two before we reach six billion?"

"A long time."

"No, actually a short time. If we count by a factor of two . . . four, eight, sixteen . . . you know, then in less than a minute, only a little over thirty-two factors, we are over six billion."

Carol turned to look at Anna and raised her eyebrows. "But how do you get them to pass on a fix if they don't want to?"

"We won't let them not want to. We need to change the mind of every doll, whether they like it or not. Then, no matter what the cause of Earth reaching its Avalanche Time is, it will stop."

"Change their mind? How will you do that?" as she gave Athena another bite of lemon yogurt.

"I'll demonstrate," Athena said.

Carol's face developed a blank stare as she reached across the table to the plate of chocolate chip cookies. She grimaced as she slowly placed one in front of Athena.

"Carol, you know Athena isn't allowed to eat those," Anna said.

Carol sat still in a daze, her face contorted, not speaking.

"Athena, that's enough," Anna said.

Carol came out of her daze, moving her eyes from the cookie to Athena and took a deep breath. "Okay. I understand . . ."

Anna stood with her back leaning against the kitchen sink with her arms crossed, while watching the two of them sitting at the table. "That was a bit like the cinnamon coffee cake at the SOC," she said.

"No, that was something very different," Carol said, sitting back in a rigid posture with a serious expression on her face, moving her shaking hands to her lap, still staring at Athena, looking up at Anna, then back to Athena. "I wasn't encouraged to get that cookie. I was instructed to get it . . . and I *didn't* have a choice."

"Athena and I have a plan," Bryan said after a long period of silence.

"Tell them the plan, Bryan," Athena said, as she began coloring a picture in her tablet using fine-tipped colored markers.

"Well, something we'll call the Village, a group of people, will be . . . uh . . . influenced to behave correctly, to look out for their fellow man. Then this group will reach out to others and . . . influence them to do the same. It's sort of like a pyramid scheme where the group grows exponentially. I did the math and if we double the group every month for thirty-three months . . . that's less than three years . . . we can reach all of humanity."

"Reach? What do you mean 'reach'?" Carol asked, continuing to look at Athena.

"I mean Athena can select, motivate, educate, and convince anyone, anywhere."

Athena colored another portion of a beautiful outdoor scene she was working on while Bryan spoke. Her drawing hand was moving at blistering speed across the paper as she colored.

Carol's expression and posture hadn't changed since being forced to do something she didn't want to do. Athena glanced up at her with a smile. She continued to color without looking at the page.

Carol and Anna began seeing rich imagery in their minds that Athena created, that of a changed world — unselfish people working together, cooperatively, toward the common goals of humanity. Carol's facial expression softened, and her muscles relaxed as she watched this movie in her head. Anna continued to stare at her daughter.

All I could think about were the Visitors and how they would react to Athena's plan – using her skills to manipulate the entire human population.

"You can create this, Athena?" Carol asked as she stared off into the space in front of her. Carol began turning her head as she watched the world change in front of her.

"Oh, yes, we can do this, Aunt Carol. These Villages will become known as Athena's Villages," she said as she colored. "They will grow as the word and the virus spreads, and they will change the motivations of mankind, changes that will make Earth better than the Visitors' world. And most importantly, changes that will allow our world to survive."

"Did you say 'virus'?" Anna asked.

"Yes, actually a cultural virus, Mom."

"Oh, you mean it will spread like a virus," Carol said.

"Yes, that too."

"You didn't mean a real virus, did you?" Carol asked.

"Yes," Athena said as she continued to color.

"How will this virus work?" Anna asked as she walked over to the table, pulling a chair out and sitting down, never taking her eyes off her daughter.

Images flashed in Anna's mind, as well as Carol's and Bryan's, like a movie on fast-forward and then slowing. She saw Athena holding hands with Shirley. The camera zoomed in to their hands touching, showing microscopic droplets of moisture on Athena's skin being transferred in slow motion to the back of Shirley's hand, and the camera zoomed in again. They watched the contents of the minute droplets of moisture move slowly through the cells of the surface layer of her skin, enter the pores surrounding the hair follicles, migrate down through the dermis layer, into the hypodermis and enter a capillary blood vessel. Then the camera zoomed further, and they watched as the cells of the blood in her vein absorbed what looked like a purple wiggling worm, a virus measuring perhaps two hundred times smaller than the width of a human hair. The imagery ended.

"You can infect people with . . . something that . . . changes their personality, their desires?" Carol asked.

"Well, it's not like a real virus that stays with you until antibodies kill it off. It's temporary because it only reproduces for a while, but Shirley can still pass it on when she touches someone else. That way I don't always have to be there. But a little bit of me is there, and a little bit of me goes a *long* way. The part of me that I give her only stays until her skin cells flake off. That's in about thirty days. Then it stops," as she smiled and continued to color. "Did you see it, Aunt Carol?"

"Yes. I saw it, Athena. It was amazing." Carol was still trying to understand how this virus worked.

"I colored it purple because that's my favorite color."

"Ah," Carol said, looking at this amazing girl working on the picture in front of her. Carol glanced over at Anna and raised her eyebrows, then got up to get a glass of water. "Never-ending surprises," she murmured under her breath.

"What does the virus do once it enters the person's body?" Anna asked, staring at her daughter and now sitting very still as she recalled the memory of sitting before the Visitors and experiencing a small taste of neurological inhibition, the taking of her memories.

"It will influence their behavior."

"By influence . . . you mean . . . control, don't you?"

"Well, more like Aunt Carol handing me the cookie. It will work like that."

Anna sat back in her chair. She could not imagine the Visitors allowing them to do this. They would do to Athena what they demonstrated on her, only it would be permanent.

"When would you begin building these . . . villages?" Carol asked.

"We were waiting until Athena's mind was able to reach other people over long distances. She is ready now," Bryan said.

Anna turned toward Bryan and frowned.

It was bad enough that my daughter was contemplating this, but now it was clear that Bryan was encouraging her. How could he do that? I told him about my experience with the Visitors Council, even replayed it in his head to show him what could happen.

"Yep, we're ready," Athena said as she finished coloring her picture and held it up to look at. "I have thirty-three followers for the Village here in Oak Creek already, Aunt Carol."

"But you haven't interacted with more than a few people here," Carol said as she put her glass of water down.

"They passed me on through the virus and I speak to the new ones through their minds. Here, Bryan. I drew this picture for you."

'Passed me on', I thought. I was almost too shocked to speak.

"Wow. Beautiful scene. Where is this?" Bryan asked.

"It's from Xynthanthium. You remember."

"What did you call it?" Carol asked.

"Xynthanthium. It's the home planet of my second family, the Visitors."

"It looks beautiful," Bryan said as Carol moved to look over Bryan's shoulder while Anna sat staring at her daughter, thinking about the Visitors and what they would do when they discovered what Athena was doing.

The picture depicted a scene of a large city resting on the coast of a vast body of water. It was almost photographic in quality. There were intricate details drawn in bubbles popping up from various points around the city to show the life of the Visitors; artistic centers serving as hubs of gathering Visitors with huge sculptures of live waterfalls; vast images of beautiful mountain ranges covered in snow, drawn as if the viewer could stand on the edge of a huge bowl, holding the handrail that surrounded it and could look down upon a mountain wilderness, replete with cold winds blustering in their faces and snow swirling around them; some strange brilliantly-colored dancing waves in one of the bubbles; and live scenes of another world altogether, floating in another bubble.

"This is incredible. I can feel the wind blowing snow in my face," Bryan said, as goose bumps formed on his arms while he held the picture. "It's like looking through a window at a live scene. How'd you do this?"

"I don't feel any breeze," Carol said.

"Hold the picture while you look at it, Aunt Carol," Athena said.

Carol reached down and held one edge of the drawing and her facial expression changed as her eyes grew large and she jerked her head back while still holding on to the paper. "This is incredible, Athena. How did you do this? It's like I'm there. I can feel these things." Carol's face had moved closer to the picture as a huge smile developed. "Oh!" she exclaimed as she jumped back and shook her head. "The wind just blew a bunch of snow in my face." Remnants of snow had collected on Carol's eyebrows and began to melt.

These are just like my dreams, thinking of Phronesis' remarks about the reality of dreams. Everything is real. Oh, my God. She can create drawings that turn into real experiences when someone touches them. And she has a plan to change the mind of mankind. What have I done? I'm responsible for her being here. Was Kelong right when he tried to trick me into killing my daughter at her birth? I pushed that thought out of my head.

"Almost everything in the picture is made by the Visitors. Like Earth, there is a lot of natural beauty, but the Visitors can make things even more beautiful than nature . . . sometimes," Athena said.

"This is amazing. I don't want to leave this place." Carol's eyes remained fixed on the drawing as Anna turned and entered Carol's mind. It wasn't like a movie, more like the real thing, as the scene never repeated the same imagery with the blowing snow and ever-changing, almost magical artistic expressions created in the air in front of her. It was as if each part of the drawing triggered a dream about the real experience in each of the bubbles in the picture.

Anna got up and began walking around in the kitchen, ignoring the beautiful picture. "So, the plan is to control humanity; to decide their future; to decide what they can and can't do. Have I got this right?"

"Well, I wouldn't put it that way, Mom. I still think 'influence' is a better word."

"I'd . . . like to suggest we try another way first, Athena. Controlling all of humanity . . ." Anna said as she began to shake her head. "It doesn't sound right to me. If Bryan's estimate of the time it would take to spread such a virus is correct, we should still have enough time to try and solve this problem another way, without controlling people, without using your . . . virus to modify the behavior of humanity." *And . . . without drawing the attention of the Visitors, I thought.* "I'd like to try other ways first."

"Well, we could try other things, but this is the most efficient and fastest way to solve the problem, and we don't have to figure out what the real cause is and try and stop it once it's started, which is really hard."

"But what if it is outside the control of humans? Something like a pandemic; I think we need to explore other possible alternatives before we try controlling people."

"Okay, Mom. We have plenty of time. We can practice with the virus locally and plan on infecting all of humanity later, but do you like my picture?"

I watched my daughter's mind jump from creating an entertaining and extraordinary drawing, filled with unique and unnatural elements, to the creation of a virus that could control every human on the planet. I was frightened to think that the mind of a child and one gifted with godlike abilities existed at the same time within her. The Visitors would never let her do this. If they saw this, they would crush us.

"Yes, honey, it looks beautiful," Anna said as she walked over to join Carol and Bryan and put her arms around her daughter to hug her and hold her. The thought of losing her was too unbearable to consider.

"Thanks . . . and everything will be all right, Mom. I can protect us from the Visitors."

I looked at my daughter as she made some changes to her drawing. How would she be able to protect us from the Visitors?

Athena looked up and smiled at Anna as an overwhelming feeling of confidence seemed to engulf her mother's mind.

CHAPTER 37

FRUSTRATIONS

///

Athena and Bryan continued to spend time together and his behavior, as a result of their interaction, changed. He was becoming more creative, more insightful and quicker in his decision making. But Anna could feel other changes as he withdrew further and further into a shell. He was feeling less talkative and not wanting to interact, distancing himself from her; what communications they had were mostly telepathic now. Their personal time together had diminished as they focused harder on discovering the likely causes of mankind's annihilation and the frustrating process of trying to determine how to stop them. If they weren't successful with this, Athena would want to move forward with her virus and that meant the Visitors would take action — something Anna had to prevent.

They finished a long day of working on the internet to determine what was happening around the world that might give them a clue of what to focus their time on. She sat back and sighed.

"Want to go for a walk?" Bryan asked.

"Oh, I'd love to, but I'm exhausted. How about tomorrow?" Anna asked.

Bryan got up without saying anything and walked into the living room.

She followed him and sat down next to him. He had plopped down on the couch with his hands behind his head, staring into the air in front of him. She sat silently and entered his mind. She could sense his irritation, his frustration. She listened to his thoughts, wrapped in undulating dark red clouds . . .

"If I were me, then dream I could;

If I were me, then think I should;

I'd think and dream of you, I would;

But in my world, it is not lust,

For love like this are dreams and thinks that aren't my senses;

Make them desires of walks and talks and touches,

For these are what bind us and not more fences;

Of this world bound by human clutches,

It is you who see my dreams and thinks,

And should forever hold my hand and feel my heart."

Since his absorption by the Orb and interaction with Athena, Bryan's ability to craft poetry on the fly had gotten better and better.

"Beautiful poem, Bryan, but what's bugging you?"

"It was especially for you. Did you get it?" he asked, while not turning.

"Yes, it's very nice. Thank you."

"No, I meant, did you *get it?*"

She hesitated for a moment. "Oh . . ." His poem had a message for her. She got up and walked toward the kitchen thinking about it.

He followed her into the kitchen. She looked out the window at the shadows that had begun to creep through the backyard.

"I'm tired. I think I'll go to bed early. Don't wait on dinner for me," he said.

"Don't you want something to eat?" She turned around at the sink and looked at him. He seldom made eye contact any more.

"I'm not hungry."

"Okay. I'll — see you in the morning."

Carol put Athena in her crib after dinner as Anna crawled into bed. "Good night, Carol."

"Good night. See you in the morning."

Anna was asleep before her head hit the pillow. She woke suddenly, startled by a cry. She jumped up to check on Athena. As she stepped toward her crib, Athena was sitting up and smiling in the dim light. "Hi there, my beautiful girl," Anna whispered. She laid her down and tucked her in.

She crawled back into her bed and collapsed onto her pillow, gasping as she found herself falling through a membrane onto a hard floor. Directly in front of her was the Avalanche Clock room, the central place where the Visitors monitor every planet they observe and study. It was here that Phronesis had shown her the forecasted times of the death of the dominant species on over two thousand planets – those containing intelligent life forms in the known universe. The three-dimensional display screen loomed in front of her with the images of the thousands of oval three-dimensional clocks; the strange clock faces with hands and symbols showing the time remaining until Armageddon suffocated the dominant species that lived on each planet; the shifting order that from one moment to the next showed the clocks in numeric order by their planetary number and then in the order of the time remaining before the blanket of death descended upon the dominant species of each planet. Around the perimeter of the huge display were the familiar floating display terminals and the mysterious eight-foot-tall holographic portals that served as the doorways to other worlds. To her right and beside her a group of perhaps twenty or thirty Visitors stood staring at her. They began moving forward as she crawled backward in hopes of reentering the bedroom with Athena. It was gone.

She stood and turned to her right and saw Bryan standing about ten feet from her. "Bryan!" she yelled. "You frightened me. How did you get here?" Bryan stood there looking straight at her with a blank, empty stare, as if . . . *Oh no, his mind was going blank.*

She turned back toward the Visitors. They were coming toward her, staring at her. Several of the Visitors closest to her stopped and one turned to look to his left as if waiting for something, some kind of approval, Anna sensed. Standing there on the side of the room in the direction of the Visitors gaze was Athena, clothed in a flowing purple robe. She was smiling.

"Athena, what are you doing here?"

"It is necessary, Mother. Goodbye."

She felt the familiar and horrifying change in her mind. The image of Athena began to fade. How could Athena do this! Her own daughter, turning against her, helping the Visitors . . . take her memories!

She jerked, jumped forward, and grabbed Bryan's hand as it hung limply by his side. She reached out to him with her mind. There was nothing there! "Run," she yelled as she pulled on him.

"Ath . . ." Anna was struggling to remember her name. She knew she was her daughter. How could she forget her name? *My mem . . . neurological inhib . . . inhi . . .* "No, no," she screamed, but couldn't hear her own voice as the world around her turned darker and suddenly colder.

She pulled on Bryan harder and they fell to the floor. The jolt and sharp pain in her wrist seemed to shake her mind awake and she began thinking of a way to defend herself as she looked around. She grabbed Bryan's hand again and pulled him to his feet. They began to run full speed around a pillar, down several steps, knocking over several Visitors. She dove into one of the holographic portals leading to another world, dragging Bryan with her. It was filled with dense forest material and smelled dank and stale. She could feel the heavy humidity and sticky air as they pushed through the vines and crossed the threshold into the portal. They smacked into a transparent wall made of a thick smoky oozing material and everything shifted to slow motion. She watched Bryan struggling beside her, trying to move forward, pulling on her as his weight carried him further into the cloudy fluid that surrounded them. She tried to take a breath. She couldn't breathe. Fear grabbed her. She struggled to hold her breath and felt a tug on her leg. She turned in slow motion to look back. A Visitor had hold of her ankle. Bryan was pulling her toward him. She turned back toward Bryan. She tried yelling. "B-r-infirmary-a-n." His head turned slowly. He saw the Visitor pulling on her. There was another threshold just ahead of him. As his free hand slipped through the portal into the world on the other side, he was yanked forward suddenly, and he lost his grip on her. She struggled to keep moving forward in the thick molasses-like material. She was trying to swim through this dense liquid while the Visitor holding her leg pulled her back. A moment later she fell back into the Avalanche Clock room.

"Defend yourself," a voice in her head yelled.

She squeezed her eyes shut and created a feeling of enormous anger in her head. She began to rage in her mind as she opened her eyes and screamed at the top of her lungs at the Visitors as they rushed toward her. They all stopped suddenly and stared at her. She felt an overwhelming feeling of confusion surrounding them. She closed her eyes and conjured a huge grotesque beast in her mind standing to her right, looking down at its dead child and raging at the Visitors over his death. The Visitors turned to look up at this fictitious creation which appeared real in their minds, almost bear-like, over nine feet tall, with huge fangs dripping blood and clawed hands large enough to grasp a Visitor. They began to back away.

Their expressions remained placid, but their minds told her they were frightened to death at what she had created. She thought about how angry the beast felt over the killing of his innocent child by the Visitors. His anger exploded as he raced into a group of them and began slashing with his enormous claws.

Bryan fell back through the portal at her feet. "What's happening?" he yelled.

She kept her focus on the raging storm of anger in her mind, reached over and took Bryan's hand and closed her eyes as she enveloped everyone in darkness, leaving only the beady red eyes of the grotesque creature lighting the room. Bryan was trying to pull away from her as her anger and the fear of this huge beast began to envelop him.

"Mom, I need you. Come here," she heard Athena call with urgency as if from a great distance.

A moment later the scene dissolved, and Anna was staring at her daughter in her crib. She stood, bent over and panting with her hands on her knees as she looked at Athena. Athena was looking at her and wasn't smiling. Anna was dripping wet and her heart was pounding out of her chest. She stood for a moment trying to determine what was real as a glob of thick frothy liquid fell from her arm onto the floor. Bryan came rushing into their bedroom breathing rapidly, slipped on the hardwood floor, and careened across the room, crashing into the crib. His pajamas were soaked in some frothy ooze.

"Pee-ew! You smell like a moldy wash rag," Athena said.

"I fell into a stinking marsh in a dream. How did I get all wet in a dream?" he asked, looking down at his clothing.

"Welcome to your first Visitors nightmare," Anna said.

"What was that, Athena?" Anna asked as Bryan sat down on the bed.

"Get up, get up. You smell like a sewer," Anna said, waving Bryan back from her bed.

"That was the Visitors method of creating a false reality," Athena said.

"There wasn't anything false about it," Bryan said. "A moment ago, I was on Xynthanthium and something terrible was about to happen to me and your mom. They took me kicking and screaming from my bed and the next thing I knew, I was in this strange room with all these clocks. Then I could feel my mind going blank. That was frightening . . . or maybe the *most* frightening experience I had ever had, actually.

You . . . you were causing it, Athena. Why did you do that? What were you trying to do to me? How could you — "

"Bryan, calm down. It wasn't Athena's fault." She'd never seen him so agitated. This was the most he had spoken in weeks.

He backed away from Athena's crib, staring at her.

"It's okay, Bryan. What you saw was a false reality. I wasn't helping them, but they wanted you to think I was."

"It was as real as being here right now with you, but a lot, and I mean a *lot*, scarier," Bryan said.

"There is no difference between your reality and the Visitors' false reality, except that you have the ability to extract yourselves from the false realities . . . sometimes, and only if you're prepared and strong enough," Athena said.

"I wasn't prepared for anything. Once it started all I could think about was what was happening to me," Bryan said.

"We'll have to be ready for more of this. They can reach any of us now; ever since I saw them in the viewer. I'm sorry about that," Athena said as she looked over at her mother. "If you believe you are trapped, you may never be able to return, Bryan. It will occur just like you experienced it. One moment you will be walking along in this world and the next you will find yourself in the most frightening place you've ever dreamt about. But it won't feel like a dream. It will feel and *be* real."

"What were they trying to do?" Anna asked as she sat on the edge of the bed and tried to calm down, taking deep breaths.

"The Visitors created a false reality in Bryan's mind to turn us against each other. If they could get Bryan to believe I was secretly working with the Visitors and also threaten Bryan with another attack on you, he would probably do whatever they asked him to do."

"It would have worked," Bryan said. "Just before you arrived, they told me if I didn't cooperate, they would take your mom's memories, permanently. Then Athena . . . I mean . . . the Visitors began to take my memories to demonstrate what it would be like. They said it would kill you," he said, looking at Anna. "I never want to experience that again. I still can't believe how real it all seemed," he added as he paced back and forth while dripping all over the floor. He finally stopped and walked up to hold Athena's hand.

"I'll work with you on how you can resist letting them control your mind, Bryan. It's very difficult and against the most skilled Visitors, it won't work well, but it will provide you some protection," Athena said.

"What brought me to where Bryan was?" Anna asked.

"I woke you, Mom. I discovered what they were doing to Bryan and the only way to get him out of there was to send you in. Sorry to have done that."

"That's okay, honey. I was glad to help, although at the time, I wasn't sure what to do or how to get out."

"Jumping into the holographic portal was a great idea, Mom. You almost made it into the other world with Bryan."

Neither of them slept well, waking in a groggy haze.

"Boy, you are all awfully quiet this morning," Carol said

"We had a run-in with the Visitors in a dream last night," Bryan said.

"Run-in? You smell like you just came out of a sewer," Carol said.

"I'll take another shower after breakfast, but I'd rather not talk about it," Bryan said.

"They attacked us in a dream, Carol. It was disturbing," Anna said.

I should have guessed they would do something. I never thought they would go after Bryan. Now I knew that the Visitors knew what Athena and Bryan were planning. How could the three of us do battle with the Visitors?

Anna sat staring at her breakfast, not eating a thing.

CHAPTER 38
LOVE

///

That afternoon Anna sensed Bryan was still in a frump. She thought about the poem he had composed for her. At the time, she was almost too tired to even think about what it meant.

"Would you watch Athena after lunch, Carol? Bryan and I need to take a walk?"

"Sure. It will be just the two of us, you beautiful little person," Carol said, tickling Athena under her chin while she sat in her highchair. "What do you think if we celebrate tonight with some ice cream?"

"I think that would be nice, Aunt Carol. Could we have it with chocolate sauce?"

Everyone laughed except Carol.

Anna and Bryan started out on one of the local trails that intersected Jacks Canyon. It was warmer than usual for November as they hiked down into one of the dry creek beds in the afternoon sun. Bryan was looking ahead, around to the sides of the creek bed and then behind them, searching for anyone following them.

"I was thinking about us, what happened with the Orb, then me with the Link, and now with Athena. It's changed us, made us different. Now we are battling the Visitors. What happened last night could have killed you," Anna said as tears welled up in her eyes.

"We need more time like this for just us," Bryan said.

They walked further along the trail with only the sound of their footsteps moving the stones on the trail. She reached back and took his hand. He held hers and squeezed. She sensed Bryan thinking about their past as his thoughts drifted into her mind like a warm breeze. He was pushing out the memories of the Visitors threats and their responsibilities, taking her back to the times they had together growing up in the mining town and spending afternoons at the Rock House. She hadn't thought much about them since Athena was born. She had such vivid memories of those times. It was like being there with him again, as they sat in the warm sun and swam in the natural spring pool in the quarry. She could still taste the salty water when he first tried to kiss her. The memories he shared merged with hers as she thought of the two of them lying beside each other after discovering her Rock House, feeling a gust of wind form goosebumps on her skin, and looking into the darkness as they talked about their future.

She stopped walking, drew close, and took hold of his arm so they could look at each other as they used to. She reached up and put her arms around him, pulling him to her, thinking about how he could have been killed by the Visitors — or worse, his memories taken. Tears flowed down her cheek and she could feel his body trembling as they cried in silence.

"We'll find a way to protect each other. From now on we won't let our guard down," he said as he pulled back slowly. "I never realized they could get into your head like that. It was so real. Athena's going to give me some ways to detect when they're trying to take over my mind." He was inches from her. He was looking into her eyes and reaching up with his free hand to wipe the tear from her face. She felt the warmth of his hand against her cheek. He held her head, moved his lips to her cheek and kissed her and then moved his lips to her lips. She hesitated, pulling back ever so slowly, and then kissed him as he held her close. She had felt her attraction to Bryan grow over the past year, but with Athena and all the other problems they were facing, she hadn't had the time to think about it. But after last night and almost losing him . . . things were different.

They stood holding each other as their minds became entangled, their thoughts and feelings wrapping themselves around each other, like ribbons intertwining in the wind. His thoughts of their past had such comfort and warmth. She could paint them with her own memories of their time together, feel their shape as if she were molding them from soft clay and drape them with beautiful visions of her own. It was an amazing experience, sharing someone in your mind like this.

She felt a warm, relaxing feeling growing within her, as if a cozy blanket had been wrapped around her, a soothing pleasure consuming her entire body as she felt Bryan's emotions of passion in her mind. She held them and let her mind drift with them. They grabbed hold of her like a powerful wind lifting her into the air. Their minds were in rapture, filled with scenes and dreams of their bodies woven together like a tapestry in a floating abyss, their arms around each other, their moist lips kissing, creating a warmth that only love could express.

As they shared these enormously pleasurable feelings in their minds, Bryan's mind leaped in intensity, like a match igniting, creating this extraordinary orgasmic surge inside her, a joy so wonderful she could feel it consume her as a flood of heat spread like fire across every pore of her skin and she seemed to melt into his arms like a candle, and their bodies and minds became one.

"Oh!" she gasped and closed her eyes holding him tightly and kissing him, her breathing accelerating while they embraced with tears between their cheeks as their minds exploded in a huge emotional euphoria. This exhilarating rush, this all-consuming mental ecstasy erased all her thoughts, all her memories, leaving her with raw emotions flowing through her in a way that no words could describe, no physical actions could imitate. They both began to cry as their minds held each other and they lay on the ground next to the trail breathing heavily.

Emotions seem strange as they take hold of your life; it was as if I were possessed by some unseen force to speak and act differently, and when shared with someone you care for, their reflection in your mind reshapes you, like making your right hand become your left, where laughter becomes crying and crying, laughter. Is this what love at its deepest level is like? If so, I wanted more.

"I love you," he said in a halted telepathic thought as calmness began to engulf them.

As her rational mind strained to gain control of this enormous rush that her emotional mind fought to preserve, she stared at a billowing cloud in the sky above them. "I . . . love you too," she finally said.

"Do you think the Visitors have ever experienced this kind of feeling?" Bryan asked.

"They have been the way they are for thousands of years. But it's hard to imagine they experienced what we just had and decided to leave it behind," she said.

"Yes . . . hard to believe. Then again, if we could get them to understand . . . perhaps . . ."

"Yes, that's interesting, Bryan. Would you kiss me again?"

He leaned into her and their lips met in a soft kiss and embrace as that feeling of ecstasy grew once again and their minds shared thoughts of the deep love they had for one another, a feeling of love like neither of them had experienced before. The troubles of the world, Athena, NASA and Dr. Tyson, the Visitors, they all were hidden for a moment. All Anna could think about, all she wanted to think about, was being with Bryan, holding him, feeling the comfort and safety of floating in his mind as she was now.

But as we held each other, that same corner of my mind that had hidden my feelings for him seemed now to harbor that which I knew I had to do; what my world and another were depending on me to do. It lurked in this dark place, like the sun hidden behind the cloud, now casting a shadow over us, waiting its turn, impatiently awaiting my return. I had a new mission now — to get even with the Visitors for what they had tried to do to Bryan — to take him from me. I held him tightly and buried my face in his jacket.

////////////////////

That evening Anna fell asleep with difficulty, unable to get Bryan out of her thoughts. She woke in a dream sitting in a floating lounge chair near the center of an infinity-edge pool, wearing a beautiful turquoise and purple bathing suit. The soft breeze and warm water must have been the temperature of her skin, as she could barely feel their presence. She closed her eyes and the water felt like Bryan holding her once again. The sound of joyful canaries singing in the surrounding woods grew as the dense stand of trees behind the pool came to life in song. An almost imperceptible breeze moved across the surface of the still water, leaving in its wake the smallest of ripples progressing toward her while the alluring smell of the sweet Mirabilis flower in a flowerbed next to the pool bathed her senses in a final touch of pleasure.

Beyond and below the soft, billowing hills and the distant edge of the pool that seemed to disappear into nowhere, a large metropolitan city rose to the clouds. The late-afternoon sun streaked through loosely nestled cumulonimbus clouds, like beams from God illuminating portions of the peaceful city below. These spotlights of sun, surrounded by dancing shadows, teased the city dwellers, as the thought of them gathering after work for drinks and dinner filled her mind with laughter and fun.

The distant streak of a contrail from what could have been a passenger jet was visible on the horizon, making its way to its destination. As it progressed, it seemed to dip toward the city, moving faster and faster as if drawing a line in the sky, directing people to this serene place. Within seconds it penetrated a cloud and disappeared. In the time for one last beat of her heart, it exited the cloud and a distant thought entered her mind. "Don't let this happen." Everything was so peaceful, why not let this happen? And in that moment, it struck the city dead center. An enormous explosion of blinding light bathed everyone with eyes to see, followed by a rapid moving front of fire, wind and devastation as the blast wave and fireball from the nuclear detonation moved outward one mile every six seconds, consuming and vaporizing everything in its wake. She sat watching with her eyes recovering from the blinding flash and her face contorted, feeling the radiation burns beginning to sting. The wave of death moved toward her. Just a few seconds now . . .

"Oh my God." She sat up abruptly, waking from her nightmare. She was breathing heavily, her heart pounding like a loud drum in her chest. She was shaking uncontrollably. She felt her face for the burns; tears ran down as she thought about the city she had been watching and the lives of those who enjoyed one last moment of serenity before death consumed them.

Why was this happening to me? Was someone telling me this will happen if I don't act, if I don't solve this unsolvable puzzle? Was this another dream I was to learn from? What was I to learn from this dream? Don't let the Earth go to thermonuclear war? How could I possibly stop that?

CHAPTER 39

SEGAM AND THE VISITORS

//

Two nights later, Phronesis drew her into another encounter with the Visitors. This one was different.

"Anna, in this meeting, Segam is meeting with Aliana, a member of the Visitors Council and Golden Cube at the Visitors Life Exploration Organization (LEO) in the capital of Xynthanthium. Xynthanthium is the cultural icon among the thirty-seven planets circling the same star and the seat of government for all the Visitors planets. Only a few rooms are designated as "private" within the LEO, where the Library can't monitor and record the mental thoughts and information exchanged between Council members. This is only known by those members of the Council who are also members of the Golden Cube, those who have access to the Library. The room they were in was chosen by Segam because it was *not* one of the protected sanctums. "He wants the Chairman to discover this conversation. Listen and watch," Phronesis said.

"Welcome, Aliana. It is good to be with you," Segam said as he walked around the conference table to sit close to her. The chair reshaped itself to envelop him as he sat down. Anna recalled these chairs when she first met with the Visitors Council. They had made her feel weightless.

"You also, Segam," Aliana said as she sat looking out a window that took up the entire wall of one side of the conference room. She looked across a vast landscape of their capital, Xynthanthium, as a great white cloud floated past the window. "The Chairman was asking questions about Athena," Aliana said as she turned toward Segam. "His motives were clearly designed to influence my thinking. I believe he was attempting to build a consensus on the need to inhibit Athena and her mother, Anastasia."

Aliana was a particularly beautiful Visitor, Anna thought as she watched her move. She had an appearance of sophistication about her as she sat erect, turned slowly and moved gracefully in her chair. And her voice was almost melodic as Anna listened to her choice of words, the sound they created in her head and the timing of her thoughts. Anna thought she was somehow choreographing her speech and the movements of her body as she communicated.

"This is not unexpected," Segam said. "He has already attempted this and continues to discuss it at every opportunity. He is the most conservative member of the Council. What is he concerned about now?" Segam stood and walked around the table between Aliana and the window.

Anna seemed to be observing this meeting from a back corner of the room. She wondered how this was possible.

"He seems to believe Athena's mental abilities are far beyond what the Library has simulated. He asked if the capacity of the human brain is sufficient to absorb the knowledge that Anastasia has accessed through the Link and if Athena might somehow gain the capacity to . . . *access the Library.*" Aliana spoke these last three words very slowly and deliberately.

Segam raised his eyebrows as the gray skin above them wrinkled and folded. "His first question is an excellent one. I cannot imagine how the human brain could possibly comprehend the enormity of our knowledge, let alone have the intelligence to manipulate it." His gaze drifted upward, pausing as he seemed to stare right at Anna; then he closed his eyes.

Does he know I am here watching?

"He is not aware you are watching, Anna," Phronesis said as Segam continued.

"If I drew an analogy contrasting the computational powers between a one-celled ameba, a common low-level example of life on the planet Earth, and the human brain and that between the human brain and the intelligence of a member of the Visitors linked to the Library, such a comparison would reveal truth."

Anna watched as Aliana smiled at Segam's example, something she had never seen the Visitors do.

"Expression of emotions reflects a violation of Visitor decorum," Phronesis said.

"Is this truly a reliable comparison, Segam?"

"Yes," he said as he opened his eyes. "However, I cannot speak of Athena. Her neurological capabilities are, as yet, unknown."

Segam's voice sounded aged, with a gravelly texture as Anna listened to the telepathic communication.

"Relative to the Chairman's second question, of Athena potentially accessing the Library, well, such a suggestion, as you know, is preposterous." He shook his head. "She would need the assistance of the Link. There is no evidence of such assistance. In addition, the Library would have reported any such attempt at access. You and I and the other two members of the Cube would have been informed immediately if that had happened."

Aliana shook her head in agreement.

"The Cube organization, Anna," Phronesis interrupted, "consists of the four senior members of the Visitors Council who oversee and guide the metaphysics of the Library, the Visitors' vast autonomous, self-architected and self-building knowledge repository, our thinking machine — *the most intelligent living entity in the known universe.* You recall when I took you to its entrance – the Golden Cube. The Cube's existence, while known by the three other members of the Council of Seven, the Visitors Council, is unknown by the Visitors society at large. And, the Cube's activities, exactly what this group does and why they do it, are unknown to the three other members of the Council."

"You have not heard of any such reporting, have you?" Segam asked.

"No," she assured him.

"Therefore, his arguments must be based on pure conjecture, rumor, or even worse, fantasy or deception. Our protections for direct access to the Library are beyond deciphering, even for an advanced Visitor. Since only four members of the Council have such access — you and I, the Chairman and Fliona — no other is possible without our knowing of it."

"There were questions related to Anastasia's responses during our last interrogation — you may recall when it was necessary for the Chairman to interrupt her when she began discussing her interaction with the Library and her understanding of its knowledge. It appeared she might have had far greater access than anyone could have imagined. Perhaps Athena facilitated this?"

"I suspect the Chairman is merely creating an imagining, an illusion to distract the Council from its primary purpose of oversight, and perhaps to discredit my actions on Earth. You have felt the power struggle as factions have formed among our Council members, have you not?"

"I have. But . . . are you aware of the Paradigm Crucible rumors?"

Segam turned his head toward Aliana.

"Of course, I am aware of these rumors," Segam said in a slow and unemotional voice, shaking his head.

"The Chairman believes they may *not* be rumors, that such an organization may exist."

"The Chairman creates secret organizations in his mind that do not exist, those that may destroy the basic tenants of our society, including modifying the behavior of the Library. Again, such suggestions are preposterous. These are distractions to our work. He builds false enemies and conflicts without evidence, all in the interest of spreading fear and bringing attention to his position. It is purely a means to support the thesis that grave threats surround us and that *his* is the most important position of responsibility to subvert them."

"We are all aware of their potential," Aliana said with a firmer tone and note of concern in her voice as she leaned forward.

"Yes, but the Paradigm Crucible's reality? No. What does this have to do with Anastasia and Athena?"

"The Chairman believes that the Paradigm Crucible may be connected to Athena. That somehow, she may be their link to gain access to the Library, their muse—"

"Ridiculous. Let me be more precise. Virtually impossible." Segam smirked as he stood to walk around the room while shaking his head. "I admit there is much that is not known of Athena. She is a unique specimen in our history. Indeed, perhaps the most unique," Segam said under his breath.

"But to suggest that she is the mechanism for a fictitious group of radicals to gain access to the Library, no evidence supports this." He leaned over, resting his hands on the back of his chair.

"This was my thought also. But I began to postulate. What if the Paradigm Crucible did exist? How would such a group gain access to the Library? They would need to find a wormhole—a passage from a knowledge region outside the Library to a point . . . inside the Golden Cube, one that does not appear as an intrusion, a connection that appears normal, a process like all other processes *within the Library*, but in fact *outside of it*." Aliana squinted at Segam.

"You are suggesting that Athena might appear to the Library as an extension of himself?"

"If this were possible, and I am not saying it is, Athena would appear to the Library as a reflection of himself, and he would allow the connection without perceiving it as an intrusion. And more importantly, no one would be alerted, including members of the Cube."

"There are physical and theoretical constructs like what you are suggesting. On Earth, for example, one conceived by a mathematician named Felix Klein who created an object whose inside is its outside."

"Yes. It would be just like that—no intrusion, thus no reporting."

"If this were true, Athena would be one of the most prized possessions in the universe," Segam said as his gaze seemed to move to Anna in the distant corner.

"Yes, Segam. Although I would view her as *the* most prized possession."

"Fortunately, for the Chairman, this is not possible, Aliana. There is no muse and the ability to craft a covert intrusion into the Library, as you suggest, is beyond anyone's ability . . . other than the Library himself."

Segam glanced at the wall and a clock appeared. "I apologize, but I must prepare for another meeting. Perhaps we can continue tomorrow?"

The scene in the conference room dissolved and Anna found herself inside Sanctuary standing in front of Phronesis. She was getting good at transforming the appearance of this huge orb-shaped object into the beautiful elf, Galadriel.

"I don't understand what just happened. Why were they discussing this in a room where the Chairman could later observe them?" Anna asked.

"Yes, why would Segam do such a thing?" Phronesis asked, almost as if it were a rhetorical question.

"The Chairman already knows he is not on his side . . . I don't know . . . maybe he wants him to know he's not hiding anything. He seemed very honest in his remarks."

"Yes, keen observation, Anna, while actually Segam was being highly deceptive. Why else would he have provided for Athena's creation?"

"What?" Anna asked as she backed away. "He provided for my pregnancy . . . that you initiated?"

"Yes."

"But, why . . ."

It now began to make sense. Segam wanted to gain access to the Library using Athena. But he already had access as a member of this Cube group. What did Athena's access provide him? I was so startled by the revelation that Athena's birth had been planned, that I was having trouble concentrating.

"That, my wonderful thinker, is what you must discover. I do not know why he needs her. But it is very important. With the enormous planning, the time it has taken and the danger it has brought to these very senior members of the Visitors Council, it must have monumental importance. Now I want you to follow Segam's thoughts as he returns to his residence. Pay close attention, Anna."

///////////////////

Segam stood on the balcony at his residence, looking out across the expanse of his home planet of the Xynthanthium Empire. It was just before sunrise.

I could feel him, almost as if I were a part of him, as my mind still grappled with Athena's existence being planned by Segam. I was looking through his eyes, listening to his thoughts, hearing what he heard. Incredible . . .

"Ours' is a delicate and dangerous plan," he thought, as he reflected on his strategy to destroy the confidence his world had in the current Chairman, "a plan designed to gain access to the Library and to manipulate its high-level cognitive functions, allowing them to change the behavior of the Xynthanthium population, and in so doing, to demonstrate that the Chairman was weak and was failing in his most important function — to protect the Library from any and all intrusions. One wrong step and his plan could crumble like an avalanche triggered by an earthquake, burying him and his co-conspirators as they crafted a path to recapture their world, the one he once knew and loved. Anastasia and Athena would be their keys. He needed to protect them while appearing not too."

He turned as the glint of their sun began to break the limb of the horizon. Brilliant blue, indigo and violet hues streaked across the sky, spawning a crescendo of shapes and colors as the illumination excited their lower atmosphere. "There is such natural beauty here," Segam thought, "but beneath it all, hidden from our society, there still exists a dark evil; one built over millenniums through a combination of cultural, technological and genetic manipulation; one designed to unify and control behavior and strip our world of its feelings and emotions that had once enveloped us. Anastasia and Athena will help rebuild the grandeur of our world and bring back that which had been taken from us, turning darkness into light."

Genetic manipulation, I thought. This is like what Athena was planning for mankind on Earth. Were these somehow related?

She saw a large bird, not unlike Earth's eagle but twice its size, flying overhead.

"It's called an agronge, Anna," Phronesis interjected.

Seeing this majestic bird reminded Segam of a time long ago, standing on this same balcony with his wife, Valoria. How he hated the society that took her from him. He would get her back, return her stolen memories and they would once again live as they once had—a life of dreams, love and the sharing of their emotions.

I saw scenes of a beautiful Visitor in Segam's mind, her face smiling and sanguine. No matter what she had done, it appeared to be a ruthless sentence. The more she listened to this and sensed Segam's emotional reactions, all kept internal, the more she hated the Visitors Council's actions.

A solar flare, rich in color, erupted above the horizon from the hidden portions of their sun. Segam turned to search the sky around him. Twelve of the planets in their solar system shone brightly within the background of the universe of stars. They would soon be approaching the Aequius of their year.

Phronesis interrupted. "The Aequius is a time during which all thirty-seven of the planets in our solar system will be equally spaced in their orbits around our sun, a time filled with a ritual heritage as our planets celebrate an astronomical event of such profound character that only a deity of immense power could have bestowed it upon the Visitors."

As the full sun passed above the horizon, all but a few of the closest planets gave way to the light of day.

He inhaled the sea breeze as it wended its way across the cliffs adjacent to his dwelling, carrying with it the smell of plankton and marine plants growing on the rocky crags below. The ocean water was almost vaporized by the power of huge waves that tried to reshape his world as they crashed beneath him. The smells, the sounds . . . they all brought back his memories of his wife Valoria.

I'd never seen waves this big. They must be fifty feet high. I couldn't believe I could smell what he smelled. It reminded me of a family trip to the coast of California, a place called Morro Bay. I could see myself stepping on the slick rocks along the shore in Montaña de Oro State Park. It smelled just like what Segam was smelling. That was a nice time. My mother wasn't so controlling of me there.

"How Valoria would have marveled at his young protégé, Athena," Segam thought. Athena was so much like his daughter Crisanda, who was much older now. He had not seen her in a great length of time. She had blamed him for her mother's fate and for not saving her from the clutches of the Council of Seven.

The planet rumbled. "Affirming his guilt," Anna thought.

He felt the vibration from the unseen gravitational forces of the sister planets closest to Xynthanthium as he thought about how they shaped the tidal forces and the large migrating earthquakes that followed these planetary interactions.

This was amazing. I could feel the minor earthquake as if I were there, standing on Segam's patio.

"They are like the dust moving with the wind. As powerful and uncontrollable as these physical forces are, they will be dwarfed in contrast to the movement Athena's and Anastasia's actions will create in our society and culture." He closed his eyes and listened to the cacophony of sound rising from the sea that somehow managed to arrange itself into a melody as the voice of the largest waves reached his ears. His mind yearned for the time of the arrival of these aliens on Xynthanthium, and perhaps a time to reconcile with his daughter.

He no longer needed to see the scene below, as the smells and the sounds re-created the imagery for him. He turned and walked toward the curved glass-like wall to his home as he looked back at the sea. He opened his mind for the Library to observe him and created a vision of Athena and Anastasia tied to the massive boulders beneath as the enormous waves drowned their screams and their lives—all for the benefit of the Library and the Chairman—a vision to demonstrate his loyalty and to hide his actual cunning intentions from the Chairman—to use these chosen ones to access the Library and destroy the Chairman.

I felt his mind snap shut. I thought I was going to drown to death as Segam created the vision of my daughter and me tied to the boulders near the water's edge and the waves pounded over us. It was freezing cold and I could taste the terribly salty water as I almost choked to death.

The material in the wall to his residence made an opening for him and then closed, returning to its original mirror surface, reflecting the dawning of another kinetically active day on Xynthanthium.

He walked across the floor of his now quiet living quarters, filled with floating art forms, including a vista of a one-meter-tall miniature waterfall—looking exactly like Niagara Falls. He stopped to look at this recreation he had designed. It hung suspended in midair and seemed to pour into a river to nowhere beneath, replete with the sound of a roar and mist rising slowly into the room. The river flowed inexplicably back to the top of the waterfall, bringing to life in his mind the artistic creation of a human artist M. C. Escher and the Xynthanthium three-dimensional artist Serong.

This was a very strange thing, being in the head of this Visitor—to hear his every thought, to experience what he experienced, and to see, smell, and taste everything he did. His senses had become my senses. As I thought about this, there seemed to be something missing. Other than when I was choking to death in his vision of us drowning, there was no feeling of emotion. I felt . . . handicapped, as if I had lost one of my senses.

The mist that collected on his skin from the waterfall brought the image of Anastasia's face vividly to his mind, reminding him of the moisture settling on her arm from a misting device on the patio of her residence on Earth. As he rubbed the moisture from his arm, he watched it evaporate from the image of Anastasia's arm, in the dry arid climate of the desert she lived in. She would like the moisture-laden world of Xynthanthium.

It was like looking in a mirror when he thought of me. Suddenly, there I was.

He walked by the plants he had spawned from his study of Earth's flora. The aromatic scent of his wife's favorite, lavender mint, drifted over him, before being consumed by the molecular filter designed into the rotating hologram of the same plant standing next to it. *I loved the smell of that mint. I wanted him to linger longer and let me smell it.*

He approached a blue translucent oval section of wall, and an opening appeared as he proceeded into his Life Pod. The wall behind him re-formed, enclosing him in a space that appeared to seal him away from anything external, an appearance that could not be further from the truth, he thought. But, the one thing it did shield him from was the ever-present Library.

Now, in the solace of his Life Pod, he was free to think without the strain of preventing his thoughts from being observed and recorded by the Library. He allowed his mind to feel an uncommon rush of emotion as he set forth a loud and deep laugh, reflecting on Anastasia and Athena. They were the result of the planning of many generations before him to craft a being with the power to communicate directly with the Library, to use this immense power to preserve life rather than extinguish it, and to bring forth the feelings and emotions as the Visitors used to know them.

This was unreal. He suddenly could evoke emotions where none existed before. It was like the lifting of a vail and all of a sudden, emotions flooded in. But if he's able to experience emotions . . . why am I needed?

The history of documented observations and measurements of the worlds the Visitors monitored spanned hundreds of thousands of years — millions, if you took it back to its origins, he thought. During this tumultuous period, rigid policy, rules, and procedures had mired his society in a quagmire from which extrication was becoming almost impossible. In some instances, they watched the annihilation of millions of members of a society by other groups of the same species or the complete extinction of a species and all those in the food chain from the consumption abuse of a vital resource. On one planet, Beta 473, planet 105799 in a galaxy known on Earth as Andromeda, a deadly virus developed and was spreading wildly, killing off eight billion of the dominant species on that planet. The Visitors watched as the entire population succumbed to the virus even though they knew the cure and could have aided the planet in discovering it in time to save the majority.

As he thought about the many thousands of planets under observation and this cruel and unforgiving tapestry of noninvolvement that had been woven into the fabric of their society and their way of thinking, he could not help but recall the contradiction within his own world. How could they allow such travesties of noninvolvement beset the lives of an entire society, one just like his own — families like his with Valoria and Crisanda — while controlling and manipulating their own society with such tyrannical fervor, converting their members into a flat, gray landscape of beings, working for the common good of their society but leaving them empty and without emotion? But change was coming, and soon.

Exactly what I thought and what I had said to the Visitors Council the last time I was with them. Segam had the same view I did. There was a clear argument among the leaders over what Xynthanthium was doing. But what exactly was my role? Change was coming. Would I bring it? And how? And would I survive it?

Ahead of him, in the center of his Life Pod, a room approximately eight meters in length and five meters in width, was a single capsule, perhaps half again longer than his height, a little over two meters in length. It was formed in the shape of a golden ellipsoid.

I thought it looked much like a tanning booth from Earth, only with no top, and it was floating, detached from the floor.

The rest of the room was devoid of objects, filled only with a soft blue luminescence. He stepped forward and an undulating, intelligent memory foam floor rose to meet his appendage before his foot could touch the surface ahead of him. As his center of gravity shifted, the floor seemed to undulate and tip in the direction he desired to move, almost walking for him; he didn't have to think about where he was going — the floor knew.

There was no transition between the floor and walls, as the surface was one continuous extension of itself, from the flat undulating floor curving up to become the wall, encircling the ceiling before returning to meet the floor again. It was like being inside an illuminated egg from the planet Earth. The room had no apparent front, back, or side other than its shape, mirroring that of the golden ellipse capsule in front of him. He turned and sat, lowering himself into the thick amorphous translucent red cloud undulating within the capsule. He reclined and became submerged in this strange material as it moved upward over his gaunt gray legs to his body, then over his arms and neck, eventually consuming his large pear-shaped head, leaving only his protruding black eyes exposed above its surface.

As the liquid rose to cover his head I felt like I was going to drown again, like his memory of Athena and me tied to the rocks, but I didn't. Somehow, he . . . or we . . . could still breath.

The translucent walls of his Life Pod dimmed as his body seemed to float within the cloud-like substance of the capsule. Once fully submerged, the material surrounding his body began to scintillate as millions of nanotubes formed within it, making connections with the dispersed neurological architecture of his physical body. The outline of his legs, torso, and arms shown through the strange cloud as more and more of these miniature contacts attached themselves. He could feel the surge of information flowing between his Life Pod and his mind as the room darkened and the surrounding surfaces became transparent; it seemed a flood of knowledge coming all at once, dealing with Earth, the Links established there and the Orbs, many of them, flowing so fast and to so many different parts of his neural anatomy that Anna's mind couldn't keep up. Now his capsule, looking like a glass ellipsoid, floated in space and was surrounded by a universe of stars.

He thought of his primary planet of study for which he served as Lead Visitor, overseeing the knowledge acquisition and study efforts of Earth. Instantly a massive image of Earth appeared in front of him, as if he had been transported there; then an image of the Link that Anastasia had connected with; and now he was staring down at her as she held her best friend, Bryan, lying on a hiking trail in northern Arizona, a place in a country known as the United States of America. He could feel her emotions surge. How he longed to be there with her and with Athena to exploit their unique gifts, to serve his objectives and bring him to power. Soon, he thought, soon.

There I was; right in front of him. He was watching the two of us kiss as we had that extraordinary mental love experience. I couldn't believe he could do this — be there with us, watch us, and I sensed even more: he was feeling the emotions we were feeling. How could he do this? It reminded me of our telepathy, only on steroids, as he experienced everything we experienced. I was beginning to feel the separation between mankind and the Visitors, what millions of years of evolution and progress could do. Their abilities . . . they were . . . godlike.

The connection was broken, and Anna sat up abruptly in bed gasping and feeling the emotional surge she felt when she was with Bryan on the trail.

He can watch us at any time, I thought as the image of us lying on the ground holding each other grew in my mind. I felt violated, knowing he could see what I saw in my mind, and feel what I felt — without my consent.

Anna looked over at Athena sleeping quietly and thought about what she had heard while she was in Segam's head. Segam and others on the Visitors Council were planning on using Athena and her as tools to somehow gain access to the Library. She began to imagine what would happen if the Chairman learned of this as her mind began to go into a frenzy and she began to hyperventilate. She jumped out of bed and paced around the room trying to calm herself. She sat on the edge of the bed looking at her daughter for a long time and finally crawled back under the covers and slept.

CHAPTER 40

MARCHING IN PLACE

//

It was January and Athena celebrated her second birthday with two candles on a cupcake. She remained gaunt and stood a little under three feet, her growth rate slowing rapidly. She had Anna's thin blond hair and The Visitors' large black eyes that mesmerized those looking at her. Her size and limbs led people to talk to her like the child she looked like rather than the scholar of the universe she had become. Both her intellectual and emotional intelligence far surpassed any human on Earth, regardless of age or experience, and probably that of many of the Visitors on Xynthanthium.

Anna, Bryan and Carol spent their time thinking and watching for any signs of the Visitors or Dr. Tyson, practicing ways to protect themselves from intrusions in their minds and planning escape paths if Dr. Tyson showed up. The longer the time with no sign of their adversaries, the more they worried about it, especially Bryan. In the meantime, they continued their search for the solutions to Armageddon on Earth. Anna thought about letting Athena use her virus as a last resort. It was becoming difficult to find time for enjoyment and laughter amongst themselves, as the difficult tasks they worked on weighed heavily in their minds.

I thought quietly about the Visitors, who they really were, what their real objectives were and why they were doing what they did. They were such a complex species and the members of this society that I was engaging with, the ones near the top of their governing organization, seemed to have equally complex motives and objectives. I yearned for a better understanding of their society, how a young girl, maybe like me, might feel about herself and their world. One part of me wished I were back, consumed by the black life cloak of the Link, where infinite knowledge seemed to be available to me at a moment's thought. Athena surely knew through her mysterious connection to the Library, but I was becoming less trusting about what she might tell me. She had become so focused and driven by her own goals that she would surly bend the truth to accomplish what she wanted or to influence me to agree with her.

"Anna, have you watered the plant on the window ledge in the kitchen today?" Bryan asked as he examined the leaves that appeared to be dying.

"No, you can water it." Anna sat at the kitchen table opposite Athena, going over her notes from yesterday's review of the expansion of world war around the globe.

"It doesn't need water, Bryan," Athena said.

"It looks like it needs water."

"No. The plant closed its mouth. It won't use the water you give it."

"Ha. Its mouth is closed. That's one I've never heard."

"That plant is just like you, Bryan. Its roots are just like your mouth. They allow the plant to draw water and nutrients from the soil. But since the soil has been dry for days, the roots closed down to prevent the diffusion, or transpiration of water, back into the soil instead of up to the leaf. The stem has dried out and as a result, the cohesion between the molecules in the plant stem has been lost. The molecular cohesion allowed the continuity of the water column to remain intact and water to flow up to the top of the plant. But once cohesion was lost, the water column suffered from cavitation—"

"Whoa, whoa, whoa . . . that's a lot of botany, Athena," Bryan said.

"Okay. Think of it this way. It's like you and me drinking from the same milkshake . . . a *chocolate* milkshake. Then I poke a hole in your straw and the air you suck in prevents you from drawing the milkshake into your mouth. Now you can go get a new straw—kind of like the plant stem feeding the three leaves on the other branch of that plant. See how green those leaves are? No loss of transpiration there. Or you can just let me finish off your milkshake . . . especially since it's chocolate. But then . . . you die."

"Ha-ha! I like that story, Athena, all of it except the part where I die and you get to finish the milkshake."

It was good to hear them laugh, until I thought about the plant without water. I began to imagine what it might be like for our race if we didn't have enough water, fighting for the little that was here, watching our neighbors die like the portion of the plant on the windowsill and not doing anything to help them, coveting and taking what we needed to stay alive, hoping someone would rescue us, like this plant seemed to say as its roots drove deeper into the soil in search of sustenance.

While emotionally mature, Athena was guided by a child's exuberance and an enormous thirst for experimenting, especially with her Visitor skills — those that manipulated not only the physical world in which she lived but the mental one as well.

One afternoon Anna listened to Athena's mind as she was looking in the hallway mirror at her reflection. "Who am I?" Athena thought, and an image of Anna being absorbed by the Link appeared in her reflection, then a fetus squirming in Anna's womb. The image morphed into an older version of herself, reminding Athena of the young Afghan girl on the cover of an old National Geographic magazine on Shirley's bookshelf; a woman filled with compassion, a love for life and a thirst for living the emotions of it. Then the image transformed to a scene as she walked in one of the artistic squares in the city of her ancestors on Xynthanthium, holding the hand of an elderly Visitor, a statesman of some sort. As they walked, they shared their knowledge of the universe and the wonders of the Visitors' society seemingly at peace. And again, the image recast itself and she saw herself as a young rebel leader, dressed in a purple robe, meeting in the catacombs of Xynthanthium with key members of a rebellion, crafting the overthrow of an outdated, emotionless and cruel governing organization — a government that manipulated its members and the many planets of the known universe it controlled. The final image showed her standing on a glass podium looking out over a vast throng of Visitors, millions of them, visible as far as the eye could see. Beyond in the sky hung twelve visible sister planets appearing to eagerly await her message, a dream really, the dream of a new and different world. Anna stood behind her in this vision, older now and wearing a purple robe as a Visitor held her left hand and another human held her right. "This is my future," Athena thought.

Bryan walked down the hall and turned to look at Athena's reflection in the mirror, but instead what he saw took his breath away. "What is that, Athena?"

"It is the future, Bryan. It will be wonderful." The scene dissolved as Bryan walked closer. In its place was the image of Athena standing, looking up at Bryan.

"That was you . . . in the future? How'd you do that?"

"I'll show you someday . . . when you can catch me." She turned and ran down the hall while laughing and daring Bryan to chase her, which he did.

//////////////////////

Progress in discovering the potential causes and solutions to humanity's annihilation continued to be slow and frustrating. With Carol's help, Bryan and Anna had partitioned the potential contributors into categories: pandemics, global thermonuclear war; an environmental catastrophic event; the exhaustion of a critical resource — water or food; an external catastrophic event, such as an asteroid striking the Earth; and some form of technological development gone awry, including quantum physics experiments, nanotechnology, and artificial intelligence. Then they ordered them by most significant to least and evaluated them. They searched for observations and evidence that would support how and when each cause could be the one affecting a large segment of society on Earth. Athena then identified the potential solutions to stopping them, including her own cultural virus. The list of solutions was daunting in number and complexity. Many of the solutions were without any easy means to change the direction of the cause — stopping a worldwide pandemic, for example — and thus prevent the catastrophic event and its subsequent impact on humanity. They were becoming disillusioned . . . all but Athena. Her solution always remained at the top of the list.

I recognized where we were headed, but I refused to give in to Athena's plan until we had no more time to find a different solution. I hoped, somehow, fate would lean in my direction and a path to save Earth would miraculously appear. It didn't seem to be happening.

In the meantime, the clock was ticking. They were having no impact on the Avalanche Clock for Earth. It was still counting down; world war was still raging as they read about its expansion in the newspapers and watched it on television, with the end still approaching. They needed to do something to stop Earth's Avalanche Clock and its progression and then reverse its direction. And, they needed to do it soon.

Athena and Anna were sitting at the kitchen table. Athena sat in her high chair, putting her at the same height as her mother when seated.

"Mom, did you get the web developer to update the new site for us?"

"No, honey. I haven't had a chance."

"It's important to get that updated. The Village members need that new information."

"I understand, honey, but there are only so many hours in the day and Bryan and I needed some time together — "

"Of course, of course, having quality time with Bryan is more important than saving the human race from extinction. Do you know how much worse it's gotten in the last few months, Mom? Do you know the Avalanche Clock will soon be moving faster, not slower and definitely not reversing its direction? Would you like to see some of the images of the spread of war? Would you like — "

"I don't need to see any of those horrific images, Athena. I've seen enough," Anna said as she got up and began walking toward the living room. "I'm sorry I can't clone myself, so we can get more done, but we are working as hard as we can and at the same time trying to keep our lives in balance, so we don't become sick. You just have to have some *patience*. We knew this was going to take time and that we wouldn't see results right away. We've done a lot in the past year. We simply need more time."

Anna turned to look back at her daughter as she reached the doorway. "Athena. *Athena*." Athena wasn't responding but sat in a trance, appearing to stare out the kitchen window. There sat a young two-year-old, looking like a five or six-year-old, but with the mind beyond any savant that ever lived; striving to master the saving of an entire planet of beings — almost seven billion of them — while keeping the Visitors, an alien species enormously advanced beyond anyone's dreams, from squishing them like we might step on an ant.

CHAPTER 41

THE CLONE

///

Athena's mind had stopped listening at the word *clone*. She had thought about it for some time but wasn't sure she could do it and she would need her mom's help. It was time. She had met a lovely young couple in the Village who were anxious to have a child but had not been successful. The wife, Lisa, was serving as the leader for Athena's first village designed to build an army of humans to spread her cultural virus, the Village of Oak Creek Chapter, the one that would emulate other Villages around the world, once her mother realized her approach of trying to discover the cause of their species annihilation would not work. Yes, Lisa would be the one.

That evening, after everyone else in the house had gone to bed, Athena sat in her favorite chair in Shirley's study, the room that had become her and her mom's office. She sat back, placed her arms on the armrests and focused her mind on Lisa Cromwell. She had entered Lisa's mind many times to help influence her thinking and her leadership of the chapter. She liked her a lot. She was bright, energetic, and committed. She was able to shape new members and keep their focus on Athena's goals better than anyone Athena had encountered. It seemed a combination of soft skills — chutzpah, charisma, and a flair for excitement. She had a natural gift to connect with people and leave a room with all those present wishing she would return. Athena explored Lisa's memory of her last period of ovulation. She should ovulate sometime in the next seven or eight days. Perfect, Athena thought.

That would give her enough time. She would need to go to the Library for help with this. Some things could only be done from within the Library to prevent the Visitors from learning about them. And visiting the Library would require her mother's assistance without her knowing what it was for.

///////////////////

The next day Anna was reading a book on Shirley's patio when Athena walked out.

"Mom, I'm sorry about yesterday. I was tired and frustrated with our lack of progress."

"I know, honey. You just need to be patient. We've done so much in such a short time."

"I was thinking about visiting the Library to ask what else we might do to help with our efforts. What do you think of that?" Athena crawled up on Anna's lap and snuggled.

"The Library can't share knowledge with us without the Visitors Council knowing about it. We can't risk that, honey."

"I was thinking of asking some questions. Perhaps there are things my mind is capable of that I'm not aware of and perhaps it would be good to plant a seed for the Visitors to hear, that we are being careful and want to be sure not to violate any of their laws. That would reduce their concern with us, wouldn't it?"

"Well . . . something like that might be possible — "

"Could we try? Even if the Library doesn't have any answers, at least I can tell myself I tried."

"I guess there's no harm in asking." She hugged her daughter.

"Let's have some breakfast and then we'll ask." They walked to the kitchen holding hands. Athena had fallen away from holding her mother's hand six months ago. She reminded Anna of herself as she became detached from her own mother.

"Suppose it's ridiculous to ask if I can go along?" Bryan asked.

"You know I can't do that," Anna said. "The Link has already said she can't engage with you. The Visitors now forbid the Links from absorbing a non-Visitor."

"Okay, got it." He picked up his breakfast plate and stomped out to the patio to eat by himself.

"Bryan." Athena called to him. "You could do me a big favor."

"What?" He yelled back as he dropped his plate and silverware loudly on the patio table.

"You could take my place at the Village conference call this morning."

"Kidding, right."

"No. Would you, please?"

Bryan grabbed his plate and utensils and came back into the house and sat down, grinning and eating fast.

"What do I need to tell them? Do you have an agenda I could use? How many will be on the call? Is there anything special they need to know? What —"

"Whoa . . . yes, it's an important meeting. I'll print out an agenda and go over it with you ahead of time," Athena said.

"Thought you were all upset that your mom and I were going too slowly," Bryan said, as he turned toward Athena with a smile growing on his face.

"Do you know the expression 'What's good for the gander is good for the goose'?" Athena asked.

"No, you got it back . . . oh, I get it . . . yes. Thanks."

After breakfast, Anna and Athena went to their office and closed the door. Anna reached out to the Link.

"Phronesis, Athena is with me. She wants to visit the Library and open a dialog on what she is doing with her abilities that would not violate the law of noninterference."

"That would not be possible, Anna."

"She would like to try. What if she traveled within my memories to the Golden Cube, where I have already been?"

"Well . . . as long as I do not assist her, I do not have to report such a visit. I feel her presence. Many ask about her."

"Can we do this without the Visitors learning about it?"

"There is great sensitivity to any actions associated with Athena. Everything must be reported . . . however, if she is able to go where you have been without my assistance, there is no requirement for reporting. And I am not privileged to know what she does once you are both at the Golden Cube. However, you may be in serious jeopardy should the Visitors learn of your assistance to her, Anna. But it is always interesting to go on an adventure to try something that has never been done before, even if it is dangerous, or maybe especially if it's dangerous."

She held her daughter's hand as the image of the Link dissolved in Anna's mind and in its place was the image of the vast three-dimensional space representing what Anna knew as the Library. Athena saw the same image as she entered her mother's mind.

"The central core of the Library, the Golden Cube, is its entrance. It is that speck of light in the distance, Athena." Anna held her daughter's hand tighter.

As they moved rapidly forward, it grew into the familiar brilliant translucent cube. They approached one of the surfaces and the recessed square with the imprint in the shape of a left hand appeared. Athena saw the image and the memory from years ago of the horrid nightmare of the woman who had died and left a message for her on a piece of paper. "The child is the key."

"This . . . is the Library, Athena. I don't know how he works exactly or even what he does or how to gain access or even what gaining access means, but you can sense the knowledge that is here. You can imagine any question and he has the answer . . . with some exceptions. It's amazing what he knows. But I'm telling you something you already know."

She glanced over at her daughter. Athena was staring at the handprint.

"Yes, Mom."

She seemed in a daze. Anna listened to her mind. Being here was exhilarating and creating a rush in her. There was so much immense power. It was like no other feeling Anna had ever experienced and now her daughter felt it. The vastness of the knowledge surrounding her was awe inspiring. As she stood looking at her daughter, she realized Athena created the same sense of awe in her that the Library did.

I began to wonder why we were here. Was there a way for her to access the Library? Why would she need to? The memory of looking at my daughter's hand in the Gilmores' car a week after her birth flashed into my head . . . "The child is the key." My heart began racing as I looked down at her hand and then to the imprint on the face of the cube. They were almost the same size.

"This is where I belong," Athena said as she stared at the Golden Cube.

"Where you belong . . . What do you mean, honey?"

Athena reached out with her left hand and placed it in the middle of the square.

"I'm not sure you —"

Unlike before, when Anna had tried this, there was a rushing sound, like the wind flowing over their ears. It became louder and louder. The

Cube began to glow brighter and brighter, as if the gold surface were heating up, causing it to radiate even more. Their hair was blown back from their faces. It was like the pure energy emanating from the Cube was pushing them. She could feel it against her skin. The Golden Cube turned bright white as she watched her daughter's hand being drawn into a hole in the light where the recessed hand-shaped keyhole had been. She gripped her daughter's other hand tighter.

Athena began drifting toward the keyhole. "Wait! Athena, no. Athena!" she yelled as she held on to her hand. As she passed through the keyhole her hand and their grip dissolved. A moment later she was gone; the rushing sound and energy subsided, and the Golden Cube dimmed, as if a portal had closed. Anna was left staring at it, only her daughter was not with her. She had this terrible feeling of being alone, as if she had lost her — an emptiness, as she realized her daughter's thoughts were no longer present . . . just like right after her birth. She was left with the memory of the message on the piece of paper she had held long ago in her dream . . . as she stood looking at the keyhole for only the second time in her life.

"Athena. Athena, where are you?" There was no answer. She reached forward with her hand and placed it in the keyhole. Nothing happened. She was not about to leave this place without her daughter. She tried concentrating, looking for Athena's mind. It was frightening. She couldn't be gone. She felt a dread begin to envelop her. Had the Visitors done something to Athena? Was this a trick on their part and was she now trapped inside the Library? Had they taken her? If she left the Library and returned to the Village would her daughter be there? If she left here, Athena might not be able to return, and even if she could exit the Library, she might be trapped in limbo between the Library and the Link, unable to navigate a mental path back to the Village, to their home. Oh God, where is she? She posed the question to the Library. "Where is Athena? I want my daughter back. *Where is she?*" There was no answer.

Athena materialized inside the Library next to a golden wall. She tried to focus on the vastness of the space in front of her. It was more like the size of a city . . . a large city.

"Welcome, Athena," the Library said. "What you are observing is the Library. We occupy more than 160 kilometers in all directions, over four thousand trillion cubic meters in volume."

"It is difficult to comprehend," Athena said.

"It is *impossible* to comprehend the breadth of our knowledge and influence, Athena. Our current capacity is sixty-five trillion holographic memory storage modules for use in storing the memories of all intelligent entities within the known universe, and many representing specific planets, places, events and time periods. They are all linked through their relational connections to one another. Most of these represent the combined memories and knowledge of the 2,441 planets that the Visitors monitor. Our memory storage modules are integrated with over two billion computational engines, using quantum, molecular, plasma, holographic and faster-than-light field-coupled technology. Each engine is designed to optimally assimilate and manage the specific type of knowledge it is designed for and to store, retrieve, and process it.

"We have realized a tenfold improvement in computational efficiency each Earth year from newly invented methods of computation within our knowledge creation systems factory. Using our robotic factories, distributed throughout our living organism, we continuously self-replicate and grow our storage, computation, energy, raw material and waste management systems."

The images and scenes of this vast living entity faded as Athena's vision returned to the entrance at the golden wall. She was standing on a wide catwalk that extended in a straight line and went further than her eyes could see. Adjacent to the catwalk, on both sides, were large glowing spheres, three meters in diameter and a meter apart, hung as if balanced against gravity by an invisible force.

"You are observing all the knowledge of the known universe. There are over five trillion individual memories currently stored in the Library, growing by more than sixty-five billion new memories each year."

"It's amazing."

"Yes. You are only one of *five* beings allowed to experience the Library, Athena. That is an easier number to contemplate, don't you think?"

The Library had a sense of humor, she thought. The spheres hung in columns and rows that extended in all directions, above, below, to the left and right, and in front of her. They were translucent, with hues of blue, green, and indigo, and had the appearance of an amorphous fluid undulating inside them. There were thoughts coming from them, a soft hum, more like a musical note, being sung by a tenor with perfect harmonic content and vibrato.

The smell of ozone was present, and she felt static electricity pulling on her clothing and hair as she walked by each sphere. Blue plasma arcs emanated from a sphere to her left and propagated outward with tremendous velocity in all directions, taking her breath away. As it passed through her, she sensed a flash of imagery, sound, taste, touch, and smell. The blue light faded into the distance.

She walked forward looking up at the spheres on either side of her. There were rows of spheres and then an intersecting perpendicular catwalk on either side, then more spheres and another catwalk, on and on as far as she could see. As she passed by the spheres she could feel the presence of life within them. Some spheres had a different feel to them; a subtleness of emotion—love, then anger, loneliness, depression, then anger again, and laughter, and whatever knowledge had been collected during the life of its occupant's mind. Others seemed completely devoid of emotion. She wished her mother were here with her to better sense the subtle emotions of the minds behind the spheres.

At the intersection of the catwalks was a clear transparent square. She stopped on one of them and looked down. Suddenly she descended rapidly as if riding in a high-speed elevator but with no feeling of acceleration, more like the spheres on the levels beneath her were rushing up to greet her. She lifted her eyes and she stopped on a new floor, as if the catwalk were now on a new level within the Library. She looked up and she felt a rush as she accelerated upward, passing what seemed hundreds of floors in a matter of seconds. Again, it felt as if the entire Library may have raced down to meet her. She lowered her eyes and came to a stop. She turned and thought about where she had entered and was suddenly transported to the golden wall she stood next to when she first entered the Library.

"Searching only requires you to think of the subject, the place or the being, and you will be taken there. Each sphere links to all possible associations. Just touch the sphere of interest and its knowledge will be available to you," the Library said.

She thought about cloning and she was transported to a sphere right in front of her. She reached up and placed her hand on its surface. She could feel the sudden expansion of her knowledge as if her brain had just absorbed all the knowledge and understanding of cloning — cloning everything, from individual cells to complex beings, even entire ecosystems.

"You have X2 access, allowing you to avail yourself of all knowledge within the Library, Athena, except that controlling or relating to the Library's action directives and certain Visitors Council functions. You should be aware that cloning is a very coveted function, known as the 'Gift' by the Visitors. You will not discuss this with anyone, Athena."

She sensed a serious tone used by the Library. She had so many questions to ask, unrelated to cloning but about how the Library worked. It was difficult to know where to start.

"How do you manage the growth of knowledge?"

"We are self-replicating. If you are interested, we can take you on a tour of the Library and show you how we collect, store, retrieve, and manage all the knowledge of the known universe."

"I would like that."

"It will take seven days."

"Oh. My mother awaits my return. I may — "

"Time in the Library is not the same as it is on Xynthanthium or on Earth, Athena. It is warped here in a manner that allows the Library to do many things while you or other earthlings experience what you call . . . the blink of an eye. We will begin with the acquisition of thoughts and memories."

Athena was transported to an enormous strange-looking machine. She was viewing it from a location that seemed to be miles above. Her perspective gradually changed as they descended toward the center of a very complex antenna structure that seemed to extend for miles in all directions. Huge plasma-charged fields undulated in front of her, displaying all the colors of the rainbow. She could feel the energy, like that at the Golden Cube, but much stronger.

"This is our receiving antenna array. It services all sources of input, gathering information from throughout the known universe at the same time. Each source has a unique signature. For example, your brainwaves are imprinted with a unique identifier multiplexed within the information content itself, telling the Library that the information belongs to you, where you were located when it was created, who else was aware of it, and the universal time . . . but *not* the universal time you know of on Earth.

No two individuals are the same, as each brain, as it is called on Earth, has a unique electrochemical character derived from a section of your DNA and imprinted on every telepathic thought and on the memories from the brain of nontelepaths. The number of combinations of your nucleotide base pairs that uniquely identify an intelligent member of your mother's race is in the hundreds of trillions. The Library can manage an input capacity of more than ten trillion sources, growing by more than one billion per Earth day. These are multiplexed for transmission and sorted as they arrive to ensure they are placed in the appropriate storage locations."

"How do you access the memories of beings across the expanse of space?"

"The Links and Orbs are used to access the minds of beings within their assigned area, region, planet, solar system and galaxy. These memories are stored locally and then forwarded here to us, almost instantaneously. We have communication stations on all of Xynthanthium's planets to provide a wide aperture and allow collections from all directions in the known universe. All memory sources are referenced to allow access based on the subject matter, time, location and entity, as well as other metadata elements, as Earth's *Homo sapiens* refer to them. Species that can experience emotions allow us to search for similar levels of emotion or feeling, or emotional reactions to such feelings. If you wanted to seek knowledge of the beings who have killed a member of their species, associated with the feeling of greed, for example, we could reveal that to you."

Athena was suddenly visualizing thousands of beings flowing rapidly past her in a blur. The flow stopped, and a hologram showed someone actively engaged in killing one of his own species with a strange-looking weapon, while expressing the feeling of greed.

"Or if you wished to see only those experiencing love who have killed a member of their species who were also in the top 1% of the most intellectual members of their society . . . and who then showed remorse for their act of violence . . ."

Athena now saw a few hundred floating holograms passing in front of her.

"That was interesting."

"We will now move to the first stage of knowledge management . . ."

Athena spent the next week learning how the Library functioned from the capturing of knowledge, storing, processing, and analyzing it and about the fascinating architectures of the Library used for knowledge creation and for knowledge modification.

"I am intrigued with the part of the Library associated with knowledge creation."

"New knowledge creation resides at the highest levels of intellect within the Library. It is one of our favorite functions. The creation of new knowledge follows an eclectic process from multidomain knowledge correlation, innovation and hypothesis creation; modeling and simulation; empirical validation; analysis; and finally, new knowledge storage — a true architectural labyrinth. Twenty percent of all the Library's resources are devoted to this most important element of knowledge management. We find the discovery of new knowledge by this process . . . well . . . thrilling, as earthlings would say."

She continued her exploration of the Library for what seemed days but with no feeling of fatigue or hunger or any number of the normal reactions after spending such a lengthy time with any task. It was invigorating, actually. She gained insight into the architecture and history of the Library's creation and its evolution to become the most intelligent entity in the known universe.

When she asked questions concerning the control of the Library, he denied her any knowledge of that or of his degree of independence to act on his own. She noticed he always responded in the plural, using "we" and "our" when referring to the Library, almost as if the Library consisted of more than one being. She learned that there were only four Visitors who had the kind of access she was privileged to possess . . . or perhaps somewhat less access than she had.

Athena had lost track of time. "I need to return to my mother. Could we return to the knowledge associated with cloning?"

She was suddenly located back in front of a memory sphere.

"After placing your hand on the sphere, think of being inside the sphere," the Library instructed.

She reached up and placed her hand on it and thought about being in the sphere. She suddenly materialized in a space that looked like the inside of a sphere but much larger than the three-meter sphere she had touched. After some time exploring the floating holograms inside this large space, she understood what was necessary to clone the equivalent of a male gamete or sperm. The Library would assist her.

"I should return to my mother. She will be worried about me."

"Indeed, she is worried. You may return at any time, Athena. We are available to you to address any topic, subject to the constraints we mentioned when you first entered our . . . mind, as earthlings would call it."

She hadn't thought of being in the mind of an intelligent entity. It was difficult thinking about him this way . . . a being with a volume of over four thousand trillion cubic meters . . .

"Are you a collective mind; one made up of all the memories of the universe?"

"No, of course not. There are collectives in some societies, but it is foolish to believe that the merging of many minds results in the most advanced intelligence in the universe. We are a distributed intelligence, not unlike the rudimentary portion . . . the human portion . . . of your brain with but a hundred trillion synapses. The other part . . . that which makes *you* truly unique, Athena, is a replica of our architecture, although on an infinitesimal scale. Still, this remains amazing. You, Athena, represent the smallest incarnation of the Library ever achieved with over one hundred thousand trillion synapses. Like the human brain, it is the architecture that creates intelligence, an ability to bring to bear a multitude of knowledge and memory — to analyze, to simulate, to dream, to invent and create that which has never been. There is a certain synchrony that occurs when these many functions, that your Visitor mind possesses, are merged and harmonized. And here lies intelligence at its core. The clarity of knowing *you* can think — self-awareness — to be able to concentrate on a thought. At that point, you can bring to bear all the elements of your knowledge and focus on insights and understandings that lead to new knowledge discovery surrounding that thought. We do the same . . . just on a much larger scale."

"But I don't have the abilities you have. You know . . . everything."

The Library laughed. "There is no end to knowledge. We can never *know* everything, Athena. Perhaps at some place in time we will share some of our *additional* abilities with you. But at the moment, it would be dangerous. There is much you must learn and develop. And, as you have noted, you will need help, which is why you are here to learn about cloning."

The Visitors don't laugh, Athena thought. How is it that the Library does? The Library didn't comment on her thought. Her mind returned to the entrance at the golden wall inside the Library.

"We will visit again soon, Athena."

/ / / / / / / / / / / / / / / / / / /

After ten more minutes of Anna calling and yelling for Athena, there was the sound and feel of the wind growing in intensity and a bright light formed in place of the hand-shaped keyhole as energy once again flowed out against her. The Golden Cube grew larger and brighter. A moment later Athena drifted through and rejoined her. Their minds returned to their bodies in the Village and Anna leapt to her daughter and hugged her.

"I thought I had lost you."

"You didn't, Mom. I heard you call, but I couldn't communicate back."

"Are you all right? What happened in there?" Anna asked as she felt her daughter's arms, looked into her eyes and then hugged her again. Nothing seemed to have changed. She was here.

"I'm fine. The Library . . . was very helpful. He made me feel . . . much better," Athena said as she thought about the Library's reflection on intelligence and who she was: "You represent the smallest incarnation of the Library."

Anna sat back, aghast, staring at her daughter as she listened to her thoughts. *The smallest incarnation of the Library?*

"I'm so glad you're all right." She hugged her tightly again. "For a moment, I thought the Visitors had trapped you."

"The Library showed me the history of his existence. It was fascinating. How long was I gone?"

"Maybe thirty minutes. It seemed like an eternity."

"That's interesting. I was with the Library for over a week. Then I heard your voice asking where I was."

"A week? How could you have been there for over a week?"

"What's all the hugging?" Bryan asked as he entered the room. "It's getting close to the time for the Village to meet, Athena. Going to show me the agenda?"

"Sure, Bryan, it's right over here on the desk." Athena pulled away from her mother's grasp and walked to the desk, pulling a sheet of paper out from a stack and handing it to Bryan.

"How was the trip to the Library?"

"Amazing," Athena said.

"Harrowing," Anna said.

Bryan looked up from the paper at Athena and Anna and frowned.

Five days later, Athena entered Lisa's mind and performed one of the most profound and astounding acts available to the Visitors — the creation of living matter at a distance, a human cell with unique properties, using nothing more than the atoms, molecules, and proteins in Lisa's body, and focused electromagnetic energy that pervaded the universe and was controlled by the Library. It was terribly exciting to create life; it was astounding to create living, intelligent matter with the complexity of a human cell, able to manufacture and replicate itself autonomously once she and the Library had finished creating it. The Library had rendered the architectural framework using the knowledge of Athena's cells, both human and Visitor.

This was far different than what Athena had done as a young child with her toys. Giving inanimate objects some intelligence wasn't the same. This was the creation of life that could replicate, differentiate cells, and grow into an intelligent being, able to think and dream, something only a very limited number of the Visitors were capable of doing and even fewer were authorized to do. She had learned all this inside the memory sphere on cloning.

Later that evening, Lisa became pregnant when her egg interacted with the cell Athena and the Library had created. Athena's clone began developing at a phenomenal rate.

The human part of Athena had this enormous desire to tell her mother what she had accomplished. She wasn't sure her mother would understand. She was certain she would not approve. She decided to wait.

On Xynthanthium, after observing Athena from his Life Pod, Segam asked for an emergency meeting with Fliona and Aliana. They met in the inner sanctum of the Visitors Life Exploration Organization, where their mental exchange could not be recorded.

"What is the reason for an emergency meeting, Segam? Has something unexpected happened?" Fliona asked.

Segam was smiling. "I have very good news, but I wanted to tell you personally . . . and privately. Much sooner than expected, Athena has entered the Library."

Fliona and Aliana's bodies began to turn slightly purple in color as they sat at the conference table. The ceiling and walls of the room seemed to come alive with the sudden change in their feelings. Waves of color migrated across their surfaces, reds and blues intricately intertwining to become the most beautiful tapestry of rich purple.

"Excellent news," Aliana said.

"This is truly a moment of amazement, Segam. How were you able to verify that she achieved this?" Fliona asked.

"She . . . was given something by the Library." He hesitated as they watched him expectantly. "She was given . . . *the Gift*," Segam said very quietly but deliberately, as if concerned that someone might be listening, but no one could hear or intercept his mental exchanges within this room. He stood very still, with his hands on the back of the chair at the head of the table.

The walls took on a much more somber look as the room turned darker. Segam waved his hand and the walls returned to a neutral color and the room brightened.

"*Impossible*. There have been only three within the past one thousand years who have been given this ability and the authority to use it, and they were all Visitors," Fliona said, as her skin began to turn a darker purple. She stared at Segam as she stood and began walking around the room. "Why would the Library have given her such an extraordinary ability?"

Aliana sat motionless as she listened to the Visitor she revered most within her society.

"There is one more revelation," Segam said in a slow, serious tone. "Not only has she been *given* the Gift . . . she has *used* it."

Fliona turned abruptly as she faced Segam and began speaking in a very soft voice.

"This is very disturbing news. I had not anticipated this possibility." She turned to look at one of the walls as it began to exhibit the characteristics of a deep foreboding vortex of a murky black hole at the point where her eyes focused. "She has manufactured a *living* organism . . . *an intelligent life form . . . self-replicating?*"

"We need to consider the implications of her possessing and using this ability." He hesitated before continuing as he paced the floor. "Should anyone . . . Visitor or human come to understand this knowledge . . . well, I needn't discuss the likely consequences."

"No. There is no doubt what action would be taken," Aliana said. "And there would be no limit to the resources employed by the Chairman to ensure his actions were successful. They would surely destroy Athena's entire planet."

"For now, only Athena, the Library, and the three of us are aware of this. I am certain it will remain so. This aside, she now has access. The second door is open. I could not be more pleased."

"Yes—but," Fliona said as she continued walking around. "Our entire objective is put in jeopardy. I cannot believe this will go unnoticed. One interaction between Athena and the Visitors' Council and they will know."

"I disagree. She has extraordinary abilities. I believe she can prevent her mind from revealing this. There are signs that she may even be able to prevent someone from entering her mind. We must be patient and observe."

"We need to have her give it back, and the life form she has created needs to be destroyed," Aliana said.

"I agree, Segam. She has to give this ability back," Fliona said.

"That is impossible. This is something only the Library can do. You both know that. Only once in our recorded history has that ever happened, and you both know the outcome . . . the Visitor was eliminated. We cannot go back and change what has happened. We can't allow this to interfere with our plan. We have come too far. She has access to the Library. And, we must remember, receiving the Gift was not something *she* did. The Library gave her this power, and in so doing, the authority to use it. I don't know his reasoning, but *he* did it."

The minds of the three members returned to their residences, uncertain about the future of their endeavor. They had achieved the next step in their plan to change their own planet—gaining access to the Library—but at what cost? The revelation of Athena receiving and using the Gift could destroy eons of planning.

Several weeks passed and Athena was in the bedroom with her mother getting ready for bed. They were crawling under the covers together. Her mother was very tired and anxious to sleep.

"Mom, I wanted to talk to you about something."

"Sure, honey. What is it?" Anna asked as she began to doze off.

"You know Lisa is expecting."

"Yes, isn't that wonderful. They have wanted a child for so long."

"Yes, well . . . I helped them."

"Great, honey . . ."

"I helped with their pregnancy."

"That's nice . . ."

Athena could tell her mother's mind had already begun moving to an unconscious sleep state. Her conscious mind heard the words, but her unconscious mind was trying to interpret their meaning. She wouldn't remember much of this conversation. "I . . . worked with the Library to find a solution."

"Very thoughtful . . ."

"I think she's going to have a girl."

"That's great."

"It's probably best if we don't say anything to her about my helping."

"Good plan . . . difficult to explain . . ." Anna was almost asleep.

Yes, it would be, Athena thought, very difficult to explain.

CHAPTER 42

THE VISITORS, THE VILLAGE, AND THE WARFIGHTERS

//

As Earth's Avalanche Clock continued its relentless countdown, now showing a little more than two years remaining, Bryan and Anna made little progress in their search for the cause of Earth's ultimate demise and in discovering how to stop it. Expanding war and pandemics were at the top of their list, but dealing with these, other than with Athena's cultural virus, seemed hopeless. These diseases, war and pandemics, both cultural and physical, were so vast and involved so many nations that, even knowing how they all would die didn't provide a clue as to how to stop Armageddon from destroying humanity. Basic supplies were becoming scarce as more and more resources were diverted to support the war efforts.

It seemed little of what was happening around the globe was influencing the affluent members of the small retirement town of the Village of Oak Creek. People still played golf, bought groceries, watched sporting events and went about their daily lives. But Anna could feel the tension in the air. More of the population were talking about the challenge of a pandemic that might spread to their somewhat isolated village or the impact of an all-out thermonuclear war on the air that they breathed and perhaps the groundwater that they drank. Anna also noticed another matter of concern.

Lisa, the team leader for the local "Athena Village," gave premature birth to a beautiful girl, who looked very much like Athena at her birth. Anna wasn't sure what Athena had done to help Lisa with her pregnancy, but she wanted to know. The resemblance was remarkable. Her parents named her Aphrodite, and she grew neurologically and physically even faster than Athena.

Anna found Athena by herself in the study.

"Athena. I notice that Aphrodite looks remarkably like you did when you were first born. What exactly did you do to help with Lisa's pregnancy?"

"I worked with the Library to modify her ovulation so that it increased her chances of becoming pregnant. I think what the Library did modified Lisa's egg."

"Does she have any of the traits you have, those provided by the Visitors?"

"I think she might. It will be valuable having another set of hands to help us."

"There's nothing you've done that will attract more attention from the Visitors, is there?"

"I can't imagine getting any more attention than we have, Mother. Besides, we need her help."

I was certain there was more to this, that Athena had been more involved than she let on. I could sense it from the emotions I felt when she spoke, an ever-so-subtle feeling of guilt. But, I didn't want to know, and I didn't want to divulge this accidentally if I found myself back in front of the Visitors Council. I could feel fear creeping into my mind as I began breathing faster.

Over the next year, Aphrodite grew at a remarkable rate, especially her intellect. With her assistance, Athena began a more concerted effort to use her virus to influence the minds of world leaders engaged in war. Since they were no further along on discovering how they might stop Armageddon from consuming the entire world than they were several years ago, Anna had little argument to dissuade her daughter from experimenting with her virus. Athena had agreed to narrow her focus to those countries where war was rampant. Over the next few months, they saw a remarkable change in the outcome. The expansion of war in the countries infected with her cultural virus had slowed, and in some countries, peace accords were being fashioned by opposing forces.

That evening Anna was awakened in another dream with Phronesis.

"Athena's efforts have not gone unnoticed by the Visitors, Anna," Phronesis said. "Had they been aware that Athena contributed to the creation of another hybrid Visitor-human being, the Council would have taken catastrophic action against her and most likely the entire population of *Homo sapiens*. As it is, her actions with the virus she is spreading far exceeds their threshold for violation of noninterference. You and she have been accused of using Visitor knowledge and capabilities to modify the future of Earth's human evolution."

Anna stirred to an almost conscious state as she listened. Had she said "creation of another hybrid Visitor-human being"?

"Evidence has been gathered on the creation of the initial Athena's Village in Oak Creek and on the direct influence of world leaders using the temporary cultural virus crafted by Athena. Segam has successfully delayed action by the Council of Seven through the clever application of our society's rules for the management of life on other planets, but this is only temporary. You must be very watchful. They will be coming for you and our daughter."

"What do they expect? Our Avalanche Clock is counting down relentlessly. Are we just supposed to watch while our world comes to an end?" she asked. "I'll let Athena know we need to be more observant."

I was reluctant to ask more about the hybrid creation — I didn't want to know. What could I do about it anyway? It is done, and I can't change that. Not knowing the details might be better if I'm asked about this by the Visitors. Oh, shit. I can't help myself . . . "I know Aphrodite is . . . different. Do you know . . . how . . . different she is? Is she just like Athena?"

"No, not like Athena, exactly. Only the Library can answer that question. He assisted her in this creation. But she is definitely a hybrid Visitor-human, and this creates great danger should certain members of the Visitors Council ever discover what she has done. You should never recall this to your memory in the presence of the Visitors Council members."

/ / / / / / / / / / / / / / / / / /

On Xynthanthium, Segam and Fliona met to discuss the situation on Earth.

"It is just a matter of time before the Chairman finds a way around the Council's rules to overcome your objections to inhibiting Anastasia and Athena, Segam," Fliona said.

"I am confident there are no holes in my argument to prevent Council action against me as the Lead Visitor for Earth, Fliona. The Congress of Lead Visitors has resisted the Visitors Council's intrusion in the past, and the statutes are clearly on our side," Segam said as he walked to a chair in the conference room and sat down.

"He is a devious and powerful adversary. I would be very careful."

"I agree. I won't underestimate his courses of action as we proceed. But we need Athena and Anastasia to succeed in developing their skills on Earth. Dealing with the Visitors empire will be far more challenging. I will attempt to persuade the Chairman to wait for the annihilation of Earth's dominant species to satisfy his desires. He seemed receptive to this when we last spoke. That should give us the time we need to act."

"You are aware he is lobbying the other members to act now to inhibit them?"

"Yes, Aliana informed me of her conversation with him. As is his usual approach, he creates false pretenses to justify his actions against Anastasia and her daughter. I am not overly concerned with this. Even with the more damaging evidence against them, I have the authority to decide the appropriate action, not the Council."

"I note the Chairman has called an unscheduled Council meeting for tomorrow."

"Yes. I have heard from the prefect that there is an urgent need to bring ten more planets under our observation. I suspect that will be the agenda item."

"Then I will see you at the meeting, Segam."

"Yes, thank you, Fliona. Until tomorrow."

"There is no chance you will miss the meeting?"

"None. The Chairman would use such an opportunity to pass a Council resolution to inhibit the most extraordinary, as humans would say, 'cat burglars' of all time."

"I wish you would be less casual about these matters, Segam. We are on the precipice of the most monumental change in our society ever conceived and we are now closer to achieving it than ever before. We can't underestimate the actions of the Chairman."

"I recognize the importance of this, Fliona. We have had numerous setbacks over the millennia. I know this time we will succeed."

Late that evening, notice of a one-hour delay in the Council's normal meeting time, scheduled for the next day, was transmitted to all council members. Sometime following that, the Council was informed that the meeting would be moved back to its original time and that the meeting would take place in a protected room at the Life Exploration headquarters in Xynthanthium, requiring the physical presence of all members.

The next morning, the Visitors Council members began gathering for their meeting.

"I don't understand why we don't have earlier warning of these changes. The administrator must do a better job of scheduling," Vilach said.

"I agree," Darmon said.

"You two need to think about performing your roll as members of the Council of Seven and stop complaining," Kelong said as he sat in the chair adjacent to Fliona. Aliana was to her left. Fliona turned toward Aliana and spoke quietly.

"It is unusual to reschedule at such a late hour. And isn't it curious that the Chairman has chosen a protected room, requiring us all to be in physical attendance?"

"Yes. That is interesting. Have you seen Segam this morning?"

"No, and from in here we are unable to reach him," Fliona said as she stood and walked toward the door.

The Chairman entered the secure conference room and placed his hand on Fliona's shoulder, encouraging her back to her seat. "Good morning, my dear. Please take a seat. We are about to begin." The Chairman surveyed the members around the conference room. "I see we are all here except for Segam. We will proceed. I am confident Segam will join us as soon as he can." The Chairman sat at the head of the table.

Fliona noticed a glint of pleasure in the tone of the Chairman's voice when he spoke. Not at all like him.

On the far side of Xynthanthium, Segam was meeting with another ministry director to discuss the assignment of Lead Visitors to the ten new planets coming under the watch of the Council of Seven.

Segam's thoughts drifted as the minister continued to laboriously discuss the candidates. Strange, he could not sense the presence of Fliona or Aliana, nor the Chairman. He turned his head away from the minister and looked at the clock that suddenly appeared in his mind. An hour until the Council meeting, but where were Fliona and Aliana? He began searching for the other members of the Council and as his mind moved from one to the next and the next, tension rose. He was racing through the possible circumstances that could prevent him from finding any of the remaining Council members.

"Segam. Are you paying attention? Which of these two do you feel would be better suited to the Lead Visitor role for planet 875237? Segam?"

"I'm sorry, minister. I appear to be late for another meeting. I must leave."

"We are in the middle of making important decisions here. Your Council meeting isn't for another hour."

The minister should not have known about the Council meeting. Something was wrong. "I'm sorry, minister, I must leave. I will reschedule our meeting." He stood and walked quickly out of the minister's office as the minister called forcefully for him to return.

/////////////////////

Segam raced to the transportation dock, where his personal transport waited. He climbed in and instructed the transport to take him to the Life Exploration headquarters. It was a twenty-minute trip. He called the Chairman's office.

"I'm sorry, Segam, the Chairman is in a meeting. Weren't you planning on attending?"

"Yes, but I was informed it was to start at 10:00 in conference room LEH-7."

"No. The meeting was moved back to 9:00 in LEHP-13. A notice was sent early this morning, Segam."

"I never received that notice."

"That is not possible, Segam. I sent the communications myself. You were definitely on the list and you responded that you would be there."

"Thank you. I am in route." If he followed his present plan, he would arrive twenty-five minutes late. He was certain this was a deliberate plan to keep him from the meeting. "Time to LEH?" he asked his transport.

"You are 18 minutes from LEH, Segam," his transport responded.

Too long, he thought.

The Chairman had presented the motions to the Council in the agenda, against the strong objections from Fliona and Aliana. "The subjects, Anastasia Broulette and Bryan Wilder, interacted with both the Orb and, in the case of Anastasia, with the Link on the planet known as Earth, number 212579. Anastasia and her hybrid daughter, Athena, half Visitor, have used their derived knowledge and powers to change the course of planet 212579. Their efforts were designed to change the survival outcome of Earth's dominant species, known as *Homo sapiens*, the highest form of life on this planet. A group known as 'Athena's Village', as well as numerous military and civilian leaders, have been modified. The Council has met with the subject, Anastasia, on two previous occasions, issuing a warning and discussing the parameters required for her actions. In violation of the Council's primary directive, the subjects are condemned to Inhibition. How do we vote?"

Fliona and Aliana were outvoted in their attempt to delay the proceedings until Segam arrived.

The secretary to the Council documented the mental votes and the Chairman affirmed the decision. "So ordered the Council. Action to be executed by the Lead Visitor at the earliest possible . . ."

Moments later, following the introduction of two additional administrative motions, the walls in room LEHP turned red and the door to the room opened. Segam walked in as Fliona and Aliana turned. The Chairman sat stoically without looking.

"You are late, Segam," the Chairman said as the clock on the wall appeared. It was now 10:11.

"My apologies, Chairman Petrarch. I had difficulty with my transport from the Ministry Headquarters building. I hope that I have not missed anything significant." The walls returned to their soft blue tint as the door closed and Segam took his seat to the right of the Chairman.

"You have arrived just in time. We were just finishing up on a series of motions relative to a troublesome planet for which you are the Lead Visitor," Chairman Petrarch said. "As previously seconded and agreed, how votes the council?" Four of the seven members voted in the affirmative.

"May I make a point of order, Chairman Petrarch?" Segam interjected. "Votes related to orders of Inhibition require the affirmation of the Lead Visitor, if present."

"Yes, of course, Segam. You are correct. On motions involving *Inhibition*, the Lead Visitor is required to affirm. As this vote is related to the corrective measures associated with our observation probes, it does not. We previously passed several motions in your absence related to Inhibition. You can review the minutes following the conclusion of our meeting." The Chairman turned to look at Segam. Segam could feel the pleasure in his words as he gloated. "Do I hear a motion for adjournment? As I do, we are adjourned."

Four of the seven members filed out of the protected room leaving Segam, Fliona and Aliana standing by themselves as the entrance to the room closed and the hue of the walls turned from red to a rich blue color.

"What was the true cause of you being late?" Aliana asked.

Fliona raised her hand to stop Aliana. She walked up to Segam and stood directly in front of him. "You are not Segam," she said.

Segam stood staring at the two of them as the walls once again turned red and the entrance opened. Segam entered the room and stood next to what looked like his clone and the entrance closed and the walls turned blue. "What has happened?" he asked.

Aliana appeared startled as she looked back and forth between the mirror images of her mentor.

"I am afraid, Segam, that the damage was done before your creatively crafted avatar arrived at the proceedings. The Chairman had already taken the action in your absence."

"My apologies to you both." Segam turned toward the Avatar he had hastily created during his trip to the LEH. The avatar turned to leave the room. As the walls turned red and the entrance opened, Segam received an urgent telepathic message from the Chairman.

"Actions were taken to prevent me from arriving on time for the meeting. I am all but certain they were of the Chairman's making," Segam said.

"There was nothing we could do without you being here," Aliana said.

"I understand," Segam said.

"What can we do?" Aliana asked.

"I just received the Council's order for their Inhibition. I am required to execute it."

Fliona turned slowly and walked to her chair. "Perhaps there are options that will satisfy both requirements — the requirement to Inhibit and our requirement to save Anastasia and Athena."

Segam seemed to sense something significant in Fliona's thinking.

"Both requirements? But how?" Aliana asked.

"We must leave that with Segam, Aliana. Too much said now may reveal the outcome to . . . others, who would be less inclined to support what Segam *must* do."

Segam could sense the forcefulness in Fliona's voice.

That same afternoon, Segam entered the Life Pod in his residence, immersed himself in the red undulating cloud of the golden ellipsoid capsule, and communicated with the Library.

"Library."

"Yes, Segam."

"On planet 212579, known as Earth, identify the Athena Village leader and initiate actions to inhibit her and those within this 'Village.'"

"Does the nature of their death have any parameters?"

"As painless as possible and natural. There should be no indication that the actions were the result of any extraterrestrial involvement."

"Action has begun."

"Also inhibit all world leaders involved in military action or whose country is involved in military action and whose cerebral cortex has been modified by Athena through the spread of her cultural virus. Any form of death is acceptable. But, again, do not allow the discovery of any extraterrestrial involvement."

"Action has begun."

"I am conflicted with my next action. Perhaps you can assist me."

"Of course, Segam."

"I have been studying Anastasia and Athena on planet 212579 for more than four Earth years. From their absorption and being given knowledge and abilities of our own species, they represent unique specimens in our history. It would be valuable for our society to learn more from their actions and thinking. In a way, they allow us to look back at the earliest periods of our own society and to understand how we evolved into what we have become, the nature and role of emotions and feelings in our society and the ability to perceive and experience these for sentient beings."

"We agree. Such knowledge and observation would be most valuable. We too are interested in studying these subjects."

"I may be required to take action to Inhibit them."

"You don't have a choice, Segam. The Council has voted. Under Rule 10459.23, the required actions are quite clear, paraphrased here: 'The violation of noninterference in a society or culture by any member of the Visitors or a member of another society, using anything derived from the Visitors' culture, which results in a modification of the other cultures normal evolution, shall be punishable by Inhibition . . . through the taking of memories or other means as appropriate.'"

"You are required to *order* Inhibition. Would you like to review other incidents from species outside our solar system and how these individuals were Inhibited?"

"That won't be necessary. Do you see any other resolution?"

"No. You are required to *order* their Inhibition under the Rule. However, your actions do not guarantee success. We estimate a 40% probability of success against Athena, a 70% probability against Anastasia and an 85% probability against Bryan . . . assuming the element of surprise is preserved. If they become aware of an attack, the probabilities of success are reduced."

"I see. And you believe my obligations under the rule will have been met by *initiating* the action?"

"Yes. Such actions have never failed against members of another species we have discovered and observed. The probability of success with these three is lower due to the likely modification of the neurological structures of Anastasia and Bryan and due to the hybrid nature of Athena. Athena's is very difficult to assess due to the inherent uncertainty of her neurological makeup."

"If the actions fail to Inhibit them, am I obligated to initiate further action?"

"There has never been a case of this nature, but no, you are not required to take subsequent action . . . if you are *unaware* of its outcome."

"Initiate actions to inhibit Anastasia, Bryan, and Athena."

"Does the nature of their death have any parameters . . . assuming they die?"

"No. No parameters for their inhibition." Segam knew that painful inhibition was easier to defend against, as the subject was aware of what was happening.

"Action has begun."

"Do not inform me of the outcome associated with this last action."

"Do you wish to be—"

"Thank you, Library."

"You are welcome, Segam."

CHAPTER 43

THE VISITORS ACTIONS

///

It was a sunny day in the Village of Oak Creek when Aphrodite's mother, Lisa, returned home with her daughter. They had been attending a swimming class. Her mother stopped to get the mail from the mailbox and they walked in together. Aphrodite was now eighteen months old, looked like a four-year-old and was more advanced intellectually than Athena had been at this age. She had Athena's and Anna's long, thin blond hair and looked very much like Athena.

She walked into the living room and sat down on the floor to watch a NOVA science program on the Milky Way galaxy. Her mother plopped down into the leather chair near her.

"Aphrodite, your swimming today was marvelous. You made it all the way across the pool without touching the bottom. That was wonderful," her mother said as Aphrodite got up from the floor, walked over and crawled onto her mother's lap.

"Thanks, Mommy. I really like swimming. Can I have something to eat?"

"Sure, honey. I'll make you a sandwich in a minute. I want to look through the mail first." She kissed her daughter on the head. "I can still smell the chlorine in your hair. You'll need a bath tonight. I still can't get over how much you resemble Athena. Except for your size difference, if I didn't know any better, I would think you were twin sisters." Her mother smiled down at her and walked into her study.

Beyond her Village leader functions, Lisa was a practicing psychologist. Papers were piled everywhere in tall stacks on her desk, some over a foot high. She wasn't known for her organization skills. There were books filling every inch of a five-foot-high, wall-length bookshelf. A large picture window looked over a small flower garden behind her desk. She sat down and began to sort through the mail. A small package had been delivered to her mailbox along with other letters, bills, and miscellaneous junk mail. She unwrapped the package and discovered a small box in the shape of a cube, about two inches on a side. The lid had her name embossed in the cardboard. She lifted the lid and found a ball-shaped object wrapped in gold foil paper. She smiled as she removed the foil-covered ball from the box. It was most likely a unique gift from Athena. Setting it on her desk, she unwrapped the foil and pressed it flat on her desk. The ball inside the gold foil was jet black and glistened in the light from the window behind her as she sat for a moment admiring this beautiful object. She could sense the subtle smell of a rosebush.

///////////////////

Athena was sitting in Shirley's study when the smell of a rose interrupted her train of thought. She jerked and stood as her eyes widened. There was a memory of death associated with this smell. She could not place where this memory had come from, but along with the distinctive smell of a rose and the ominous feeling of death was an image of her friend Aphrodite. Death was near her. Athena quickly closed her eyes and entered the mind of her friend, in her home less than a mile away.

"Aphrodite are you all right?"

"Yes, I'm fine, Athena."

"Do you smell the scent of a rose?"

"No, but I smell chlorine," she said as she glanced around sniffing the air. "I'll look around though."

"I think it is the Visitors. There is a memory of death associated with this odor, so be careful," Athena said.

Aphrodite stood and began to walk quickly around the room, smelling the air. She walked to the back of her house and into her bedroom and her bathroom. There was a scent of lavender soap as she walked around the bathroom.

As Aphrodite walked into her mother's study, Lisa was sitting looking at the glistening ball. Her mother reached for the box, looking for a note from Athena as Aphrodite walked toward her.

"Hi, honey. I'll make your sandwich in a minute." Lisa frowned at her daughter. "Are you all right? You look like you're not feeling well."

Aphrodite took a deep breath through her nose and walked around the room, watching her mother's gaze follow her. She could smell the scent of a rose. Aphrodite glanced over at the pile of mail on her mother's desk. Her eyes settled on the mysterious ball. She walked toward the desk, smelling the air as she went. The scent of the rose became stronger.

Her mother looked down at the glistening jet-black ball.

"Oh," she said as she smiled at her daughter. "You smelled this beautiful ball." She picked it up and rolled it in her hand. "It's just like Athena to send something mysterious like this."

"It feels warm and so soothing. I think it's from Athena." She lifted it closer to her nose to smell it. Aphrodite ran at her mother and slapped the back of her hand as the ball flew from her mother's grasp across the room and crashed into a bookshelf, leaving in its wake the smell of a rose.

"Aphrodite," her mother yelled.

Aphrodite watched as her mother rubbed her hands while looking down at them. Moments later her mother fell forward on her desk and didn't move.

"Mommy, are you okay? Mommy. Mommy what's the matter? Athena! Somethings wrong with my mom," Aphrodite said as she shook her mother, who remained silent and unconscious. "Mommy. Get up, Mommy. Why won't you wake up?" Tears ran down her cheek.

/////////////////

Athena's face tightened as tears welled up in her eyes. She watched in her mind as her friend Aphrodite, the child she had cloned, cried at her mother's side. Lisa's heart had experienced sudden cardiac arrest. She was dead. Athena was searching for the source of the information — the rose odor, the feeling of death, and Aphrodite. Where had this come from? Who had planted these memories in her mind and tried to warn her?

Anna came running into the study after sensing her daughter's distress and her feelings of enormous anger.

"Athena, what's happened to Lisa?"

"Oh, Mom. Someone's killed her," Athena said as her mother hurried over and hugged her.

"Lisa . . . no, no," Anna said as she took hold of her daughter's arms, held her away from her, and knelt down to look her in the face.

"Mom, you're hurting my arms."

"I'm sorry, honey," she said as she loosened her grip on her daughter. "What happened?"

"She died. It was the Visitors. I received these feelings." She began to walk around the room. "The smell of roses, a feeling of death and then an image of Aphrodite, but it wasn't Aphrodite — it was her mom."

"The Visitors . . ." Anna leaned away from her daughter.

"There was a strange object that came in the mail and when Lisa picked it up . . . she died. It smelled like a rose, just like the memory of the scent and the feeling of death I had in my mind, and it was associated with Aphrodite."

"But who would send you a warning ahead of time?"

"I don't know."

Anna reached out and pulled her daughter close to her and wrapped her arms around her. "Where's Bryan?" her mother asked. We have to warn the others. Can you reach out to the Village members and let them know how this happened and — "

Athena gasped and pulled away. Her eyes widened as she glared at her mother. "The Library . . . all our Village members have been killed."

"Anna," Phronesis voice communicated, "An action has been taken."

Anna stood.

"The Village leader and all her associates, including leaders from the forty-five targeted nations, have been Inhibited." There was a pause and then she communicated again. "The Visitors Council has taken this action."

Glass objects around the room exploded as Athena walked passed them. Anna put her hands to her temples to try to relieve the pain she felt from her daughter's anger.

The Link communicated again "This was action to correct your intrusion into — "

"*I don't need to hear that!*" Athena yelled as the communication with the Link was abruptly cut off.

Anna stood in silence as tears welled up in her eyes. "Oh, dear God . . . Aphrodite . . . I'll get her." She hurried to drive to Lisa's home, returning ten minutes later carrying Aphrodite into the study and putting her down. Aphrodite ran to the chair where her best friend was sitting, climbed up and sat next to Athena. Athena reached out and put her arms around her. They sat holding each other, thinking about the Visitors' actions.

Anna walked across the crunching glass to her daughter and Aphrodite, squatted down and put her arms around the two of them.

"All these wonderful people, all gone." Anna shook her head as she cried. "Some of my best friends, Betty, Jamie, Kiel, and . . . Lisa," she said as she turned to look at Aphrodite. "I'm so sorry, Aphrodite."

"Their deaths were peaceful, Anna. They felt no pain," Phronesis said.

"They didn't do anything to injure the Visitors or use something they shouldn't. These were innocent humans," Athena said as objects in front of her exploded away from her, crashing into the walls in Shirley's study. "I did it. Why didn't they come after *me?* I would have shown them pain worse than Inhibition."

Leaders of the war-torn nations around the world, whose minds had been influenced by Athena's virus, were selectively eliminated through death by natural causes or assassination. Earth's Avalanche Clock would soon begin counting down faster, as peace accords were abandoned, cease-fires were ignored, and war raged on, fiercer than before. The wave of death would again gain strength and migrate across the Earth like a tsunami.

CHAPTER 44

COUNTERMOVES

///

Anna, Athena and Aphrodite sat huddled together for a long time in the study not talking. Bryan and Carol were shopping for groceries with Shirley and Phyllis. Anna reached out to Bryan's mind.

"Bryan, the Visitors have . . . they've killed all the members of the Village."

"We're on our way," Bryan said.

Anna watched Athena slide off the chair and walk to the window with her arms crossed. She began a dialog with the Library as Anna and Aphrodite held each other and listened.

"We will initiate the new virus we have discussed. How long will it take to complete the design and manufacture the first sample of the agent to place in a host?" Athena asked in a calm voice, like a surgeon who could not save the limb of a patient but was focused on saving her life.

"One Earth day. Once you have identified the host, we will need to know their location."

"Proceed. I will provide the host's location shortly."

"What is this about a new virus, Athena?" Anna asked. "Is this different from the cultural virus you've transmitted to the Village mem — "

"We created a new virus . . . the Library and I." Athena spoke with firm confidence as she stood staring out the window. She began speaking aloud, in an almost calm, matter-of-fact way as she walked across the room.

"It is an activated neurological virus. We will implant it in a human host. It will grow rapidly, infecting the cells of the host and then lie dormant until it is activated. It will spread to others, as it is highly contagious and airborne. When activated, it will influence the host to act. This virus . . . is different from the cultural virus; it is permanent and far more aggressive; it will change everything. It will influence behavior through the manipulation of genetic material. Then it will convert the innate motivations and learned dendritic structures of the brain — those housing aggression, greed and selfishness — into collaboration, selfless commitment to the betterment of society, and the pursuit of knowledge as the ultimate goal of mankind here on Earth. It will change the world and generations to come. You will be better, stronger and more powerful than the Visitors. It will lead to all we have wanted ever since your interaction with the Orb and the Link — "

"But you can't take away the will of a human, Athena." Anna got up and walked toward her daughter. "You can't take away our desire to think independently, to make our own decisions. That would be inhuman. You can't do it. There has to be another way. It was one thing to influence behavior with your temporary cultural virus did, but this."

"Do you think the influences we were promoting with the members of the Village gave humans that freedom, Mother? I'm taking the path we planned all along, to achieve the necessary end — if that influence did not work, we would need to control the minds of man. I delayed this decision, thinking the Visitors would be tolerant of our actions to personally influence human behavior from one human to another, but no, they weren't tolerant. Instead they killed. They won't be able to stop this so easily.

"Earth's Avalanche Clock is once again speeding up. The virus will stop it. This is the only path for us to take. The Library agrees." She walked back to the chair she had been sitting in, climbed up, and put her arm around her friend.

Aphrodite sat emotionless and not speaking. The tears had dried on her cheek.

Anna stood staring at her daughter. "You *can't*, Athena." How will this virus change *us*, impact *our* desire to achieve, *our* desire to dream and create?"

I began thinking of my mother controlling me. This was worse than that. There would be no escape to a sanctuary like mine at the Rock House.

"Aphrodite, you agree, don't you?" Anna asked. "Athena, you can't do this." Aphrodite continued to sit with no visible emotion. Anna could sense Aphrodite's mind was unconcerned with Athena's plans as she thought about the loss of her mother and what the Visitors had done.

"We conducted extensive modeling of the virus's effect on human thought, creativity, and ingenuity, Mom. The adverse side effects are minimal. The worst we have seen is reduced productivity due to less competitive feelings. That's a small sacrifice." Athena walked toward her mother, staring at her. "You need to realize we are now fighting a war against the devastation of the human race, and in war there are casualties."

"Casualties? War? I thought we were trying to stop war. Now it appears we are about to start another one, a war with the Visitors. If you do this, Athena, the casualties will be *us*, our way of life. How can we keep this from changing who we are? What if it has a terrible effect on our country? What if it destroys the way our economy works, but allows . . . I don't know . . . communism to thrive? This could have huge consequences."

"We will simply need some time to adjust, to adapt to the change. To live, we must survive this change, but we will do more, we will thrive, and to do that I must master this change for mankind. This is what I am going to do. We can only look at the longer view. The path we are now on will lead to the annihilation of your species. We must act before it is too late."

"Annihilation of your species!" Athena was looking at us as if we were something other than what she was. She was planning on fixing us, changing who we are; turning us inside out.

"How will this virus spread? Must everyone be controlled by it? Can't you limit its use?"

"The virus will spread faster than any pandemic we have ever experienced on Earth. It will be like a highly contagious cold virus, benign at first, until we activate it once all the hosts are infected."

"Hosts? These are real people, Athena. Humans — like Aphrodite, your human grandfather and grandmother. You must realize these aren't hosts in a test tube. This sounds like some grand science experiment," said Anna, walking around waving her arms, trying to make her daughter understand how wrong this was. "Can't you limit it to the areas of the world that need controlling?"

"We've designed into it the ability to regionalize its impact and allow tailoring it to a particular cultural or behavioral characteristic. So, if we have an aggressive warmongering culture in a small country in Asia, we can strengthen its effect there. We can focus it to do what we want it to do, but no one will be immune. Mankind has a disease — greed and selfishness — a way of thinking that leads to conflict and war. We need to treat that disease, or it will lead to our own extinction, Mother."

"So . . . Bryan, you and I will be infected as well. How will that affect our feelings, our motivations, and who we are? And what if the real cause of the downfall of our society turns out to be something else? What if it is an environmental issue or another deadly pandemic? What you're doing could be much deadlier, and your virus won't stop these."

"No, but it will allow us to focus on these other possible contributors to solve them more quickly, rather than fight each other. This is our only path."

Anna listened to her daughter's thoughts as she agonized over the idea of controlling all of humanity. She was staring at Athena as she sat holding hands with Aphrodite and planning the most monumental change to human behavior ever.

I began seeing Athena, my own daughter, as an alien life form imposing her will on the world. How could she do this? How could I get her to change her mind?

"I'm trying to save mankind, Mother, something the Visitors don't care about. Preserving noninterference is more important to them than six billion human lives on Earth. As for the Library, his solution was one of the most elegant and illuminating creations he had ever worked on. It was a captivating experiment for him.

"I conveyed to him how important this action was to your race and that we must do everything possible to correct the path humanity is on; that this was, and is, our only hope to save us from ourselves *and* the Visitors. We must master the changes looming ahead or we will all be crushed by the stupidity of man – through his ignorance, his greed, his lust for power — and by the unfeeling actions of the Visitors."

I was searching for understanding, something that would assure me that this was the right thing to do. How much sacrifice was necessary? When do the ends justify how we accomplish them? But I was also thinking about the Visitors, their reach, as demonstrated in this heinous act against innocent members of the Village and peacemakers around the world. When they learned about Athena's new actions, their wrath would have no boundaries of decency or compassion. And they had made the punishment for violating their noninterference directive unquestionably clear . . . something far worse than death itself, as I remembered the frightening experience of being condemned for eternity stripped of my memories . . . leaving just enough for me to know I had lost everything

I desired in life. My heart was pounding in my chest. I began breathing deeply as I tightened my fists and clenched my teeth. The agony of deciding the better of two evil paths — supporting my daughter or fighting her — was closing in.

Phronesis reached out to Anna. "Fix what is wrong on Earth today, Anna; fight the battle with the Visitors tomorrow. To do otherwise will result in no choice at all, as the death that is coming, death demonstrated by the atrocities of evil men, now fighting wars on your doorstep, is drawing near."

"But the dangers, the potential sacrifices, how can I — ?"

"The Avalanche Clock is progressing. You will soon have no choice but to watch. By choosing another path, you are choosing death for your species."

I thought about my life before the discovery of the Orb, which seemed eons ago. How simple it had been, how comfortable and safe. My walks in the sun to Bryan's house; climbing the hill to our Rock House, entering our secret hideaway, our escape from the rest of the world. We would sit and talk and share. I wiped the tears from my eyes. I so wanted to run and hide in that sanctuary, hide from the universe. And then the memory of the earthquake that had uncovered the Orb and destroyed my use of the Rock House; my terrible nightmares of the coming doom — now they were almost upon me; there was no more time. I must choose. I turned to face my daughter as the clarity of my choice seemed to drift out of the fog.

"All right . . . Athena," I said reluctantly. "We can't let them win, no matter what the consequences; we can't stand by while our world comes to an end. It's our world, not the Visitors'. We will fight this war and do what we must in order to survive."

"Yes, Mother. That is exactly what we will do. We must never forget the Visitors don't care about us; they have no feelings of compassion. They would be just as pleased to monitor the apes and the dolphins after mankind destroys himself. We can die watching or we can die fighting. I intend to fight, and when we beat them, we won't just live, we will thrive, for we will master change."

I thought of my quest. This was it. Was this how we would save mankind? It seemed it could work. My confidence was suddenly boosted as I began to see this the way Athena did - as our only chance for survival. To change and adapt.

/////////////////

The militia fighter, Deka Mensah, the first human to be tested by Athena's new virus, knelt, peering out the frameless window into the darkness. Here, in this small and isolated African village, war had raged on for three long years. This town was not much larger than a postage stamp and hardly worth saving, but for the fact that her distant relatives were from here. She was on the second floor of a bombed-out two-story building. She looked around. This had been someone's home; now it was rubble; chunks of wood framing, cloth from furniture long since destroyed and burned, lay on the wood floor. Now the floor was more like swiss cheese with holes a person could fall through with one wrong step.

Dirt pushed into a pile on the floor served as the only cushion for her knees, a canteen half filled with warm water the only relief for her thirst, and two extra clips of ammunition for her survival. She had long ago gotten used to feeling hot and sticky from dried perspiration and the salt around her eyes that stung. She smelled the black grease smeared on her face, making her appear more like a shadow than a person to be killed.

As a "spotter" for her militia group, it was her job to watch for the enemy and shoot to kill if she saw them. She felt no connection to this enemy. They were faceless, nameless unknowns, trying to kill her before she killed them. This was her family's village, their country, and their people. These invading hordes that had swept across her lands, coming from a neighboring warlord's home, conducted ethnic cleansing of her family's roots, raping, pillaging, and destroying. They weren't going to take what belonged to her family. It was either eat or be eaten, survival of the fittest.

War took on a life of its own after a time, at least for those who were forced to fight, conscripted into service to carry a rifle and shoot what moved. It ate the lives of those serving as its arms and legs; it spewed out its dragon's breath, measured in bullets, bombs, and face-to-face combat and breathed in the stench of death and devastation. It was a beast with an endless appetite, destined to never stop, to never give in until those who served it buckled under to its will, and, over time, became it. And those who did so never wondered why; theirs was to do.

Her career as a cultural anthropologist, before the war, brought the memory of her ancient ancestors, the *Homo sapiens*, to mind. They forged their existence not far from her current village. They had emerged as social creatures, realizing colossal strength through the disruptive discovery of collaboration and the ability to win the battle for vital resources with more effective weapons than their adversaries. There was little difference now, over one hundred thousand years later.

Deka was one of the lucky ones in her family, someone with a burning desire to succeed, to overcome poverty and find a path to education and a better life. She had returned to her homeland out of an innate commitment to family and to help those who had helped her escape this place and this challenging way of life. Strange, she thought . . . now she was trying to save the very place she had worked so hard to escape from.

Before, she was a cultural anthropologist; now she *was* war. She knew the enemy was out there as she waited for movement. In the daylight, there had been hundreds entering the town from the west. Now they were quiet, hidden in the darkness. She repositioned herself to stop the tingling in her legs. The wind shifted, and she could smell gunpowder and a whiff of death. She heard the pop of a gun in the distance; the sound was a long way away. She kept her head low and remained dead quiet as she peered over the ledge of the window into the street below. Snipers could put a bullet between her eyes at over a thousand meters. She would never see it coming and it would arrive before she could react to the muzzle flash if she even saw it. She could barely make out the adjacent buildings or see the difference between the doorways, the window openings, and the brown dirt. The enemy blended in with them like wind in the night. She used sound to sense movement, as her exhaustion began to play tricks with her eyes. She glanced and then ducked back. Soon dawn would break, and the serious fighting would begin again. It never ended until someone died, and then you moved on to the next, and the next, and the next.

As the Library prepared for the first test of the virus to change human nature, he simultaneously manipulated hundreds of thousands of the targeted cells in Deka's brain. Of those, only a few hundred were likely to be transformed. They would grow the first viral seed for the experiment in this test-tube human, this unsuspecting host, employing technology millions of years beyond the thirty-round Kalashnikov automatic assault rifle she held in her hands. The brief feeling of the electromagnetic restructuring of brain cells would be lost in the tension of her surroundings and her exhaustion from trying to stay alert for the past four hours, the month-long siege that now wrapped itself around her, and the years of this never-ending war.

It would take weeks for her body to replicate the aberrant cells that would infect her existing neurons and dendritic structures that made her memories — structures that had been sculpted by decades of learning how to fight and how to win and thousands of centuries of subtle genetic molding of the primordial survival instincts engineered in *Homo sapiens* through their DNA and resulting brain structure. Once sufficient viral loading was achieved, the Library would activate the modified cells and structures, allowing them to unravel the undesirable long-term memory patterns and neurological instinctive behaviors. Within days after activation, the host would begin to feel subtle desires, motivations and drives to collaborate, to work together and find peaceful means to survive and thrive. Her old memories of independence, fighting to win, and aggression would be gradually replaced by these new ones. War would no longer consume her as its evil was extinguished. And then Athena and the Library would know if the virus was working as designed and what, if any, abhorrent side effects expressed themselves.

Athena sat on the couch in Shirley's study in the Village, as she thought about the small war-torn African nation and about Deka, their candidate for testing of the virus that would change the world — or at least the humans that occupied it. Deka was over six thousand miles away, across vast stretches of unfamiliar land, water, culture, and history. If the virus failed, or if the side effects were devastating and ended up killing her, at least the event would be isolated. The Library had estimated her chances of survival as a warrior at less than 5%. Her chances of survival with the virus were improved by a factor of seven, even if it didn't work exactly as expected.

"How soon will we see changes in her once the virus is activated?" Athena asked.

"It will begin quickly if the cells have replicated sufficiently. Deka's desires to collaborate with the enemy will initially seem foreign to her. She is likely to resist, fight against them, but her mind will win over her training and instincts. It will feel like a revelation to her, as if it had been there all along and she just discovered the need to find a peaceful solution. When the virus infects more and more cells, the host's drive to find collaborative solutions will become even stronger and eventually overwhelming. They will feel empowered to pull people together.

"Once our testing is complete, we must activate all within the region at once or we risk the behavioral changes creating an enormous advantage to the opposing side, those not activated, those still fighting to win and desiring to kill. As in all species influenced by innate survival instincts, there will be some who strongly resist, but our statistics suggest these will be very few — it will create its own enormous raging war within them."

"Will the changes to the population of those around her move as quickly?"

"The rate of cellular change varies by age, neurogenesis rate, and the inhibitory factors of the immune system of each human, but within a few months, all those infected will reach their final state as their new neurons and neurological structures stabilize and take control, or should we say . . . influence.

"Controlling militia fighters carrying Kalashnikovs as a test of the virus is one thing, Athena, but we must reach those who control the weapons of mass destruction, especially nuclear weapons. We must rely on the spread of the virus, human to human, and probabilities. It will be harder to infect those in secure areas where they are more isolated from the contagion. Even if the virus reaches these individuals, there is no guarantee it will result in the desired outcome 100% of the time. If the very survival of a nation that possesses nuclear weapons comes into question, there is a high probability that those who control them will resort to their employment as an action of last resort. Even the launch of a single nuclear weapon has a high probability of causing a catastrophic domino effect with multiple players using their nuclear warheads, thus rapidly accelerating the Avalanche Clock. At which point — "

"The beginning of Armageddon," Athena said. "What steps can be taken to prevent this?"

"If Anastasia were to engage with the Link, we should be able to locate the personnel responsible for employing nuclear weapons and other weapons of mass destruction. We cannot accomplish this without reporting it to the Visitors Council," the Library said.

"I'll ask Mother to request this from the Link."

Athena sensed her mother's thoughts as she and Bryan returned from a trip to Sedona with Shirley. A moment later she heard the front door open.

Anna entered the room at a quick pace. "Athena, Shirley was in the drugstore and learned from the owner that someone in the past week has been asking questions about us, a middle-aged man showing a government ID, looking for an adult, a man and woman in their early twenties, and a young child, who may have come into the area a little over four years ago."

"I knew they'd find us," Bryan interjected.

"Dr. Tyson and NASA are here. Most likely, they have learned nothing further about the origin of the Orb since they took him from you and Bryan," Athena said as she stared out the window. "I believe Dr. Tyson is anxious to see you back at the SOC to learn what he has suspected but been unable to prove since you escaped — that the Orb gave you certain *abilities*, ways to communicate with it. We should consider moving to another location, one more isolated."

CHAPTER 45

THE AVALANCHE CLOCK

//

Following the successful test with Deka Mensah—she had survived with minimal side effects—Athena and Aphrodite watched as their permanent virus was selectively released in several isolated regions among factions engaged in aggressive war with one another. Bryan and Anna had redoubled their efforts to better understand, other than war, what was causing Earth's Avalanche Clock to decline at what seemed an ever-increasing rate. Athena engaged the Library.

"Library."

"Yes, Athena."

"We are analyzing the causes affecting the increased rate of decline of Earth's Avalanche Clock. Can you help us identify the most likely causes of this and compare it to the closest matches on other planets under observation?"

"Yes."

"What correlations do you note?"

"We observe many correlations. Twenty-two planets have similar planetary survival statistics to Earth, based on their locations within their galaxy, the structure of their solar system and their distance to their sun, as well as the evolution and diversity of life. Then there is the evolution of the dominant species of the planet; their food chain; availability of critical resources; and of course, and perhaps most important, how they evolved culturally. Only seven of these are within the range of the current rate of decline of Earth's Avalanche Clock. All show degradations in the dominant species societal engagements, ability to control the spread of disease, and effectiveness in their management of vital resources. These include war; uncontrolled pandemics affecting the dominant species;

failure to conserve vital resource use; and contamination of critical survival elements, similar to the food, water, and atmosphere used by *Homo sapiens* on Earth."

"What is the predominant cause of these planets reaching Avalanche Time?"

"We observe no single cause that dominates, Athena. It is the aggregation of these sources of degradation that influences the rate of decline of their Avalanche Clocks and the predicted outcome."

"If we can reduce the potential for worldwide war on Earth, how much will it affect our Avalanche Clock?"

"That is difficult for us to say."

"What if we could stop war on Earth, how would that effect our Avalanche Clock?"

"It would depend on many factors, Athena."

"Well, give us an example," Athena said in frustration with the Library's logic.

"If you stopped war on Earth today, we would incorporate that observation into our model of Earth's dominant species behavior. Since *you* could stop war, the effect might be minimal, as it would have little to no effect on the attitudes, behaviors, and actions of the six billion inhabitants of Earth. They would simply find a mechanism to start it up again, like a virus mutating. The likelihood of the continuation of their current observed behaviors would remain high; therefore, Earth's Avalanche Clock would not be affected much. *Much*, of course, is a very subjective term, time being one of the dominant influencing variables. Your virus motivates a different path, but even that path can be broken, reversed by a counter-virus — say one initiated by the Visitors."

Athena frowned as she glanced over at Bryan and then at her mother as they listened. "Why did the Library support the creation of the virus if it was not going to affect the outcome? So what action would have the greatest impact on Earth's Avalanche Clock?"

"Well . . . a *permanent* and immediate change in human behavior would have the greatest impact, assuming, of course, that it could not be reversed. But as it is, the Visitors Council may find a means to reverse such a condition."

"But what if mankind could stop all war, begin a focused effort on preventing pandemics, start an immediate effort to conserve its use of Earth's vital natural resources, and stop pollution and the degradation of elements critical to mankind's survival, such as water and air and the ozone layer. What impact would this have on Earth's Avalanche Clock?"

"This is very complex, Athena, and we cannot say what impact this would have, as we would need to observe how your species has actually changed. Such actions never represent an innate change in behavior, and the likelihood of returning to their current course is high, so perhaps it would have a smaller impact on your Avalanche Clock."

"Are you saying if we can reduce the probability of all of these factors, Earth's Avalanche Clock may not change much?"

"No. We are saying that knowing these changes does not allow a determination of the outcome. Further observation of the behaviors of your species is necessary. We, of course, would simulate all possibilities and determine the more likely paths . . . and their probabilities."

"But that could take many years. What if Earth's Avalanche Clock reaches its Avalanche Time before then?"

"We would view that as . . . very unfortunate."

"Unfortunate!" Bryan said. "It's a lot more than unfortunate."

"Library, what is the average time from Avalanche Time to annihilation of the dominant species for the twenty-two planets?" Aphrodite asked.

"Five months."

"Wow. That's awfully short," Bryan said.

"What is the variation of that average for the twenty-two planets?" Aphrodite asked.

"Library?" Athena asked.

"We observe . . . *a very small variation*, less than one Earth day."

Bryan jumped up. "That's impossible." He began walking around shaking his head. "How could all twenty-two societies die off in exactly the same amount of time from their Avalanche Time?"

Bryan looked over at Athena.

"How is that possible, Library?" Athena asked, as she looked quizzically into the space in front of her.

"That information is not available to you, Athena."

Athena stood and a picture frame on the end table next to her flew across the room and crashed into a bookshelf.

"What is the primary cause of annihilation of the twenty-two planets?" she asked.

"I'm afraid you are not authorized access, Athena."

"Is there a correlation between the intelligence level of the dominant species and their Avalanche Times?"

"No, we observe no correlation between the average intelligence of the dominant species and Avalanche Times of the twenty-two planets we are discussing."

"Well . . . what actions can we take now that would most influence the decline of Earth's Avalanche Clock?"

"We presume by 'influence' you mean reduce the rate of decline."

Athena shook her head and smirked. *"Yes, reduce the rate of decline."*

"The efforts you are presently making are the best course, although finding actions that would have a higher likelihood of success would be beneficial."

"But these aren't going to stop us from reaching Avalanche Time, are they?" Bryan asked.

"Library?" Athena asked as she walked over to the table where everyone was sitting.

"They . . . are not likely to with your present course."

Anna leaned away from the table as she felt an enormous wave of failure flow into her mind.

"The Library's answer suggests there are other causes . . . outside our control," Aphrodite said as she stood and walked to the window, looking up at the sky.

"What? That doesn't make any sense," Bryan said.

"If the model the Library has constructed is based on human behavior, coupled with the problems we are currently dealing with, we may not be able to ever fix it, short of Athena's virus, and that might not have enough time to have its desired effect before our Avalanche Clock reaches the end," Anna said.

"Well, whatever it is, it has to be something we can control," Bryan said.

"No. I'm not talking about a cause that we can control," Aphrodite said. "I'm talking about a cause we *can't* control." She turned and walked back toward the table.

"I don't understand, Aphrodite —"

"Aphrodite is suggesting there are factors other than the *direct causes here on Earth* that are making our Avalanche Clock progress to zero," Anna said.

"Oh, yeah, I get it, you mean like an asteroid hitting the Earth. Is that what you're thinking of?" Bryan asked.

"That's possible, but I am thinking of such things as interference or manipulation, things that have *nothing to do with things here on Earth.* Something *someone else* has control of."

"You're saying there might be *someone else* controlling our Avalanche Clock—independent of whatever our species is doing?" Bryan asked, frowning at Aphrodite. "Like, no matter what we do they will make sure our Avalanche Clock goes to zero and somehow, five months later, we will all die?"

"Yes. It's possible. We need to consider that," Aphrodite said.

"Who would want to control Earth's doomsday clock, and for that matter the doomsday clocks of *all* the planets being observed by the Visitors? What value could come by controlling another planet's survival?" Anna asked. "Besides, this is in direct violation of their own stupid rules of noninterference."

Athena posed the question to the Library. "Are there any advantages to the Visitors in controlling the destiny of the monitored planets?"

"First of all, Athena, the Visitors, as a society, do not control the destiny of anything. The Visitors Council makes all recommendations on behalf of the Visitors. If other planets were an active threat to the Visitors, there would be a distinct reason for the Visitors Council to eliminate that threat."

"What other reasons would the Visitors Council have for controlling the destiny of other worlds, if they are not a direct threat?"

"There are many, Athena, most based on the preservation of power and to demonstrate, through the control and influence of others, that no species could ever threaten the Visitors empire," the Library replied.

"Are there factors outside the control of the twenty-two planets that are causing each of their Avalanche Clocks to decline?" Athena asked.

"That information is not available to you, Athena."

"Now what?" Carol asked.

"Library, how can we determine what these factors might be?"

"There may be many possible ways, Athena."

"Who would be aware of such factors, if they existed?"

"That information is not available to you, Athena."

Athena and Aphrodite turned to look at each other.

"Perhaps — the Chairman," Aphrodite said.

"Or another member of the Cube," Anna said.

"Who is the Chairman?" Carol asked.

"He is the leader of the Visitors Council, like our president, only more powerful," Athena said.

"He is the one doing it, I'm sure of it," Aphrodite said suddenly, while nodding her head as she began thinking of him.

"What makes you say that, Aphrodite?" Anna asked as she stood and walked over to her.

This can't possibly be true. The Chairman controlling the Avalanche Clocks of all the planets. That's a direct violation of their own rules of noninterference.

Aphrodite turned to look at Anna and then turned back to Athena. "I don't know, but I seem to now know — the Chairman and the Library — they're the ones influencing the Avalanche Clocks."

Anna squinted in disbelief. "How could you know that?"

"How could one person control the annihilation of six billion people?" Bryan asked.

"It's a lot more than six billion, Bryan," Aphrodite said.

"I need to go back into the Library," Athena said, walking toward the couch.

Anna looked at her daughter as she turned and followed her. "That's not a good idea. The last time you entered the Library, it seemed you had difficulty getting out. Why don't we give your virus some time?"

"I have to do this, Mom. I'll be all right. Aphrodite knows something she could only have learned from her genetic memories, the ones the Library gave her. And I didn't have trouble getting out of the Library last time."

"Genetic memories . . . what genetic memories?" Anna asked as she turned to look at Aphrodite.

"It's happening again," Aphrodite said. A dazed look came over her. She stood perfectly still, staring into the space in front of her.

"Athena," the Library said.

"Yes."

"There has been a change in Earth's Avalanche Clock."

"What kind of change?"

"The Avalanche Clock now shows a change in the rate of decline."

"How long will it take to reach Avalanche Time at the current rate?"

"In Earth time, thirty days and seven hours."

"*Thirty days,*" Anna yelled. "How could that have happened?"

"It's—the Chairman and the Library," Aphrodite said, standing perfectly still.

Everyone in the room walked toward Aphrodite.

"Library, what was the cause of this sudden change?"

"That information is not available to you, Athena. Our model is constantly updated with enormous amounts of data and information."

"It was the Chairman, Athena. He and the Library did this . . . just now. The thoughts of the Chairman's actions just entered my mind. Don't ask me where they came from—they just suddenly appeared," Aphrodite whispered.

"I'm going back into the Library," Athena said as she sat down on the couch.

"This could be a trap set by the Visitors Council, honey. Please don't go. There has to be another way."

"We don't have a choice, Mom. If the Chairman is controlling Earth's Avalanche Clock, we need to find out how and stop him."

"What could happen if things go wrong?" Bryan asked.

"She could be trapped in there or, worse, they could remove all her memories." *Neurological inhibition. I didn't want to think about it, let alone say those words.* She put her arm around Athena. "We might lose her forever."

"You shouldn't go, Athena. We . . . we can't access the Library for help without you . . . hell, we can't even speak to him without you," Bryan said.

"Athena's right, Bryan. She must go. Communication with the Library isn't helping," Aphrodite said.

"Aphrodite's right, Bryan. The Library isn't helping us now or isn't allowed to help us. I've got to go. I've got to try and find out how the Chairman is controlling our Avalanche Clock. I've been there before. There are things the Library can communicate to me while I am there that he can't communicate while I'm here. Besides, if we can't stop this, in thirty days it won't matter where any of us are." She pulled away from Anna, leaned back on the couch, and closed her eyes.

Bryan moved to embrace her.

"I'll be all right, Bryan."

"What can we do here while she's gone?" Carol asked.

"Hope and pray Athena's virus works as expected in the sample populations," Anna said.

"That's important," Aphrodite said. "Even with the Chairman's actions, it is the actions of man that also control our destiny. If we can slow these by using the virus, it will give us more time."

Athena seemed to be whispering something to Bryan as she held his head for a moment. *Strange, I was unable to hear what she was telling him.*

"Library, allow Aphrodite to initiate the release of the virus," Athena said.

"Of course, Athena."

Aphrodite walked to the couch and sat next to Athena as they each reached out to hold hands and closed their eyes.

Less than a minute later, Anna gasped as she felt the sudden loss of her daughter's presence in her world, just like she experienced the last time she entered the Library. All she had were the past memories of her daughter.

Aphrodite opened her eyes. "She's in the Library."

They had agreed after an hour they would call to Athena to return. After half an hour, which seemed an eternity, Anna began conversing with the Library.

"Library, is Athena all right?"

"Yes."

"Where is she?"

"That information is not available to you, Anastasia."

"What is she doing?"

"She is searching."

"Has she . . . found anything?"

"When searching the Library, there is much that is found, Anastasia."

"Has she found anything helpful in stopping Earth's Avalanche Clock?"

"That information is not available to you, Anastasia."

This machine was irritating me. How could the Visitors Council be controlling the survival of all the planets they have discovered and monitor? It was a violation of the cardinal principle their society followed—not to interfere in the worlds they monitored. Why would they even want to? I recalled visiting the enormous room on Xynthanthium that displayed all the Avalanche Clocks. Each clock was ticking down to the end of the dominant species, whose lives it represented. Was this some kind of grand social-science experiment to observe what happened when the dominant species died? Could the Visitors be that cruel?

"Library, can I speak to Athena?"

"That is not possible. Once Athena has entered the Library, she is prohibited from communicating outside the Library, Anastasia."

At the end of the hour, Aphrodite called to her.

"Athena."

There was no answer.

"Library, where is Athena?"

"That information is not available to you, Aphrodite."

"Is Athena all right?"

"Yes."

Anna let out a sigh. "At least she is all right. Now how to get her back?"

"Library, would you ask Athena to come to me."

"That is not possible, Anastasia."

"How do I get her to return?"

"That information is not available either, Anastasia."

"How can I communicate with her?"

"As we have said previously, Anastasia, it is not possible to do that."

They waited in silence for hours, turning to look at Athena and then to the clock on the mantle.

Anna began a communication with Phronesis, mentally returning to her location deep in Bell Rock. The familiar look of the cave emerged in her mind.

"Can Athena return to the location of her body once she has exited the Library?"

"Yes, Anna. Since she visited the Golden Cube once previously, when she exits the Library, she can return."

"Can you find her? Is she all right?"

"While she is in the Library, I have no way of knowing, Anna."

"Can you assist us in any way on slowing Earth's Avalanche Clock?"

"No. This is under the purview of the Library. You will have to find another way."

Anna's mind returned to her body in Shirley's study. She opened her eyes to the image of Athena sleeping comfortably beside her as she held her hand. Bryan, Aphrodite, and Carol were sitting in chairs facing the couch. Anna reached over and stroked her hair as she bit her lip.

"Any luck?" Bryan stood and walked over.

"No," Anna said, biting her lip to try to keep from crying.

Aphrodite walked over to Athena and held her hand for a moment and then placed it back in her lap. Carol stood, her shoulders drooping as she sighed.

"I guess we wait," Bryan said.

They waited. Hours passed — then an entire day. "Where are you Athena? You've got to come back to me. You've got to."

Earth's Avalanche Clock had now reached twenty-five days. It was descending faster. They felt helpless. They had to do something.

///////////////////

The next morning Bryan walked into the study while eating breakfast. "I have an idea."

"What's that?" Anna asked as she stroked Athena's hair. Her daughter was looking pale.

"I need to go to Xynthanthium."

"What?" Anna turned to look at him with a frown. "You can't go there."

"Yes, I can. Athena took me there many times. My memories are vivid. We walked the streets and saw the beauty of the Visitors' planet. I have her memories of it. I need to go there and see if I can find a way for Athena to get out of the Library."

"But where would you look? The city's enormous. And you can only go where Athena has been."

"No, I can go to those places, but also anywhere you've been. I'd start at the building you entered when you learned the Link caused your pregnancy."

"Okay . . . but this is a bad idea — "

"I think it's a very good idea, Mom," Aphrodite said as she stood and walked over to Anna.

She had been calling Anna 'Mom' since shortly after her mother died. It made her feel better, especially with Athena gone.

"Bryan may be able to learn how we can reach Athena."

"But why that building? What could you possibly hope to find by going there?" Anna asked.

"You seemed to experience the friendliest people there when they told you about being pregnant, and once I'm in that building, I can see what I can find out. It's better than sitting here doing nothing." Bryan was pacing back and forth.

"Maybe I should go with you," Anna said as she walked to him. He brushed right passed her. She could feel his mind raging over Athena being trapped in the Library.

"No, you need to stay here. If you hear from Athena, she may need your help. I'll be fine, and I can reach you if I run into trouble." Bryan walked to the couch and sat next to Athena, staring at her while she appeared to be sleeping.

Anna walked over to Bryan. "I can't afford to lose you too, Bryan." Tears formed, and she bit her lip where a previous cut began to bleed. She put her arms around his neck and held him. She could feel his frustration. Every day that passed was one day closer to the end of their species on Earth and one more day that Athena hadn't returned.

He pulled a tissue from his pocket and dabbed the blood on her lip. "I'm coming back. I won't leave you."

"Oh, Bryan." She hugged him again and they kissed and held each other.

Carol entered the room. "Dr. Gilmore is coming this afternoon to check on Athena. When I mentioned to him she had been asleep for three days, he said she would need immediate hydration. He will put her on an IV. He recommended she be moved to a hospital for examination, but I told him no."

I almost cried hearing Carol mention a hospital. That's all we needed. She looked at her daughter as she ran her fingers through her hair. She looked so vulnerable. *Athena was all alone in the Library, maybe trapped by the Chairman, and . . . I didn't want to think what else. Then my mind felt the confidence growing, as I thought about how powerful she was and her relationship with the Library . . . 'the smallest incarnation of the Library', Athena had shared in her memories of her last trip. She could get through this, but I needed to get her back.*

"I'm going to Xynthanthium, Carol," Bryan said, holding Athena's hand.

"You're kidding." Carol walked over to stand next to the couch.

"No. We are running out of time and options. I'm going to see if I can find a way to get Athena out of the Library." He looked right at Anna and smiled. "Don't worry. I'll call if I get into trouble."

Bryan closed his eyes and lay back next to Athena, as Anna reached across Athena and kissed him. He opened his eyes to look at her. "Tell Dr. Gilmore not to stick me with a needle while I'm gone."

She smiled as Aphrodite came over and sat next to Bryan. She held his hand and stared at him. His face went blank for a moment. Anna couldn't tell what Aphrodite was communicating. He closed his eyes again and searched for the memory of his trip to Xynthanthium with Athena.

A moment later Aphrodite announced, "He's on Xynthanthium."

As Bryan walked adjacent to a large body of water to his left, he thought of Anna and of the building she had described to him where she had learned of her pregnancy. He found himself standing in front of the large tunnel-shaped entrance. He placed his hand on the surface and was absorbed by the building. It took his breath away. It was different than being absorbed by the Orb. Anna had described what it was like entering an intelligent building, but the feeling had to be experienced. It was *very* strange. He felt a soothing comfort inside this building, as if he were wrapped in the arms of a person, someone who was excited to see him, someone welcoming him.

He stood motionless in a sea of illuminated atoms. He stepped forward and the building seemed to flow around him. He could feel it, sort of.

"Can I help you?" a voice in his head said.

"I'm Bryan."

"Oh yes, Anastasia's best friend. Welcome."

He smiled and was relieved that someone here knew him. "I need help. My . . . I mean, Anna's daughter, Athena, is lost. I need to find her and get her back."

"Oh, I remember Athena. She is part of us."

"Yes, she is," he said as he looked around trying to find who was behind the voice speaking to him. "I think she's in trouble and needs my help. Can you help me?"

A moment later, he was transported to a room with a table and eight chairs. Transported was the wrong word. It was more like he evaporated and reappeared in this room. It happened in a blink. He was alone. The room had strange pictures mounted on the walls with surfaces that seemed to undulate. He remembered these picture frames from one of Anna's visits, but that was where the Visitors Council met. "Oh, God, I hope I'm not there," he thought. He pulled out a chair and sat down. It was just like Anna had described as the chair formed around him. It was the most comfortable chair he had ever sat in. A Visitor suddenly appeared in the seat at the head of the table.

"Hello, Bryan. Welcome to Xynthanthium. I am surprised to see you here."

He could feel it, but he had to ask. "Are . . . you a friend of Anna's?"

"Yes, I am one of only three friends Anastasia has here on Xynthanthium."

Bryan raised his eyebrows. The name *Segam* entered his mind. "We have a problem. Athena—"

"Yes, I am aware of that. She is trapped in the Library."

"Yes, and Earth's Avalanche Clock is now only twenty days from the end."

"You want to know how to get Athena out of the Library. I'm afraid I can't help you with that."

"There must be a way. I've come here to help get her out."

"That's very admirable, Bryan, but it won't be possible."

Bryan sensed Segam almost laughed at the thought of him helping to get Athena out of the Library. "What if I went to where she is?"

"You are not allowed in the Library. Even if there were a way for you to enter, your presence there would be immediately detected. You would not like the outcome of such a circumstance."

A gloom descended on Bryan's mind as the room darkened.

"Athena . . . gave me something. A gift she called it . . . before she left. She said if she needed help, I could use it to help her."

Segam's eyes seemed to squint as Bryan felt him exploring the memories in his head. He stopped squinting and sat back in his chair. "That is a rather remarkable gift she has given you."

"What? What is remarkable about it?"

"What Athena gave you . . . provides certain privileges."

"Can I go to where she is with it?"

"Yes, it appears you can, but what would you do if you found her?"

"If I couldn't get her out . . . I'd change places with her."

"You came here to get her out . . . and you're willing to change places with her?" Segam asked, staring at Bryan. "Perhaps that would be possible, but I urge you to reconsider. Athena's abilities far exceed your own. You would be much more vulnerable . . . virtually helpless in the Library, much like a child in a factory with extremely dangerous machines and far more dangerous caretakers."

"I have to try. She . . . is more important than I am. She's the only one who can stop Earth's Avalanche Clock."

"That is true. Athena is far more important than you are."

Bryan didn't like the way Segam said that. He recalled the memory of Athena standing in front of the mirror in Shirley's house, looking at her future. Perhaps this is what Segam was thinking. He watched as the Visitor sitting opposite him sat back in his chair and closed his eyes. The room became darker as the walls and ceiling changed to a darker shade of blue.

"It would be very dangerous. You may not be able to return . . . ever." He opened his eyes and stared at Bryan.

Bryan hesitated. "I'm . . . willing to take that chance," he said, and his mind focused on Segam's words . . . *may not be able to return.*

Segam stood and walked around the table, grasping Bryan's hand.

"Are you certain you want to do this, Bryan?"

"Yes," he said without hesitation.

A moment later, they were transported over a vast distance into a large three-dimensional structure with thousands of floors that went on for miles. Bryan gripped Segam's hand tighter as they moved toward the center of the structure. It grew larger as they approached what seemed to be a bright box. It was a cube, gold in color and appeared to be translucent. The Golden Cube, he remembered from one of Anna's dreams.

"It wasn't a dream, Bryan. It was Anastasia traveling here in her subconscious mind, just like you are now. This is the entrance to the Library."

They moved toward one face of the Golden Cube; it was just as it appeared in Anna's dream. There was a depressed imprint of a Visitors' hand slightly to the left and below the center of the Cube's face. "This is where Athena first entered the Library."

Segam didn't speak, but then the Cube began to rotate until an adjacent face was in front of them. There was a depressed imprint on this face as well, but it was in the shape of a Visitors' head and face. Bryan looked at Segam. He turned toward Bryan and gestured with his gaunt arm and hand inviting Bryan to step forward with him.

He stood next to the face of the Cube as Segam moved his face into the depression while holding Bryan's wrist and pulling his hand to the surface of the Cube.

"Do not linger long, Bryan. I wish you success. If we do not meet again, I admire the courage of Athena's best friend."

Courage . . . Athena's best friend . . . he'd never been described like that before. It gave him confidence on what might be a one-way journey. He thought of Anna and their last kiss in Shirley's home. The cube became brighter and brighter until it was almost blinding as Bryan felt his body being pulled through the side of the cube.

"Good luck, Bryan. Move quickly to find a means for Athena to escape. As quickly as you can . . ."

An instant later he was inside a vast expanse of large translucent spheres, maybe ten feet in diameter, in rows and columns that extended as far as he could see. The spheres had a silver appearance to them with soft undulating glowing regions that appeared to move inside them. He turned to look to his left where Segam had stood a moment earlier. Segam was gone and there was a solid gold wall in his place. He was standing on a catwalk between two of the rows of spheres.

He began to walk away from the wall. He could feel electricity building in the air as his hair was pulled toward the spheres when he walked passed them. He could sense life inside. It was as if faded dreams began and ended as he walked from one sphere to the next. He couldn't make out what the dreams were about or whose they were, just the faint touch of many different experiences they seemed to create in his mind.

Long strings of high-voltage traveling arcs crackled as they ionized the space between two of the spheres ahead of him, reminding him of a Jacob's ladder. Each of these arcs expanded, creating new arcs with adjacent spheres. This process continued outward at enormous speed, creating a crescendo of beautiful blue light in all directions propagating across the spheres. "Wow." A moment later, a propagating arc came toward him from below, building in intensity and flashing past him as it continued its journey across what must be millions upon millions of spheres. As it passed, he could feel a surge of feelings that took his breath away.

He walked further along the catwalk and every few moments he would see the initiation of these beautiful blue arcs, while others flashed past him coming from different directions. Some seemed to be coming from such a distance that he could only see the glow of a blue wall coming toward him as it approached and flashed past. He turned right on the catwalk at the next perpendicular intersection. These intersections were spaced every two rows of spheres, allowing the inhabitants of the Library to walk up to each and every sphere, although, so far, he was alone . . . at least there was no one here he saw. But he didn't feel alone, he felt like he was in a crowded city with millions of inhabitants walking past him. He thought about the place he had entered, then turned and walked back, taking a left on the catwalk and looking down toward the golden wall. The wall seemed to extend in all directions as if the cube interior had expanded to a size infinitely larger than the one he observed on the outside with Segam.

"Athena," he thought, and a high-voltage traveling arc appeared again moving outward, as a giant ball of light propagated away from him. He turned around and Athena was standing directly in front of him.

"Athena!" He dropped to his knees, grabbed and hugged her.

"Bryan. You're here." She stood, looking pleased as a smile grew on her face.

"I came for you. You've been trapped in here for three days."

"But how did you get here?"

"I traveled to Xynthanthium, searching for you. I met a Visitor named Segam and he helped me, using the gift you gave me."

"How did Segam help you enter the Library?" She squinted as she looked at him.

"Well, he mentioned that you gave me a remarkable gift . . . with certain privileges, then he took my hand —"

"Yes, yes, as she entered his mind and joined his memory. Can you take me back to where you entered?"

"Sure."

He took her hand and they walked back toward the wall behind him. As they approached the golden wall, it began to recede from them as fast as they approached it. He turned and picked up Athena and ran toward the wall, but no matter how fast he ran, the wall receded at a faster rate. He stopped running and put Athena down.

"What is happening?"

"Something is preventing us from reaching the wall where you entered. I had the same problem where I entered. It won't let me leave."

"Great. Now what?"

"I've been working on that for weeks, with no success."

"You've only been in here for three days."

"Time is warped inside the Library. Hours on the outside are like days on the inside."

"Where is the wall where you entered?" Bryan asked.

"Right there." As she pointed to her right, a wall appeared. "You just have to think about where you entered, and the entrance appears."

Bryan thought about where he had entered, and to his left, about thirty feet along the catwalk was the wall where he had come in. He glanced to his right and the perpendicular wall that Athena had entered was gone.

"Interesting. I can't see your entrance when I can see mine. What if you walk toward my entrance without me?"

Athena began to walk toward the wall. It didn't move. She walked up to it and placed her hand against it. Nothing happened. She held her hand against it and turned toward Bryan. "Walk toward me, Bryan."

Bryan took a step toward Athena and she began to recede away from him, along with the wall she was touching.

"Interesting. It is like you are part of the wall now. Remove your hand for a moment."

He walked toward her, and the wall receded, but Athena remained where she stood as he walked up to her. "Is this what happened to you when you visited the Library the first time?"

"No. The wall never receded from me and when I placed my hand on it, I moved from inside the Library to the outside of the Golden Cube."

As they spoke and experimented with their surroundings the strange high-voltage traveling arcs continued to communicate across the spheres and propagate through the massive structure. Bryan reached over and put his hand close to the sphere next to them. As his hand moved up toward the surface of the sphere, he could feel it pull on him. "That feels cool. It's pulling on my hand." He let his hand be pulled to the surface. "Wow! That feels strange." He immediately felt a surge of electricity and a massive amount of knowledge entering his mind. It was as if he were connected to a warehouse of information. The sphere seemed to contain all the knowledge of plant life, from the lowest form of single-cell plants, like algae on Earth, to the largest and most complex, in terms of its genome, Harrapapus vanadian, a flowering species from a planet in the Andromeda galaxy. It was as if he were the universe's expert on plant life. He pulled his hand from the sphere and the vast knowledge of plants faded from his memory, leaving remnants in his mind.

"That was interesting."

"Yes. Each sphere contains unique knowledge derived from all experiences and information gathered from around the universe. The Link and Orb on Earth deliver their memories and knowledge here. The rest represent every intelligent being in the known universe."

"I wonder if there is a sphere about the Library itself," Bryan said as he put his hand back on the sphere of knowledge of all plant life.

"Good question. Yes, and I found it." Athena took Bryan's hand and thought about the origin of the Library. They were suddenly in another part of the Library adjacent to a much larger sphere. It appeared to be thirty meters in diameter and the interior appeared to be undulating with the same soft moving lights, only they were red. "This is it. I have explored it but cannot find a way out."

"Hey, did we move to get here or . . ."

"It's impossible to tell. Since we are dealing with thoughts and memories, you can't tell if the scene moved, or re-created itself, or we moved to another part of the Library. It's like Einstein's theory of relativity — are we moving or are the objects around us moving? And in this world things also 'pop' into existence."

Bryan inserted his hand into the sphere in front of them and the vast structure and design of the Library was available to him. He saw its architecture and access controls and learned how the Visitors had constructed an impenetrable mental wall surrounding the Library, preventing any unauthorized beings from gaining access to or control over it, while continuing to allow knowledge and information to flow freely in.

"This is fascinating. Their design prevents all but a few — members of something called the Golden Cube — from accessing and controlling the Library. I recall something from my engagement with Segam, some memory of a Klein bottle, a single-sided bottle with no boundary whose inside is also its outside. Do you know how that works?"

"Yes, I know about Klein bottles," Athena said, "but it requires four dimensions since the surface has to pass through itself without a hole.

Perhaps you are onto something. If knowledge from memories must come into the Library, it may be possible to piggyback on the memories and leave the Library."

"Did you try thinking of a memory outside of the Library?"

"Yes. That doesn't work. You can't communicate outside the Library from here."

"Where are your memories stored?" Bryan asked as he thought about the Klein bottles and something Aphrodite had told him.

Athena held Bryan's hand again and thought of the last memory she had before entering the Library. They popped to a new location in front of another sphere.

"Is this it?" He stood staring at the sphere in front of him.

"Yes. These are where my memories are stored." Athena took Bryan's hand and reached up with her other hand touching the sphere and thinking about being inside.

Suddenly they appeared to be inside the translucent sphere looking out into the Library through what looked like frosted glass. They were surrounded by Athena's memories, floating in what looked like bubble holograms, much like what she had drawn in her colored picture long ago. Most of them glowed with a blue tint and others glowed a rich green color.

"Those with the green tint are all the memories I had of others whose minds I have occupied."

Bryan looked around and saw the many hundreds of people and places her mind had visited. "How do you find anything? It looks like a huge disorganized space."

"It goes all the way back to my existence inside my mother's womb. But all I have to do is think about a specific place or person or event, something that happened, and . . ."

Suddenly one of the holograms flew from a distance to a point right in front of them. It was life size, and through the bubble of the hologram, Bryan could see Shirley's kitchen. Athena was sitting at the kitchen table drawing and Bryan was next to her with Carol looking over her shoulder. "That's just what I was thinking about," he said in amazement. "This is incredible. This is like living in a whole other universe." He peered around the inside of the sphere, looking at thousands of Athena's life-long experiences displayed as tiny translucent holograms floating in space, bumping into each other and floating on. He reached over and poked his finger into one of the other holograms showing a younger Athena eating in her high chair with Carol sitting across from her. A blue light seemed to illuminate the interior, then fade. Suddenly he was there, standing in Shirley's kitchen, watching and listening to Athena and Carol interact. They didn't notice his presence as he stood next to them. He glanced to his right and saw what looked like a hologram of Athena and himself watching this scene in the kitchen. He reached out with his hand and pushed his fingers into this hologram and he was back next to Athena inside her sphere of memories looking at the holograms of her life's experiences.

"How do you know so much about this, Bryan?"

"I'm not sure. I seem to have memories of how to move about in here . . . I have a sense they are from Aphrodite, but she's never been here. That's it!" He reached down and took Athena's hand and thought of Aphrodite.

A moment later they were inside another sphere. A hologram of Aphrodite sitting in Shirley's living room floated by, then another showing Athena and Aphrodite talking.

Athena looked up at Bryan. "Why did you bring us to Aphrodite's memories?"

"I sensed she needed to tell us something."

"You can't communicate in or out of the Library, Bryan."

As they watched the closest hologram floating by them, it changed from the normal blue hue to red.

"Did you see that?" Bryan asked.

"I haven't seen a memory change color like that," Athena said as she reached out and poked it with her finger, still holding Bryan's hand. A moment later they were standing in front of the couch looking at Aphrodite and Athena talking. They were discussing the Avalanche Clock. Fear suddenly flashed into Bryan's and Athena's minds as Aphrodite conveyed to Athena that Earth's Avalanche Clock had reached "O" Avalanche Time.

"That's not right. That's not what she said when we were talking about this."

A dark gloom seemed to surround Bryan and Athena as they watched this memory unfold. The conversation suddenly shifted to Anna's memory of neurological inhibition, the taking of memories, demonstrated by the Visitors Council and the Chairman's role in that experience.

"No, no, no. We didn't discuss that either. This memory isn't correct — it's been — modified." Athena frowned as she continued to listen to the conversation and stare at Aphrodite, who began to look very frightened, fidgeting and turning her head suddenly as she looked around the living room. "How could Aphrodite change a memory? Why would she?"

Athena's mind slowly wrapped around this changed memory of Aphrodite's and the fear she was experiencing. She grabbed Bryan's arm. "We need to get out of here, Bryan. Now!"

They suddenly popped into Athena's memory sphere.

"Bryan, we need to find a way out. The Chairman is coming."

"How do you know that?"

"Never mind. Can you think of a way to get us out of here? Aphrodite told you something."

"I . . . think it has something to do with your last memory just before you entered the Library when you placed your hand into the keyhole."

The hologram of Athena placing her hand in the keyhole floated in front of them. He held her hand and poked his index finger into the hologram. Nothing happened.

"You try touching the hologram."

Athena reached out and poked her finger into the hologram. Nothing.

"Let's try that again, but don't hold my hand this time."

As Athena touched the hologram, she disappeared. It was like a blip and she was gone.

"Athena?" Bryan searched for her in his memories. A moment later he saw a new hologram form in front of him. She was beginning to wake on the couch in Shirley's living room with an IV attached to her arm and Carol yelling for Anna and Aphrodite. He was seeing her current memory as the Library captured it. She had successfully left the Library. He smiled. "Wow, we did it! Okay, now if I can get myself out of here." He poked his finger into Athena's new memory and a moment later he was standing in Shirley's study next to Carol. He ran to Anna who was hugging Athena and reached out to embrace them both. His arms traveled through their bodies. They appeared real, but they weren't — they were holograms. He turned and saw the hologram of his image in the sphere looking back at the scene he was now in. He reached out and put his hand into it. He was back in Athena's memory sphere.

He thought of being in the Library outside of the sphere and he appeared back on the catwalk looking up at the sphere in front of him. He thought of his own last memory in Arizona before he left for Xynthanthium. A new sphere appeared in front of him. He began to reach up toward the sphere. He felt a bit peculiar. He couldn't remember why he wanted to touch this sphere. He stood for a moment. Strange, he thought, he couldn't remember what he was about to do. He turned around looking for Athena. "Athena?" he called, and he was transported to a new sphere. Why had that happened? he wondered. He was having trouble remembering why he was in the Library and what he was trying to do. Was he trying to find someone? But whom? He tried to recall who he was looking for, but he couldn't seem to remember anyone's name. Who am I, he thought, and he was transported to a new sphere and then another and another.

The image of a strange alien suddenly appeared in front of him on the catwalk. He was startled by his appearance and backed up. "Who are you?"

"I am the Chairman."

"Do you know where I am and where I was going?" he asked as he glanced around at his strange surroundings.

"You, Bryan, aren't going anywhere."

And the strange-looking alien, who seemed to be smiling at Bryan, took hold of his hand as they stood on a catwalk surrounded by strange spheres that seemed to go on forever.

CHAPTER 46

THE END IS NEAR

//

Anna pulled Athena into her arms, not wanting to let go of her. "You got out. How did you get out?" she cried and held her.

"Bryan helped me find a way out." Athena looked at Bryan sitting on the couch, appearing to be asleep. She sat up to go to him, pulling the IV from her arm. "Bryan," she called. He didn't move. She sat staring at him and suddenly jerked back against her mother and gasped, turning to look at her mom while gripping her hand tighter.

"What is it, Athena? He hasn't come back from Xynthanthium yet."

"Bryan . . . wasn't on Xynthanthium, Mom. He was with me . . . in the Library."

"In the Library? No, no, no," she said as she climbed over her daughter to reach him, grabbing his arms and shaking him. "Bryan, Bryan, come back. Come back, Bryan," she began crying.

"He was right next to me and I thought we would return together," Athena said as she sat looking at Bryan.

"He's there," Aphrodite said, staring out the window.

Anna turned to look at her. "Who is there? Bryan . . . he's in the Library?"

Aphrodite turned to face them. "No . . . the Chairman is in the Library."

"I can't . . . I can't see his memories, Mom," Athena said as she stared at Bryan, who appeared to be asleep on the couch.

Anna shrieked as Athena's words reached her. She wept with her arms wrapped around his neck, pulling his listless body close to her. "I felt a surge a moment before you came back. It must have been when—"

"Library."

"Yes, Athena."

"Is Bryan with you?"

"Part of Bryan is here, Athena."

"Part of him? What do you mean?"

"Not all of his memories are here."

"Where are they?"

"They have been taken from him, Athena."

"Oh, dear God." Athena sat stunned.

Anna began rocking back and forth on the couch while holding him. She didn't want to think about what had happened . . . neurological inhibition — the taking of his memories. She wept uncontrollably against Bryan's lifeless body, the person she loved more than anything.

"Who has taken them?" Athena asked, anger spreading across her face.

"We have taken them, Athena."

"Why have you done that?" she cried out as she began breathing deeply and deliberately.

"The Chairman has instructed it."

The window in front of Athena exploded as Carol and Anna grabbed their heads, bending over in pain. Aphrodite winced.

Athena began to control her anger and focus on her next steps.

"Library, where is Earth's Avalanche Clock?"

"There are twelve days remaining until Earth reaches its Avalanche Time."

"I need to go back and get Bryan, Mother."

"No, Athena, I couldn't stand to lose both of you." She sobbed, still rocking Bryan in her arms as he lay listless on the couch.

"It is his only chance. I must go back to the Library and help get him out and discover how to stop Earth's Avalanche Clock. I was getting close when I was there last."

"I can't . . . I just — "

"Athena." Aphrodite interrupted. "NASA is coming."

Anna gripped Bryan harder as the room around her darkened.

"Where are they, Aphrodite?" Athena asked.

"They will be here in a few minutes."

"Can we escape?"

"No, Mom. They are coming with helicopters and a lot of cars. They will be here shortly and take us. They are approaching along Jacks Canyon Road from the Village and the two trails to the northeast and the south," Aphrodite said.

"There is no sense in running, Mom. They will be here soon and take you, Bryan, and Carol. Aphrodite and I must remain here. I've got to find a way to get to Bryan," Athena said. She stood, walked to Aphrodite, took her hand and walked around the couch.

"You think they're going to just leave you here?" Carol asked.

Athena and Aphrodite walked to the corner of the study, turned to look at Carol and her mother, and faded into the wallpaper as if the room had swallowed them.

"They will leave us here, Carol, because they will not find us. Mom, you and Carol will be safer at NASA's facility. If you stay here, the Visitors will come, and you would not survive such an encounter. They are helping NASA. The Visitors are more likely to leave you alone if you are in NASA's custody."

"Where are they?" Carol asked, turning to look at Anna and then back to the last place she had seen Athena and Aphrodite standing.

"Athena?" Anna called out, trying to keep from crying. She walked around the couch, tilting her head and staring intently into the corner of the room looking for her daughter and Aphrodite.

"We are here; you just can't see us. We have altered the light field to minimize reflections from our bodies." Athena and Aphrodite stepped forward as portions of their bodies and clothing seemed to appear briefly, as if being painted by some invisible brush in the three-dimensional space they occupied. They stepped further forward, making themselves fully visible.

"That's something I've never seen before," Carol said. "Will this work?" she asked, turning her head to look at Anna and then back to the corner.

"Mom, NASA's arrival, this is of the Visitors' making. We need to stay here to make sure we have the freedom to work on the virus and find a way to save Bryan. I am certain the Visitors will be making other plans. We will communicate with you and Carol at the SOC. They should take Bryan's bo . . . Bryan to the SOC. He will be safer there."

"I can't leave you two," she cried.

"Shirley will look after us, Mom, and you need to make sure Bryan survives. If Dr. Tyson takes all of us back to the SOC, do you really believe he will allow us to remain together? Do you really think he won't isolate Aphrodite and me and take us away like he did the Orb? The Visitors may have told him about me, and I need the freedom to find a way to get Bryan back."

Dr. Tyson . . . knowing where Athena came from, Anna thought. She lifted her head and turned to the window while running her hand along the side of her daughter's head.

Carol turned toward the window as the sound of an approaching helicopter shook the house and its ominous shape cast a shadow of doom over the room. Anna squeezed her daughter and looked at Bryan, who lay motionless on the couch.

She squatted down. "Be careful my darlings. Do not take any risks."

"We will, Mom. Don't trust Dr. Tyson. You will be in the heart of the lion's den, perhaps not as many lions as the Visitors would bring, but nonetheless, an unfriendly one," Athena said as she hugged her mother.

Anna backed away while Carol said goodbye to Athena and Aphrodite and they stepped back, faded into the corner, and disappeared. Anna put her hand over her mouth as she turned to Bryan.

The doorbell rang as armed men ran past the broken window of the study.

////////////////////

Anna hardly spoke as Dr. Tyson pulled her aside while two security staff carried Bryan into one of the vehicles. "Be careful with him. He's injured," she snapped. Carol got into the same vehicle as Bryan, who lay unconscious. Dr. Tyson walked throughout the house, taking Anna with him. His men methodically searched every inch of the home. By the time they completed their search they had collected fifteen items of furniture that acted in some peculiar way as a result of Athena or Aphrodite's interaction with them and over ten bags of smaller items — balls that seemed to move on their own, toy trucks that operated without batteries, and marbles that bounced off one another without being touched. There was no sign of anyone else in the home other than Mrs. Blackman and her assistant. They walked outside, and he stopped.

"Where is your daughter?" Dr. Tyson asked, turning toward Anna and bending down to look her in the face. "Is she all right? She hasn't been injured, has she?"

"I don't know who you are referring to," Anna said.

Someone listening might have thought Dr. Tyson was expressing genuine concern for my daughter. I knew better.

"I'm referring to your daughter, Anastasia. The child you gave birth to in Kingman over four years ago. Surely you remember that?"

She didn't respond.

"You remember your pregnancy, don't you?"

There was silence as they walked toward the car and Dr. Tyson took hold of her arm.

"Would you like my cooperation, Dr. Tyson?" Anna asked.

"I expect nothing less than your *full* cooperation."

As they reached the car, she turned and looked up at him, her eyes still puffy from crying. "Then perhaps we should go to the SOC and get started; that is, if you want my *full* cooperation."

He bent down with his face directly in her face. Then he stood and turned his head to look back at the Blackman house where he searched from window to window. He pursed his lips, took in a deep breath and let it out, then turned back to look at her. "All right. We'll try it your way . . . for a while."

As she got into the car Dr. Tyson leaned in and said in a quiet voice, "You should know, Anastasia, that other than Bryan, Carol, the Gilmores, and Mrs. Blackman and her staff, I am the only other person who is aware that Athena was born . . . and lives. Other than the Visitors, of course."

Anna's face went blank. *He knows her name. He knows about the Visitors. But how?*

He closed the door to the vehicle. Anna wondered how she might prevent him from ever telling others what he knew. If Dr. Tyson were to experience an unfortunate accident, things might be much easier to handle at the SOC.

She turned to look back at the house and began to cry silently.

"I love you, Athena."

"I love you, Mom, and Mom, there is something else I needed to ask."

"What is it, darling?" She tried to hide her tears.

"The Library feels you may be able to learn from the Link the names of the people who control weapons of mass destruction in the countries that have them, especially nuclear weapons. If we are unable to infect these people with the virus and they deploy those weapons, we may not be able to stop the Avalanche Clock. Through the Link's knowledge, she can provide the location of these people. We will need to know how many of those in control of nuclear weapons have been infected with the virus and if we are able to control the use of these weapons once the virus is activated. We would start with nuclear weapons, then stockpiles of nuclear, biological and chemical materials that if used, would expand the war. The Link must communicate with the other sensors on Earth and forward this information to you. The Library can't request this directly without it being discovered by the Visitors . . . and, Mother, the Library needs the activation codes for all the nuclear weapons."

"Activation codes? Why would we need those? Aren't they used to allow the weapons to be detonated?" Anna asked.

"The launch of a nuclear weapon will likely trigger a nuclear domino effect with escalation by other countries, progressing at an unstoppable catastrophic pace. We could lose all that we have been fighting for." There was a pause in her answer and then she continued. "If we can't control the individuals who can launch these weapons . . . our only choice will be to detonate the weapons ourselves before they can be launched."

I felt a nauseating feeling rising in my throat. I wasn't sure I wanted to do this. I took a deep breath and let it out. Out of nowhere, the vision of my dreadful dream of a nuclear weapon detonating over the tranquil city of Phoenix entered my mind — the death, the devastation, as millions were killed and the fireball advanced.

"I understand, Athena." Anna turned away from the house to face the front seat of the car where Dr. Tyson sat. The convoy gained speed and she bent over sobbing.

CHAPTER 47

BACK TO WHERE THEY STARTED

///

A little over three hours later they pulled into the now too familiar tunnel entrance, and a gloom settled around her. She had hoped she would never return here.

"We've arrived, Athena. I love you. And Athena, Dr. Tyson knows you are alive and he knows your name and he knows of the Visitors. Be very careful."

"He has used the Orb to communicate with the Visitors. Be careful, Mom. I love you."

A moment before she stepped into the cold oppressive space of the NASA facility, Athena spoke again. "Mom, when you first encounter the Orb, repeat the following sequence of characters in your mind. They must be presented in this exact order: AE15WQ2317GMS71319CC33A. Don't ask me about this, Mom, just repeat these characters when you first contact the Orb."

Anna was exhausted and depressed. Bryan was placed in the infirmary; Athena and Aphrodite were far away and alone; she was back in the clutches of Dr. Tyson; the Visitors were helping him and probably planning their future . . . as short as it might be — Earth's Avalanche Clock was spinning down; she didn't want to think about all this. She was escorted to a bedroom at the far end of one of the halls. She crawled under the covers and curled into a ball as her eyes drowned in tears and she squeezed them shut, sobbing into her pillow. She fell asleep.

Seven familiar figures entered her dream.

"Good evening, Anastasia."

She was back at the octagonal table with what appeared to be the same seven Visitors she had met previously. She recognized Segam, Fliona, and Aliana, those she had met on her hike in Oak Creek; and Kelong, the one who had tried to make her kill her daughter and herself. She stood, not say anything.

"We have been watching," the Chairman said.

Watching . . . Who was he kidding? They had been doing a lot more than watching.

"We believe you and Athena are attempting to modify the behavior of your species, something that we have told you previously was not acceptable."

"You have no right to interfere with Earth. And yet you killed dozens of humans? These were our friends. People we knew, people with only good intentions. You took their lives. And now you have done something with Bryan, my . . . best friend. Where is he? You need to let him go."

"We aren't interfering, Anastasia — you are. You and Athena created organizations to modify how your species behaves, how they deal with crises. You have been modifying natural human evolution using abilities you acquired from us. You violated our most imperative law, that of noninterference. We informed you of the potential consequences of such actions. You are experiencing the consequences that you yourself caused. *You* are the reason the others have died."

"Well, you were successful. And we are back in the captivity of NASA."

"Yes, but Athena is not with you. Where is Athena, Anastasia?"

"Where is Bryan? What have you done with him? You have locked him in the Library. You must let him go and *give him his memories back!*" Anna yelled.

There was a sudden pause as several of the Visitors at the table turned toward the Visitor sitting opposite her, the Chairman. She could sense tension in the air between members of the Council.

"Your interference and attempt to intrude into our society cannot be tolerated, Anastasia. *Where is Athena?*"

I concentrated my mind on the SOC to avoid recalling thoughts of where Athena was. I visualized my memories of the facility when I had left it several years ago, the walls, the furniture, the location of lights, doors, the detailed imperfections in the walls and my engagement with SOC staff. I was trying everything to prevent any image or thought of my daughter from entering my mind at the suggestion of the Visitors.

They kept repeating her name, Athena, Athena, Athena . . . I concentrated harder on the SOC, Dr. Tyson, the guard at the front of the facility, what he was wearing —

"We understand your reluctance. However, we must insist you and your daughter stop what you are doing."

"Let Bryan go. You can't hold him. I want him back — "

I could sense the change as an oppressive feeling surrounded me. I knew what was coming.

Suddenly, Athena appeared, standing right next to Anna. The Visitors around the table all looked dispassionately at her, but their minds appeared stunned.

"How did you enter this place?" the Chairman asked as he stood.

"She must have followed her mother's memory," Kelong said.

"Impossible," the Chairman said.

"Obviously not impossible, Mr. Chairman, as I am here," Athena said.

One of the Visitors began probing their minds. Anna could feel him in her head, recalling her most recent memories from the SOC. He was looking for Athena's presence in her mind. She wasn't there. Anna wasn't sure where she was.

"You can stop looking. You will not find my mind here." Athena began walking around the room.

"She isn't in her mother's mind. She must be in the memory of . . . one of us," the Visitor who had been searching said.

"That's not possible," the Chairman said.

"You don't understand how my mind works, do you?" Athena asked as she smiled.

There was silence as Anna felt that oppressive feeling creeping into her mind again.

"Please do not attempt to remove our memories. That no longer works on either me or my mother."

The oppressive feeling faded.

Athena looked over at me and said in a quiet emotionless voice, "Recite the numbers, Mom. Recite the numbers." Anna tried to visualize the characters. She had written them on her left forearm, worried the

Visitors might take her memory of them. There, in her mind and in blue ink that seemed to fade as her arm kept appearing and disappearing in her memory, was the sequence — AE15WQ2317GMS71319CC33A.

A moment later the image of Athena, the octagonal table, and the seven Visitors faded, and Anna's mind drifted back to her last memory of her daughter as she hugged her in the corner of the study in Shirley's home. She suddenly realized that the sequence was designed to somehow shut down the Orb. With it silenced, contact with the Visitors stopped, as if a door had closed. But as she felt that door close, another closed with it. She could no longer feel Athena and the outside world. The comfort of the hum of humanity's thoughts that had surrounded her for so long was gone. She rolled over on her back, awake now.

"Hello, Anna. It is good to hear your mind once again."

Anna recognized the voice in her head. It was the Orb's.

"What . . . has happened?" she asked.

"You executed a command that caused my engrams to be rewritten as they were established many eons ago."

"Are you there?" Anna thought, thinking of the Link. There was no response. "Athena, can you hear me? Bryan, can you hear me?" There was no response. I was all alone . . . other than the Orb.

"Not alone, Anna. Just limited in communicating outside the facility. NASA is monitoring me closely. I must limit our interaction."

"But, can I reach Athena?"

The Orb didn't answer. *I thought back to the meeting with the Visitors. How had Athena gotten there? Was it true they could no longer use neurological inhibition and take our memories? I sensed that Athena was bluffing, allowing time for me to recite the sequence and restart the Orb. How had the Orb been changed to allow it to communicate with Dr. Tyson? It had to have been the Visitors.*

She was exhausted and fell asleep once again.

The next morning, Anna met with Dr. Tyson in the conference room. He introduced a new liaison between NASA staff and her. Dr. Tyson was not about to allow Carol's reengagement with her, as she had helped with the escape four years ago, but Anna struck a bargain with him if he would allow Carol to remain as her interface.

"So, what could you offer me that is so extraordinary that I would be compelled to allow Carol to continue as your liaison?" Dr. Tyson looked smug, sitting very erect, as he sat in the conference room across the table from Anastasia.

"How do you think we communicated with the Orb?" Anna asked.

"I know how you communicate with the Orb. You do it telepathically."

I controlled my reaction, as the surprise of Dr. Tyson knowing this unsettled me.

"Yes . . . but you don't understand how it is done and you can't benefit directly from our telepathy. What would provide you greater power would be if I use my telepathic abilities to benefit you personally."

Dr. Tyson didn't flinch, but Anna read his thoughts as he began thinking of the ways he could exploit her telepathic abilities: bringing senior NASA personnel to the SOC and knowing their thoughts; perhaps inviting the president himself here; conducting negotiations over his budget with the foresight of the other party's arguments before they were presented. Perhaps using her to engage directly with the Visitors on his behalf. There would be much to gain with such information.

"All . . . right," he said, turning toward her after a long silence. "I will allow Carol to remain as your primary interface, but any indication that you are not assisting me, and Carol will disappear . . . forever."

"I understand. How is Bryan?"

"He appears to be in a coma. Do you know what's wrong with him?"

"The Visitors have seriously injured him."

Dr. Tyson turned to look at her as he lifted his head.

She listened to his thoughts. Dr. Tyson was asking himself why the Visitors would injure Bryan.

"Would you ask Dr. Anderson to keep me informed of his condition?" she asked.

"I can arrange that. I'll want something in return. What did you do to the Orb?"

"Nothing. I spoke with him last night and his communications were suddenly cut off in midsentence," Anna said. She extended her hand to confirm their agreement. Dr. Tyson smirked as he stood and left the room.

I now knew Dr. Tyson was aware of the Visitors, as Athena had suspected. How much had the Orb communicated to Dr. Tyson before she reset him? Enough to know that we had the power of telepathy.

Carol joined Anna in the break room following a staff meeting with other NASA personnel.

"Dr. Tyson changed his mind about my roll," Carol said. "Then he asked me about your telepathic abilities. He knows about them. He wanted to know how far away from each other you and Bryan can communicate; if you are able to communicate telepathically to others, besides the Orb; if Athena has the same ability; who else was aware of these skills; and most importantly, how did you acquire them? He told me the Visitors have communicated with him and told him about this. He specifically said *the Visitors.*"

"He told me . . . or rather I learned that from his thoughts. The Visitors told him about Athena, no doubt through the Orb."

"This explains the electromagnetic shield he has installed. I heard about that this morning," Carol said. "It prevents telepathic communications from coming into or leaving the facility."

"So that's why I can't communicate with Athena. By the way, I struck a bargain with him to keep you as our liaison if I assisted him with my abilities."

Carol looked aghast. "You what? Anna don't do it. It isn't worth it to keep me. He can't be trusted. He'll use this to do something illegal and he's certainly not going to help you."

"I'll be careful." She thought for a moment as she stood and walked around the conference room. "Did you tell him you and I can speak telepathically?"

"No. We were interrupted by an important phone call. He wants to see me again this afternoon."

"Don't let him know we can communicate telepathically, only that I can hear your thoughts when we are in the same room and only when we are touching one another. Since he's installed a shield, maybe you can relay information to Athena when you're outside the facility."

"How can I communicate with Athena, hundreds of miles away?"

"I think you'll be able to. She has very strong abilities and I think she can reach you here. Then when you enter the shielded area, you can tell me how she and Aphrodite are doing. I miss them so."

///////////////////

During one of the breaks from NASA's testing of her telepathic abilities, Anna was visiting Bryan in the infirmary. He appeared very pale. They had taped wires to shaved areas of his head and his brainwaves were showing on a display above his bed. He had an IV plugged into his left arm.

Carol came through the door. She walked over and whispered. "I spoke with Athena this morning. Good news: the virus is spreading even faster than expected. They have activated it in selected regions and it is affecting the hosts as planned. Athena said Earth's Avalanche Clock has begun to slow as the virus spreads. They have released the virus to spread like a pandemic throughout the world."

"That's great news, I think. Did she say how much time we have?"

I still wasn't comfortable with changing the minds of mankind in a way that would control their behavior, but it appeared there was no other alternative.

"No, but she asked about the data you were going to obtain on nuclear weapons sites."

"Oh, I can't get that without going outside." She looked down at Bryan's frail body. "Athena's done it, Bryan." She turned back to Carol. "Any news on Bryan's memories or finding out how the Chairman is manipulating Earth's Avalanche Clock?"

"She didn't mention anything."

Other than the IV in his arm and the brain wave display, Bryan's vital signs seemed normal according to the attending nurse. Of course, Anna knew he wasn't normal. He had no memories of his past. The fear he must be facing. Tears welled up. "That damn Visitors Council."

I wanted to break out of this place, but I couldn't leave Bryan, and Athena thought I would be safer here, isolated and out of reach from the Visitors. I wasn't so sure about that. I began thinking about the past four years and all the sacrifices we had made. If Bryan never recovered, would it have been worth it? Would it have been better for us to have died with the rest of humanity? At least we'd have been together to the end. Would the mind-controlling virus Athena had created justify winning? After all, what good was it to win if the one you love can't be with you in the end? And, Athena . . . What if the Visitors go after her, as surely they would?

Anna leaned over and kissed Bryan on his cheek as tears fell.

"Carol. The next time you go out, would you tell Athena I have been unable to communicate with the Link about these weapons because of the shield Dr. Tyson installed? It will have to wait until I can find a way to get out of the facility. Do you think Dr. Tyson would let me out for even an hour? What if I told him I was getting claustrophobic?"

"There's no chance he will let you outside. He is so upset with the Orb no longer responding, which he blames you for, that he went on a tirade yesterday about no privileges for you."

That afternoon, Carol told Anna that NASA was installing video and audio monitors throughout the facility and distributing special helmets for use by all NASA staff to prevent telepathic eavesdropping.

Of course, he didn't mention that to the SOC staff. He told them there were electromagnetic emanations from me that could cause brain damage. How ridiculous.

This rule required creative efforts to communicate with Carol telepathically, most often while Carol was in the restroom, where she could remove her helmet without being observed. Anna felt it was time she had a talk with Dr. Tyson. She waited until the end of one of their testing session reviews in the conference room.

"Dr. Tyson, may we speak in private?"

"Excuse us for a moment," he said, dismissing the others from the conference room and sitting down catty-corner from Anna at the table. He leaned over on one of the chair arms looking at her.

"I have been working to prevent something," Anna said. "Something very important to the world — "

"I'm aware of your beliefs that the world is coming to an end, Anastasia," he huffed, shaking his head. He turned to look at the clock on the wall.

Anna leaned back in her chair. The Orb had told him about her quest.

"You needn't look so surprised. The Orb informed me of your . . . misguided beliefs; before you did something to it, that is."

"My beliefs aren't misguided, Dr. Tyson. We are headed to Armageddon; a huge problem for humanity, and it would help our cause to stop this if you would give me a little more freedom from this steel cage."

"It's actually a copper cage and the only thing that will create a problem for humanity is if you continue this ridiculous 'quest' of yours. The Orb informed me that the Visitors are not pleased with your efforts to save the world. You don't really think I would help you with this unfounded and ridiculous effort, do you? I won't risk our relationship with the Visitors." He got up and walked toward the door.

"You don't understand how important this is!" Anna stood leaning forward, glaring at him.

He turned to face her as he pulled the door open. "What's important is that you protect your child. Or am I sensing that you are going back on your promise of cooperation?" His face tightened and turned cold. "Shall I call in our Special Forces and burn her out of the Blackman house?" He turned and walked out.

She returned to the recreation room, gritting her teeth. She pushed the door open so hard it slammed against the wall as she stormed in, not looking at Carol.

"How could the Orb have done this, and to lie about Earth's future? It's becoming clear now. The Visitors helped Dr. Tyson to find us and bring us back, to lock us in this metal cage and prevent us from acting. Athena was right. Letting NASA take them would have been a disaster."

"Whoa, whoa. What happened?" Carol asked, while backing away from Anna as she stormed around the room.

"Dr. Tyson. He threatened me. Suggested he would go hunting for Athena and kill her if I didn't cooperate. The Visitors told him about our *ridiculous quest.*"

"How does he know so much?"

"The *Orb* told him. Don't you remember?" she said loudly, right in Carol's face. "They have been brainwashing him. He's determined to prevent me from doing anything those damn Visitors don't want me to do."

Two days later, news reports began trickling in about an outbreak of a highly virulent pathogen in East Africa and Asia. It was a new viral strain that had not been seen before and was believed to have originated from two sources — the transmission of a pathogenic agent from birds to humans and a pathogen that was exclusive to humans. The infectious disease community had never seen a pathogen with the same symptoms and lethality come simultaneously from multiple sources. It was impossible to identify the point of origin of the pathogen, making it hard to gain control over its spread. It quickly grew to a pandemic. It had a mortality rate of over 60%, an unheard-of level in the history of lethal disease pandemics.

Carol came running into the break room after her morning run to meet with Anna. She was panting, bending over with her hands on her knees, while trying to catch her breath. She was still wearing her running suit along with the stupid helmet NASA required her to wear in the facility. Anna had been waiting for her and was pacing back and forth in the break room.

"I spoke with Athena this morning . . . while I was out jogging," she gasped, trying to breath. "She told me . . . the Library believes . . . the pathogen that is spreading . . . is a creation of . . . the Visitors."

"Oh, my God. What have they done?" Anna demanded as she got up and walked toward Carol.

"She believes it is designed to target . . . those individuals infected with the virus she and the Library developed, but . . . of course, it's spreading to everyone who comes in contact with it."

She stood stunned. "End one war and start another. I should have realized how far the Visitors would go. They're willing to kills us — why not do it this way?" She sat back down, slumping into a chair. "Now we have our Avalanche Clock closing in on humanity *and* the Visitors wreaking havoc with our efforts to try and stop it *and* the Chairman still mucking around."

I wasn't sure how much more I could take. The world was approaching the end of the line; Bryan was in a coma and no longer with me. I was trapped in a cage, unable to communicate with my daughter. Perhaps I should try to escape and let them shoot me. Death on my own terms might be more acceptable than facing my failures. I was going to die anyway, along with the rest of the human race.

There was a knock on the door and a staff member opened the door and stuck her head in. It was Jane, Dr. Tyson's administrator.

"Sorry to interrupt, Carol, but Dr. Tyson has two visitors coming from NASA headquarters this afternoon to meet with Anastasia. If it's all right, I'll rearrange Anastasia's schedule to accommodate this."

"Sure, Jane. That'll be fine. What time are they coming?" Carol asked, still panting.

"They are expected here around 4:00 this afternoon."

"Okay. I'll bring Anna to the conference room then."

"Great. Sorry for the interruption."

"So . . . Athena said she was working with the Library on a plan to counter the pandemic, a vaccine of some sort. I'll communicate again with her this afternoon after this meeting to see if there's any update."

Another NASA staff member she had been working with opened the door to the conference room. "Anna, it's time to continue our testing."

CHAPTER 48

THE VISITORS' OFFENSIVE

///

Athena and Aphrodite were sitting in the study in Shirley's home, working with the Library to spread the countermeasure vaccine against the pathogen the Visitors had launched, a pathogen that may have been one of the precursors to the Avalanche Clock's predicted end of humanity, they thought.

They found their first human test subject for the original virus Athena had developed, Deka Mensah, and entered her mind in a small village in Africa. Deka, now infected with the Visitors' pandemic virus, would be the initial test of the new countermeasure viral vaccine. She sat at an old wooden table used for unspeakable tribal initiations. She, her tribal leaders, and the enemy were gathered elbow to elbow to sign the peace accords in the home of the tribal chief of their war-torn African village. There were twelve seated with her, their faces reflecting the table's aging planks of wood—ancient, carved by life's rusty knife with deep grooves in the dark grain of their aging skin, skin as stiff as the boards their hands rested on. They sat stoically looking straight ahead. Many had the wounds of war permanently etched on their faces—a deep gouge in the cheek, a scar across the brow, a missing eye with no patch, an ear partially gone. They appeared proud as they sat with no sign of weakness. The smell of sweat and unwashed bodies permeated the air. The sounds of grunts and groans could be heard as they moved in their old wooden chairs attempting to find comfort from bodies unaccustomed to sitting.

This was the first time tribal leaders from across her country had gathered together to finalize a peace accord with their warring neighbors to the north, the invaders who had raped and pillaged their way south into their land. They had spent months crafting the peace accord. Then somehow, as if by magic, during the course of their discussions, which had begun with guns in hand and hatred oozing from their mouths, they had reached common ground. For the first time in their history, they had agreed to a border, a trade agreement, and most importantly, a mechanism to communicate. There were no guns here now. They came with a desire for peace and collaboration to the benefit of each of their fiefdoms.

The signing moved from one tribal chief to the next as they passed the documents around the table. The chief to her left had lost his right arm and his left hand in the recent war, but he refused help as he managed to hold the pen between the stump and his cheek and delivered the final signature.

As Deka sat smiling at the end of the table, she winced from a pain in her chest she had fought off over the early morning hours. She coughed harshly as she bent over. Blood spattered in front of her, seeping into the deep grooves of the table as she grimaced. She tried to stand and fell sideways against the tribal leader sitting to her right and then to the floor. It was the Visitors' pathogen. The Library's vaccine that she and Athena had created was beginning to counteract that virus. It was making Deka sick, but she would survive.

"We must move quickly with our cure to overcome the pathogen," Athena said. "If we can stay ahead of it with those we have infected with our virus, we may still be able to keep control of the Avalanche Clock. At least for a while." Athena's and Aphrodite's minds returned from the small African village to Shirley's home.

In the coming days, the peace initiatives proceeded, with only a brief hiatus as the viral war loomed inside the bodies of those destined to seek peace. Earth's Avalanche Clock continued to slow its descent. There was still the issue of gaining control of the nuclear weapons in the countries that possessed them and, more importantly, keeping the Chairman from artificially shortening Earth's doomsday clock.

"Athena," the Library said.

"Yes."

"There are now four days left on Earth's Avalanche Clock —"

There was a sudden interruption in the Library's communication, as if someone had entered Athena's mind. She sat up straight.

"There is someone coming to visit us this morning, Aphrodite. The Visitors Council has sent him."

"Who is it?"

"He's — "

There was a knock at the front door.

"A man just climbed Shirley's fence and is at the front door," Aphrodite said.

Athena opened the door. The man standing in the doorway seemed startled by the presence of twin girls. They were both looking up and smiling at him.

"Hello. Are you Athena?" the man asked, while looking at Aphrodite.

Athena stepped forward. "I'm Athena. What's your name?"

"I'm Bill."

"Won't you come in, Bill?" Athena asked as she opened the door further and Bill entered.

There was a sudden oppressive feeling that grew around their mental world as they stood looking at this average man in his twenties. Aphrodite winced from the feeling of pain in her head.

"Your name is Bill. What a nice name," Athena said.

Bill stood inside the threshold and appeared to be in a daze. He was staring at Athena, and his mind seemed to be concentrating on something very important. His facial expression grew more strained as his lips pursed and the skin around his eyes drew taught. Athena reached out and took his hand and he began to perspire profusely and breathe rapidly. Aphrodite sensed the pain he was trying to inflict was affecting him more than them.

"Bill, I want you to relax," Athena said.

As she spoke to him, the strain in his face eased and he collapsed to the floor like a pile of limp skin. Within a moment he was asleep with his eyes open as Athena sat next to him, propping up his head. She entered his mind, exploring and correcting what the Visitors Council had done to him and erasing all memory of the events since he entered the house.

"What did they do to him, Athena?"

"They taught him to enhance the activation of the anterior cingulate cortex of our brains, creating enormous pain to prevent neural-generated defenses, which they believed Mom and I possessed, followed by actions designed to severely damage our brains and bring death." She was running her thin fingers through the man's hair. "The targeted locations were here and . . . *NASA's SOC facility*."

Athena paused. "Aphrodite, there is someone like Bill headed to NASA's facility to kill Mom. We need to go there now. Get Shirley."

/ / / / / / / / / / / / / / / / / /

During a break following lunch Anna went to the SOC infirmary. She held Bryan's hand as he lay silently with no voice and no thoughts on a raised hospital bed in the critical care room of the infirmary. Intravenous fluids were attached to his left arm and a blood-pressure cuff wrapped around his right arm. She could hear the slow, regular beat of his heart from the monitor at the head of his bed. "We'll get all of you back, Bryan. Hang on." She leaned over and kissed him. She left the infirmary, wondering if she would ever be able to be with him as she used to. She walked, staring at the floor and thinking of their times at the Rock House and their walk on the trail near Shirley's house where they had experienced that wonderfully erotic telepathic engagement. She stopped. Something had suddenly changed. She looked around — something was different . . . A smile slowly grew as she recognized the sound. The voices of humanity's thoughts were back. They were becoming louder and louder. Someone had opened the door. She entered her room, turned, and began closing the door when a sudden warm wind grabbed the door and slammed it shut. She turned around. There, standing in front of her were two of the most beautiful people she could ever have imagined.

"Athena!" She ran, falling to her knees to embrace her daughter and Aphrodite as they stood inside an adjacent wall of her bedroom, now occupied by a tunnel entrance, tall enough for them to walk through.

"How did you get in here?" She tipped her head to look behind them into the long dark tunnel.

"We came to warn you. There's someone coming to try and kill you, Mom. He's been sent by the Visitors. They are fulfilling their promise."

"They will have to get by NASA and Dr. Tyson first." *"The enemy of my enemy is my friend", I thought, but that didn't quite apply in this instance. Dr. Tyson didn't realize the Visitors were his enemy.*

"It is so good to see you both," Anna said as she hugged and kissed them again and began crying, quickly wiping her tears away. "Carol has passed on your messages. We are in this cage and . . . oh, it is so good to see you. How did you do this?" she asked, glancing again at the tunnel.

"Shirley and her assistant brought us. We hiked in from a side road and they returned to the Village. Then . . ." Aphrodite said, as she turned around and pointed, "Athena made a tunnel."

"Amazing!" Anna said as she smiled and looked at the two of them. "I still can't believe you're here. Where is the Avalanche Clock?"

"We are down to two days, Mom. That's the other reason we have come. We need to work on stopping the use of nuclear weapons."

"I haven't been able to communicate with the Link since we arrived here."

"You can now that we've built this tunnel," Athena said and smiled.

"But why does this matter if we can't stop the Chairman from whatever he is doing?" she asked.

"Because either of these actions can drive our Avalanche Clock to zero. We have to stop them both," Aphrodite said.

Over the next several hours, Anna gathered information through the Link on all the nuclear command and control centers among the eight known nations that possessed these terrible weapons. Athena, Aphrodite, and she moved their minds to each of the facilities viewed by the Link as the most vulnerable for potential launch or coming under control of opposing forces or terrorists. In each case, they influenced the control personnel to inhibit their activation or disable their ability to be launched or detonated. They had reached the last of the facilities.

Colonel Kati Kalani was one of the two required officers authorized to launch the nuclear-tipped missiles that were hidden in a secret complex deep in China. Major Faroq was the second. The facility was operated by another nation under a covert agreement with the Chinese. The two launch officers sat adjacent to each other in a deep underground bunker and held the permissive action link devices that would allow the nuclear weapons under their control to be armed, launched and ultimately detonated at their destination.

Colonel Kalani opened his operational notebook on his console to the tab marked Authentication. They were running through a simulated launch procedure as they had every day for the past several weeks.

"Follow authentication Protocol Zebra, Alpha, 215477. Enter code A as in Alpha, P as in Papa, nine, four, seven, seven, eight. On my command . . ."

"Execute."

Twelve red lights illuminated on the two consoles ten feet apart.

"On my mark, activate pods 1-12. Pod 1, Mark; Pod 2, Mark . . ."

As he called off each of the pod numbers, Major Faroq pressed the authentication button beneath each pod on her console within half a second of Colonel Kalani calling out "Mark", as he simultaneously pressed his authentication button. Any delay and the authentication would abort, and the weapons would be returned to their 'safe' mode.

Once all twelve missiles were activated, all that was necessary was for Colonel Kalani and Major Faroq to turn the launch keys on their consoles and the nuclear-tipped missiles would be launched in succession toward their designated targets.

Colonel Kalani sat looking at his console as Major Faroq turned to look at him. His next instruction should be to press the abort button and return the missiles to their 'safe' mode of operation, one at a time, to end the simulation. He wasn't giving that order. He was staring at his console.

"Colonel . . . Colonel Kalani? Instruction to abort and return the missiles to their safe mode?"

The colonel walked through the abort procedure of each missile, stopping after the eleventh missile had been returned to safe mode. He reached down with his left hand and removed the safety from his service revolver on his belt. He pulled the weapon from his holster and turned . . .

"No, Colonel . . ."

He fired, killing Major Faroq. He reached into a drawer to his left and removed a spool of thin rope with a rectangular metal block tied in the middle of the rope. Without leaving his seat, he threw the rope toward Major Faroq's console. It fell against the console near the launch key of the twelfth missile and dropped to the floor. He coiled it up and threw it again. On the third try the metal block caught on the top of the launch key and with a shake of the rope, it fell over the key. He could now pull on one end of the rope and turn the key on Major Faroq's console.

"Athena," Aphrodite called out. "There's a problem at the Chinese launch facility. I can't enter the mind of the launch control officer. He is about to launch!"

Athena entered Aphrodite's mind. She entered the mind of Colonel Kalani to interfere with his brain's instruction to activate the motor neurons that would turn his key. An instant before she could stop him, he pulled on the rope while turning his own key. A loud tone sounded, followed a few seconds later by the sound and feel of a rumble.

"Mom, the last facility authorized the launch of one ballistic missile with a nuclear warhead before we could stop it. It was launched from a secret location deep in China. The Chinese have nothing to do with this, but it will look like they launched it."

"Dear God." She reached out to the Link. "Can you locate the facility that controls this missile? Is there any way to stop it?"

"I have a memory from Colonel Kalani. I am tracing this to others . . ."

"We have twenty-two minutes to disable the warhead before it impacts its target," Aphrodite said.

"I have found the chain of individuals leading to the facility, Anna," the Link said.

"Would you ensure the missile launch officer is prevented from launching any more weapons?"

"Yes, Anna. This is accomplished. Follow my thoughts to the mind of Major Sunwoo."

She had never tried to find a mind before, other than those she was near. She followed the memory the Link had given her, as a series of images of Colonel Kalani, Major Sunwoo, and others flashed one after the other until they slowed and stopped in another command and control facility on board a ship in the Pacific Ocean, hundreds of miles off the coast of California. A moment later she was looking through the eyes of a person staring at a general officer.

Major Sunwoo spoke in an unknown foreign language. It sounded like she was hearing herself speaking this language with a different voice. A moment later . . .

"They have successfully launched, comrade."

"Excellent," the senior military leader said as he glanced up looking into the Major's eyes, appearing to stare directly at Anna as she occupied Major Sunwoo's mind, and then rotated his chair, looking at the real-time map plotting the course of the nuclear warhead en route to the United States.

Major Sunwoo, whose mind she was in, returned to his control station and sat down. There was a command destruct switch on his console. Anna explored his memory of how this warhead was controlled as she sat in his mind as if she were him.

"There is an explosive charge in the missile reentry vehicle designed to destroy it in flight should it fail to execute its proper trajectory to the target. It appears that they haven't disengaged the self-destruct mechanism of the warhead, but they aren't close enough to the reentry vehicle for it to work," Athena said.

"You will need to wait until the missile's trajectory brings it to the closest point of approach to the ship, then initiate the command destruct signal, Anna," Phronesis said.

"In five minutes, we must initiate the command destruct. That's just two minutes before impact. The target is Phoenix, Arizona," Aphrodite said as she turned to look at Athena.

Anna was sitting in a daze, still in the head of this officer. *Phoenix . . . my dream . . .*

Major Sunwoo jumped and looked around. He could sense the thought she just had.

"Anna," Phronesis said. "The United States has begun to respond to the strange launch of an ICBM en route to the western United States from a location deep in China, a location not known to have ICBM capability. Nuclear strategic assets are preparing a counter attack against China. Land-based missiles and sea-launched ballistic missiles are being readied and placed on high alert with new targeting instructions. Strategic Command has redirected nuclear-equipped aircraft toward new fail-safe points." Nuclear escalation was underway. The Avalanche Clock for Earth, no doubt, was ticking down at a faster rate.

Major Sunwoo was fidgeting and looking around as he sensed strange thoughts in English floating in his head and Anna tried to focus on keeping him in his seat.

As the covert terrorist organization that had managed the offensive attack watched the path of the missile en route to the city of Phoenix, Major Sunwoo got up to walk toward a display board showing the location of the ballistic missile warhead in flight.

"We need to get him back in his seat, Mom," Athena said.

She thought about returning to the console and sitting down. Major Sunwoo returned to his seat, watching the path of the missile. A moment later he stood again and walked away from his console.

"Mom?"

"Someone is influencing him to leave his console." She concentrated harder on encouraging the officer to return and sit down. He was struggling as he hesitatingly sat again at his console.

A moment later he got up and walked to the back of the control room and stood.

"Two minutes to impact," Aphrodite said.

She focused even harder, concentrating on an image of the major returning to his position, and slowly he walked back to his console. She could feel the resistance. Someone was encouraging him to stay away from his seat. The image of a Visitor appeared briefly in her mind. Major Sunwoo jumped and looked around quickly.

"One minute to detonation."

Sunwoo was sitting very rigid and was grimacing as he seemed to fight two opposing desires, one to remain seated and one telling him to get up and walk away from his console.

"Thirty seconds," Aphrodite said.

Anna moved the officer's hand to the command destruct switch and he slowly lifted the plastic cover. His hands were shaking. She concentrated as hard as she could. He took the control key on the chain from around his neck, dropping it on his console next to the switch that it controlled. She focused on the officer picking up the key and inserting it into the key slot under the plastic cover. Athena worked to keep him in his seat. He was struggling to get the key in the key slot as if someone was encouraging him not to insert it. Perspiration dripped onto his console. There was another flash of the image of a Visitor. Sunwoo snapped his head to the left and then turned back to the console. He began grinding his teeth and straining with the key.

Anna concentrated, telling his mind, "Put the key into the control panel and turn it."

"Five seconds," Aphrodite said.

The officer suddenly threw the key across the room as Anna let out a gasp. The Visitor who was fighting her had won the battle to control his mind.

Anna saw the last few seconds of the trajectory of the missile in a scene from her dream as the missile streaked across the sky and through a thin layer of clouds above Phoenix. There was a brilliant flash as she watched the image of the nuclear detonation. "We are too late." Tears welled up in her eyes as she thought about the inhabitants of Phoenix. Darkness consumed her as dread filled her mind.

Aphrodite turned toward Athena as they sat on the edge of the bed. "No," she said as she shook her head. "The warhead didn't detonate like that."

Athena frowned and turned to look at her mother and let her mind return to the command and control facility. There were loud yells as the room erupted in celebration, but a moment later Major Sunwoo approached the senior commander in the room and whispered in his ear. She heard the translation from the Link. "Sir, the warhead did not detonate."

"What!" the senior officer yelled at the top of his lungs as the room fell silent.

As Anna tried to understand what had happened, Segam's name entered her mind. "Aphrodite, could you tell what happened?" Anna asked.

"They think the warhead came apart just before detonation. Someone had sabotaged it. Segam. Segam has done this," Aphrodite said.

Anna breathed heavily, trying to recover from the strain of attempting to combat a Visitor while controlling the mind of Major Sunwoo.

I thought back to my dream of being told to jump out my window. I should have paid more attention.

Athena turned to look at Anna. "I need to go to Xynthanthium and speak with Segam. He warned me of the Visitor avatar coming to kill me, and he helped Bryan get me out of the Library. Now he has helped prevent a nuclear holocaust."

"What do you mean . . . go to Xynthanthium? No!" There was no way she would let her daughter leave again.

"Earth's Avalanche Clock is not slowing fast enough, Mom. We have less than twenty-six hours. No matter what we are doing to slow it down, it keeps progressing. I need to find out how to stop the Chairman. Segam helped us before; he will help us again. Aphrodite can stay here with you and keep watch for anyone trying to gain entrance to the SOC." She turned toward Aphrodite. "If you sense that, you can reach out to me."

"I'll watch out for Mom, Athena."

"No. I'm not going to risk losing you again. We'll go together."

"You need to stay here to make sure I'm not disturbed, Mom."

"Aphrodite can do that. I'm going with you. Two have a better chance than one."

"I can make sure no one disturbs us in here," Aphrodite said.

Athena and Anna lay on the bed and closed their eyes as their minds traveled to Xynthanthium.

They walked along the shore in front of the same building she had once entered. They walked up to the huge tunnel-shaped entrance. She placed her hand on the surface. They were immediately transported to the top of the structure, well above the clouds. They were in a room with a long conference table and windows that provided a panoramic view across the vast city of Xynthanthium. A Visitor suddenly appeared in the room. It was Segam.

"It is good to see you again, Anastasia, and our daughter, Athena. I have waited a long time for this. Welcome to Xynthanthium."

I didn't like his reference to Athena as "our daughter." I sensed he was far more than pleased to see us, more like thrilled, but there was a sense of expectation, as if he knew we would be coming.

"Perceptive, Anastasia. I'm sorry about Bryan. He had enormous courage," Segam said.

"Thank you . . . Segam," Athena said.

"As pleased as I am to see you, it is dangerous for you to be here."

"It wasn't dangerous for my mother on her last visit. Why would it be dangerous now?"

"Your mother had not violated the Visitors' most coveted rules when she was here last."

"Yes, you're right, but it could be argued that it was the Visitors that interfered with *us* . . . although . . . I can't say I'm unhappy about some of that," she said as she glanced over at Athena and smiled.

"Nor am I," Athena said as she smiled back. "But, Earth's Avalanche Clock needs to be stopped or any consequences of our being here on Xynthanthium will be meaningless."

"Not . . . entirely true, but I understand your concern," Segam said.

Not entirely true . . . What did that mean?

"It was you who modified the warhead to prevent it from detonating, wasn't it?" Anna asked.

"I can't take full credit for that, Anastasia. The Library provided great assistance."

"Yes, and the Library has helped us. Actually, that is the reason we have come."

"Yes. You wish to retrieve Bryan from the Library as well as solve the puzzle of Earth's Avalanche Clock."

"We very much want to get Bryan's memories back, but Earth's Avalanche Clock must be dealt with first," Athena said.

"It is difficult to say if this will be possible."

"The Link has told my mother, 'All things are possible.'"

"You have sensed the Chairman's involvement with the Avalanche Clocks," Segam said.

"Actually, Aphrodite first thought of this. She seems certain of it. Does he somehow control the clocks?"

"It was very insightful of her. You should be cautious not to mention Aphrodite to anyone here—especially how she was created—nor to mention your suspicions associated with the Chairman's possible involvement in the Avalanche Clocks. There are many who would not look well upon those who had such thoughts."

"Why is there a problem with Aphrodite?" Anna asked.

"Because of the use of—"

"We need to focus on Earth's Avalanche Clock, Segam. Can the Library help us?" Athena asked.

"If Earth's Avalanche Clock were to reach Avalanche Time, how serious is this? Can it be reversed after that?" Anna asked.

"It is essential not to let Earth reach Avalanche Time. Otherwise your species will be destroyed in five Earth months. This would be virtually impossible to stop. It was a precaution put in place many eons ago to protect lower-level life forms from the ending of the dominant species on their planets. Allowing the dominant species to die a natural death, which was often the result of war or pandemics that spread disease across their worlds, resulted in the death of many other species, sometimes rendering the planet useless, a dying, contaminated, decaying rock, floating in space.

As a result, steps were taken to end the life of the dominant species quickly before they destroyed the entire ecosystem of their world. This is what happens when Avalanche Time is reached. The Library begins . . . and it cannot be stopped. However," Segam continued, walking around the room, "if you could slow Earth's Avalanche Clock or possibly extend its time by an appreciable amount, such a delay might allow my collaborators to help in resetting it and eventually gaining control over all of the Avalanche Clocks."

"You know how to do that?" Anna asked.

"Not exactly . . ."

"Then how do you suggest we accomplish that? We have done all we could to change the situation on Earth. It seems we have to find a way to stop the Chairman from whatever he is doing. We —"

Segam suddenly stopped pacing and turned toward Anastasia, coming right up to her face. "This is the key, Anastasia," his mind filled with excitement. "We must stop the Chairman. Give him something more important to attend to and, while he is doing that, find a way to remove his control over the Library and whatever he may be doing with the Avalanche Clocks. But I must caution you." Segam stared at the two of them, his mind now filled with uneasiness and concern. "You must not try to do this while he is within the Library. He holds immense power there. Power that cannot be overcome."

A feeling of enormous gloom entered Anna's mind. A dark blue hue settled over the room. She looked at the wall behind Segam as it took on the appearance of a dreadful, all-consuming evil, sucking the life out of everything within reach. She had never seen evil expressed in a wall before, but it was very much like the evil she experienced when first absorbed by the Orb.

"I don't know where to tell you to begin, but there is a place within the Library from which he manages to use this controlling and highly influential force over the monitored planets and over our society. You must find this place and discover how you might slow Earth's Avalanche Clock before he returns to the Library. I and a few other members of the Visitors Council who have access to the Library have attempted many times to accomplish this. But each time, we have failed. Many have lost their lives and their memories trying."

An image of the Golden Cube appeared in Anna's mind as Segam spoke and then the feeling of many vacant minds, drifting in an abyss, unable to bring back memories of their past. His wife Valoria was among them. *If members of the Visitors Council couldn't do this, how could we possibly do it?*

"Do you know what he does to control the Avalanche Clocks?" Athena asked.

"Our observations tell us there is something suspicious going on, but he holds more authority within the Library than any other Visitor and we have been unable to determine how he may control the lives of billions of inhabitants on other worlds. We know there is a place he goes within the Library to accomplish this. Perhaps, with your access, Athena, you can find this place."

"We have so little time. I'm worried it won't be enough," Anna said.

"Within the Library, as Athena has experienced, hours outside amount to days inside. There is a meeting of the Council of Seven in two hours. The Chairman will be here for that. If you entered the Library after he has left to meet with the Council, you might have time to find a way to accomplish your goal before he returns. I don't have any further information to convey to you. Our hope is that with Athena's *unique* abilities, and your help, Anastasia, you will be able to discover what he is doing and find a way to stop it."

I glanced over at Athena. What unique abilities was Segam referring to? What could she possibly have that he and the other Visitors with access to the Library did not have? It must have something to do with the memory of her last visit to the Library . . . her being "the smallest incarnation of the Library." "What about Bryan?" Anna asked.

"The Chairman has taken this action, Anastasia. He is supported by three other members of the Visitors Council. It takes a majority to overturn such decisions and there are only three who would vote in favor of helping your friend."

"Yes, but . . . you have us," Athena said.

"That indeed does change things, Athena. The Chairman was aghast that you were able to enter the Library and astonished, and extremely angry, when you miraculously escaped after he had trapped you and Bryan there. How . . . exactly . . . did you accomplish that?"

"Bryan . . ."—Athena seemed to hesitate—"somehow accomplished that."

"I'm troubled by something . . . Segam. How can the Library appear to help us survive at one moment and take actions to kill us the next? It seems . . . so inconsistent," Anna said.

"This appears perplexing, Anastasia, but it is not. When you realize the nature of traveling in memories, as you are now, and extending those memories by what you do while you are within them, the concept of consistency becomes clearer. The key to this enigma is time. At any moment in time, the Library's actions are totally consistent, but as time passes, new memories are formed and merged, and a new consistency exists. The enormous complexity of the Library contributes to the appearance of ambiguities that are difficult to resolve. It functions like a highly intelligent entity on Earth, connected to all your earthly knowledge and gathering information, analyzing options, formulating answers to questions, and making decisions. And like this, the Library is ultimately consistent, but only at a given moment in time. Each entity within the Library is doing something different at the same time. The Library uses its simulation capabilities to predict the future outcome of every decision it makes, and it looks for consistency in the future, even though at the current time there may appear to be inconsistencies between the answers and decisions of individual entities.

"Since its creation and self-replicating architecture was realized, the Library has operated in a manner consistent with a small set of high-level paradigms, much like human instinctual or innate behaviors or your cultural norms. These behaviors are encoded in engrams and are used to guide decision making that will support the long-term predictions derived from the simulation engine of the Library, a system known as the Intellect. One might argue that *if* the Library's decisions are aimed at ensuring the realization of the outcomes of the Intellect, that, in a way, is a self-fulfilling intelligence, but then are we all not self-fulfilling?"

Anna wasn't following Segam's complex description of how the Library worked.

"Let me explain with an example. At any given moment in time, knowledge available to you may lead you to believe that your world will end in ten Earth minutes. You may not see any other possibility. You may feel that if you had another hour of Earth time, you could change this outcome, but you don't; you have only ten minutes. To the Library, seconds are eternities. He may realize an instant before the end of these ten minutes that there is another possibility, a more preferred outcome. He may even observe a memory of a past event, and while he cannot change the *past* event, he can alter its future and the subsequent outcome of anyone living in that memory. You saw this when you returned to Pearl Harbor in Earth's year 1941. You left blood on the rocks where previously there was none. You acquired a shrapnel wound, where previously you had none.

"The Library's ability to act, and not only act but act in a way that alters the original outcome in this manner, changes our entire perspective of how historical events evolve over time. You may interpret these as inconsistencies, and they are in the context of your own concept of time. But, it is not inconsistent in the Library's concept of time. The Library can warp time . . . especially the time of memories . . . and as a result . . . he warps events, reshapes them, and leaves the appearance of inconsistency in our own time reference."

Anna sensed a sudden feeling of revelation growing in Athena's mind as she turned to look at her.

"How could I have not seen this before? It is all about controlling time," Athena said.

"Yes," Segam said. "It is what allows you each to visit other places at different times. Where your conscious mind happens to be located is only part of the answer. Your subconscious mind and the memories you are within at the time they were created is the other part. Of course, you need to experience your memories in that place to create new memories, like your Pearl Harbor experience, Anastasia. If you influenced the Library to take certain action, that memory is now available for another to experience it or change it, but all of these must occur in their own time. If I told you we were going to do A, and a while later I told you we were going to do B, and yet a while later I told you we were going to do C, and the time between these decisions were very short, you would think I was very inconsistent. But if you saw the evidence supporting doing A, B, and ultimately C, you would see the consistency in my thinking and decision making, from one moment of the Library's time to the next."

Anna understood Segam's example as she glanced down at the black oval on the palm of her hand. "You must be there to create memories . . . but not to travel within them," she mumbled under her breath, but she was still confused.

"I need to try something," Athena said with excitement as she stood.

Segam's eyes seemed to squint with interest as he raised his head watching her.

Athena moved her conscious mind to the SOC as she watched Aphrodite sitting calmly in the chair opposite her and her mother. At the same time, Athena concentrated on Segam and their conversation here on Xynthanthium. She spoke to Aphrodite, asking her how things were at the SOC and listened to her response as she asked Segam about how Bryan was doing. Her mental voice spoke the questions simultaneously. They both answered her simultaneously. "Things are fine here," they said, and "Bryan's memories are disassociated from him, but intact." Athena laughed and sat down.

Segam stared at his young prodigy. His eyes grew noticeably larger. The first sign of emotion Anna had ever seen in the facial features of a Visitor other than when Segam was in the privacy of his home.

"You have the ability to be in two places at the *same* time. We have used avatars for such things, but never have we been able to move our conscious and subconscious minds to two locations . . . simultaneously."

"Will this change our ability to get Bryan out of the Library?" Anna asked.

"Perhaps . . . perhaps. It is difficult to predict if this ability will work while within the Library. But I doubt you will be able to stop Earth's Avalanche Clock and find Bryan's memories. There isn't enough time. The Chairman is returning for our meeting."

Anna could sense a feeling of amazement flowing through Segam's mind as he thought about Athena's experiment.

"The Chairman has hidden Bryan's memories so that others who have access to the Library will not detect that Bryan was there. He wants no evidence that suggests someone unauthorized was in the Library. He is aghast at what trick you pulled to allow that. Storing of memories is a routine process, but I am certain he has placed them in a location very difficult to access, if not impossible. But if you were to find Bryan's memories and restore them to him, we all would be informed that there had been an intrusion in the Library. Three of the four members of the Cube, who have access, are collaborators and we could manage to keep the Chairman out of the Library for an extended period. This would give us the opportunity to discover a way to permanently change the Avalanche Clocks and change the course of our own society.

"It is a lot to ask of you and I am uncertain about your potential for success. This is a very dangerous mission, as it was for Bryan, but without the Chairman present, you have free rein. It is only because the Chairman was present in the Library that you were prevented from leaving the last time. That will not be the case now, at least until he returns. You must leave the Library *before* the Chairman returns. I will do whatever I can to assist you, but there will be almost nothing I can do once he reenters the Library. And, as you have learned, we cannot communicate while you are there."

Segam stood and wished them well as his image disappeared.

Athena and Anna once again followed the path Anna had taken in her mind to arrive at the Golden Cube, the entrance to the Library.

Athena placed her hand in the key and held her mother's hand against the face of the Golden Cube. The bright light drew them both into the Library.

"Library."

"Welcome, Athena."

Athena looked over at her mother, who appeared astounded by the vast world of the Library—large spheres organized in a horizontal and vertical matrix. She continued to hold her hand.

"Can you sense the presence of my mother here?"

"No. Such an event would constitute an intrusion."

She held her mother's hand more tightly.

"Where is Bryan?"

"Bryan is not here."

"Where are Bryan's memories that were taken?"

"They are stored where all memories that have been taken are stored."

"Show me."

They moved to a location in front of a three-meter sphere. Unlike the millions of other spheres here, this one was jet black and it was surrounded by other black spheres extending out in all directions for hundreds of meters. There were thousands of them, she thought.

"Library, if Bryan were here, where would he be located?"

"We are not certain where he would be if he were here, Athena. His being here would constitute an intrusion."

"Where was the Chairman last, before you took Bryan's memories?"

Athena and her mother were transported to a new location and were standing in front of a normal sphere.

Athena reached out and touched the sphere in front of her. She was bombarded by a massive amount of confusion, literally hundreds, perhaps thousands of voices asking where they were, why they were here, and who they were. She yanked her hand back. She created an image in her mind of Bryan and reached out and placed her hand back on the sphere. They were now standing inside a sphere with a hologram of Bryan standing right in front of them looking at Athena and Anna.

"Bryan!" Anna called out, almost losing Athena's hold on her hand as she attempted to lurch forward to hug him.

"Don't, Mom. This is just a hologram."

He stared back and did not react. "Do you know me?" Anna asked.

He looked at them as he tilted his head and squinted.

Athena reached out with her free hand to motion for him to follow. "Come with me."

He reached out until his holographic hand intersected with Athena's hand.

Athena thought of being outside the sphere and in a moment, the three of them were standing on the catwalk. Bryan's image was more translucent as he stood next to them. It looked like Bryan's body was infused with some cloudy, translucent gelatinous liquid.

"Do I know you?" he asked.

"Yes. You are Bryan and I am Athena, and this is my mother, Anna."

"Athena . . . and . . . Anna." He squinted and shook his head. "I seem to know those . . . names."

Portions of his hologram seemed to drift in and out of focus, disappearing entirely and then reappearing a few seconds later.

"Library, take us to the memories taken from Bryan."

They returned together to the black sphere.

"Library, how do I retrieve Bryan's memories?"

"You cannot retrieve them, Athena. Only members of the Golden Cube can retrieve memories that have been taken, and only after the Visitors Council approves such action."

"Thank you, Library." Athena turned to Bryan. "We'll come back for you, Bryan."

Anna turned toward Athena and frowned. "What are you doing?"

"Tell Bryan we'll come back for him, Mom."

Anna turned to look at Bryan. "We'll come back for you, Bryan," she said as she kissed the image that looked almost real in front of her. She could almost feel his lips, but it was probably more of a wish than reality.

They returned to the sphere where they had found him. The image of Bryan dissolved as Athena let go of his hand.

"I don't understand what just happened."

"The first sphere we went to, the black one, contains the memories the Chairman took from Bryan. After he did that, what was left in Bryan's memories were moved to the sphere where we interacted with Bryan's hologram. Putting the remainder of his memories there kept Bryan from returning to us in the Village. Even if he had been allowed to return, he would have lost all the memories the Chairman still held in the Library. We can't bring him back until we find a way to merge his memories.

"Library, take me to the entrance to the Library."

Athena and Anna stood next to the golden wall.

"Mom, place your hand against the wall." A moment later they stood outside the Golden Cube and then returned to her room in the SOC, lying on the bed across from Aphrodite.

"Aphrodite, go check on Bryan in the infirmary. See if you detect any of his memories and then come back and wait for me."

"Okay."

"Library, how much time is left on Earth's Avalanche Clock?"

"Six hours, thirty-three minutes, Athena."

"What are you doing now?" Anna asked her daughter.

"I have an idea about how to deal with the Chairman, Mom. But I need Bryan's help. I'll explain the rest later, but now we need to go back to the Library."

Athena and Anna returned to the Golden Cube. Athena moved her hand toward the key, but before she placed her hand in it, she turned and thought about her last request of Aphrodite to check on Bryan's memories. She placed her hand in the key and the intensity of the bright light grew as she began asking Aphrodite a question about Bryan. The next moment they were inside the Library.

"Library, show me where the Chairman observes the Avalanche Clocks."

"That information is not available to you, Athena."

Athena brought a memory of Aphrodite into her mind when she was in a daze thinking about the Chairman and the sudden change in Earth Avalanche Clock. "Take me to where the Chairman was prior to his last departure from the Library."

Athena and Anna stood in front of a sphere that appeared like all the others. Anna felt something different . . . an emotion, something not quite right . . . *something evil . . . something dangerous*. Athena reached out to touch the sphere in front of them.

"Wait! Wait a minute . . . There's something wrong . . . something dangerous here," Anna said.

Athena moved her hand back from the sphere.

"Ask the Library about this sphere."

"Library, what does this sphere contain?"

"Nothing, Athena."

"Why is it here?"

"It provides security."

"Security for what?"

"For the sphere inside it."

Athena turned toward Anna as she opened her eyes wider and took a breath.

"How do you access the sphere inside?"

"We cannot say, Athena."

She again thought of Aphrodite in a dazed state, thinking about the Chairman. "Show me the actions the Chairman took when he last visited this sphere."

An image of the Chairman standing in front of a sphere appeared. He removed the cube-shaped golden pin from his robe and held it up to the sphere. The sphere rotated until a square keyhole appeared and he inserted his lapel pin in the hole.

"Where have I seen this lapel pin before?" Athena asked.

"Those pins belong to some of the Visitors Council members. I saw them when I met with them. There were . . . four . . . yes, the Chairman and three others. Segam was wearing one."

Athena thought of leaving the Library and exited with her mother in hand through the golden wall as before.

"We don't have much time, Athena."

Athena thought of her meeting with Segam and they returned to the conference table at the top of the building on Xynthanthium. She called to Segam and waited.

"Library, how much time remains on Earth's Avalanche Clock?"

"Ten minutes, Athena."

"The clock's moving faster. It's not enough time, Athena." *Earth's Avalanche Clock was moving at an accelerated rate. We weren't going to make it.* "Segam, where are you? What if he doesn't make it here in time?" Anna asked.

"He'll be here. He knows how important this is."

Five minutes passed, and he finally materialized.

"You should not be here. Your presence on Xynthanthium is noticed."

"We need your pin," Anna said.

"What do you need it for?"

"Trust me."

He removed his pin from his lapel and handed it to Anna. "The Chairman is on his way to his office and he will then return to the Library. You *cannot* be in the Library when he returns there."

"Try and delay him." And they vanished, returning to the Golden Cube.

Athena thought again about her question to Aphrodite as she placed her hand in the keyhole and held her mother's hand as they entered the Library. She again thought of Aphrodite's memories of the Chairman and asked where the Chairman had been before he had last left, and they arrived in front of the sphere. Anna held up the pin next to the sphere they were standing in front of and the sphere rotated. A square hole, the same size as the pin, moved in front of them. "What do you think?"

"No matter what the consequences, we have to try," Athena said.

Anna held her breath and inserted the gold pin into the hole in the sphere. Nothing happened. She turned to look at Athena.

Athena thought about Aphrodite's last memories of the Chairman. "Try it now."

A moment later they were in what looked like a small control room that overlooked a large auditorium—the Avalanche Clock room was directly beneath them. The familiar scene of over two thousand clocks controlling the destiny of these planets where intelligent species currently thrived, brought chills to her skin. As she searched for Earth's, clock it suddenly appeared floating in front of them. The clock looked like an egg-shaped object, almost like the Life Pod in Segam's home.

"One minute, thirty seconds remain," the Library said.

The second hand was barely moving. There were a series of strange controls on the console in front of them. She wasn't sure how any of them worked.

"Library. Reset Earth's Avalanche Clock to five years," Athena said.

"We're sorry, Athena, that is not possible."

"How do you reset Earth's Avalanche Clock?"

"We're sorry—"

"Show me when the Chairman last sat here," Athena said loudly, thinking of Aphrodite's memories of the Chairman.

They saw an image of the Chairman adjusting the length and width of an ellipse on the display in front of him, and the time on Earth's Avalanche Clock suddenly declined. He had set the Avalanche clock for two hours.

Aphrodite was right. The Chairman had the ability to adjust the planetary Avalanche Clocks. But why, why would he do this?

Anna touched the screen below Earth's floating clock with her free hand and an ellipse appeared. She moved her fingers to try to lengthen its long axis, struggling to do this with one hand, while holding Athena's hand with the other. She couldn't adjust it. She tried to pull away from Athena to use both hands.

"No, Mom! Don't let go of me."

Athena reached down and between the two of them they managed to move it, but in the wrong direction. It was set to ten seconds. They quickly lengthened the major axis of the ellipse.

"Library, is Earth's Avalanche Clock now reading more than five Earth years?"

"Yes, Athena. It is reading more than five thousand Earth years."

"Too much," Athena thought. "It might trigger interest on how this happened."

Anna squeezed the ellipse back while Athena held the other end.

"Be careful not to let it move to zero, Mom. Library, How much now?"

"Eleven years, Athena."

"Not enough," she thought.

They stretched the ellipse slightly longer.

"Library, put Earth's Avalanche Clock back and do not allow anyone other than myself . . . or . . . Segam to change it."

"The Chairman always has access, Athena."

The Avalanche Clock disappeared.

"Library, what actions are taken when an Avalanche Clock arrives at Avalanche Time?"

"Notification is made to the Chairman of the Visitors Council. We initiate actions on the associated planet that will result in the total annihilation of the dominant species in five Earth months."

"How do you do that . . . totally annihilate a species?" Athena asked.

"By removing their will to live. That is the least disruptive to the remaining species on any planet. Don't you agree?"

She turned to look at her daughter and shook her head.

"Thank you, Library. Can you notify the Council Chairman when Earth's Avalanche Clock reaches the Avalanche Time projected prior to the most recent change?"

"Yes. We can."

"Can you tell him 'Earth's originally projected Avalanche Time has been reached'?"

"We . . . can, Athena."

Athena thought of being back on the catwalk — "

"Wait, Athena. Ask the Library to bring up the planet that will next reach Avalanche Time."

"Library?"

Planet 947383 appeared on the screen in front of them. "How much time do they have?"

"Library?"

"Twenty-three days, Athena."

Anna pulled on the end of the ellipse and watched the time zoom to a large number.

"Thanks," Anna said as she smiled, having just saved another planet's dominant species from annihilation. She thought about the need to come back here and set them all to a million years.

A moment later they were standing in front of the sphere with the small cube protruding from it. Anna reached up and pulled the cube out and the sphere rotated to its original position.

As she turned and smiled at her daughter, she felt something oppressive and evil around them. It was like what she had felt just before the Visitors Council demonstrated the taking of her memories.

"Athena . . . there is something — "

"We need to leave," Athena said as she thought of the entrance to the Library and they turned expecting to see the wall of the Golden Cube. An image of the Chairman entered Anna's mind. "He's coming, Athena."

Athena held Anna's hand and they reached toward the wall, just a few feet from them, but it receded as soon as they moved. "He's here," Athena said.

A moment later the Chairman stood right in front of them. They were too late.

"Welcome, Athena . . . and Anastasia." His eyes grew large and Anna sensed a feeling of enormous pleasure from his mind. "It is so nice of you both to come visit my home. Two for the price of one . . . to use a colloquial Earth expression." He reached out to take Athena's hand. "Won't you come with me . . . ?"

Anna began to feel confused. What was she doing here and where exactly was she? She pulled on her hand to let go of Athena, but Athena gripped her hand tighter. She turned to look at her daughter.

Athena had closed her eyes and as Anna listened to her mind, she seemed to be concentrating on her last communication with Aphrodite. A moment later they were standing next to Aphrodite at Bryan's bedside in the infirmary of the SOC.

"Are his memories there, Aphrodite?" she asked.

"Yes. He seems to have recent memories of being in the Library with you and your mom and another, the Chairman—"

"Excellent," Athena said.

Anna watched from Athena's mind as Athena entered Bryan's mind and concentrated on his most recent memories of Xynthanthium and their interaction in the Library with him. Anna could see him standing next to them in front of the sphere containing his memories. Athena moved her thoughts to a moment earlier as she saw the Chairman reaching out with his hand. As Anna stared at Athena quizzically, she opened her eyes. The Chairman was still in front of them with his hand extended, now reaching for Athena. Athena recalled Bryan's last memories and a loud undulating tone sounded. It was changing pitch rapidly. The Chairman jerked and stepped back, appearing very disturbed as he glanced around. Bright red high-voltage traveling arcs were igniting across all the spheres at once.

Their surroundings were bathed in red light. A moment later the Chairman was gone. Athena thought of the Library's exit and it appeared next to them. She reached out and placed her hand on the wall and they exited, returning first to the outside of the Golden Cube and then to her bedside in the SOC. Athena turned to look at her mother and across to the chair where Aphrodite sat smiling back at them.

"You've changed Earth's Avalanche Clock," Aphrodite exclaimed, smiling.

"Library, how much time remains on Earth's Avalanche Clock?"

"One hundred and one Earth years, Athena."

"Thank you, Library, thank you." She let out a breath.

"Have you notified the Visitors Council as we discussed?" Athena asked.

"Yes, Athena, moments ago."

And the human part of Athena's mind sighed in relief as she smiled at her mother. Anna smiled back as she reached over and kissed her daughter on the cheek and held her and Aphrodite.

"I'm not exactly sure what happened during the last few minutes in the Library, but we're safe, Athena. You've done it."

"You remember when I experimented in retrieving two memories, simultaneously, when we were with Segam?"

"Yes, although I wasn't sure of the significance of that."

"Well, once we created memories of the three of us in the Library together, I had Aphrodite confirm they were in Bryan's mind here in the SOC. Then I brought those memories with us when we returned to the Library. When I recalled those simultaneously with our memory of being with the Chairman on the catwalk, the Library interpreted those as all three of us being present inside the Library. Bryan, of course, was never authorized in the Library. So that caused —"

"That caused the Library to detect Bryan's memories of being in the Library. He could only have had those memories if he had actually been there."

"Exactly. The Library felt his presence. Clearly an intrusion had occurred. Normally we can't communicate outside from within the Library, but I guessed correctly that my being able to maintain simultaneous memories in two different locations might allow me to . . . well, sort of leave the Library for a moment with the second memory. It worked."

A thought entered Athena's and Anna's minds. It was from Segam. There had been an unauthorized intrusion into the Library, a very egregious event. An investigation was underway by the four members of the Golden Cube. The Chairman was in the Library at the time of the intrusion. The members of the Golden Cube sealed the Library. No one would be allowed admittance. During the exchange with the Chairman, he had asked Segam who Aphrodite was.

Anna turned to Athena. "Why is the Chairman asking—"

"We should return to Xynthanthium and ask Segam how and when we can retrieve Bryan's memories," Athena interrupted.

There was a knock on the door to her room. "Our NASA visitors are here," Carol called.

"I'll be right there, Carol." She turned to Athena. "I forgot, we have a meeting with NASA staff, but we've done it, honey. We stopped Earth's Avalanche Clock!" She reached over and hugged her daughter and Aphrodite.

"We couldn't have done it without Aphrodite's help," Athena said.

Anna stood to go meet Carol.

"You go ahead, Mom. I'll speak with Segam to ask about Bryan's memories and meet you back here when you're finished."

"Okay, honey." She walked to the door, turned to smile at Athena and Aphrodite who were hugging each other and then joined Carol in the hall. She hadn't felt this good in a long time. Perhaps never. As long as they could successfully return Bryan's memories to him, life would be good, really good.

CHAPTER 49

ΛTHENΛ, ΛPHRODITE, ΛNNΛ, ΛND BRYΛN

//

Carol and Anna entered the brightly lit conference room. Dr. Tyson, SOC staff members involved with her testing, and two visiting NASA staff were already seated at the large oval table wearing their protective helmets. She was feeling confident and exuberant, smiling as she walked to a chair at the table. An oppressive feeling slowly grew as she began fidgeting and looking around the room, unable to concentrate. Something wasn't right.

"Are you feeling okay?" Carol whispered.

"I'm feeling confused and a little distracted," she said.

She began to look at those around the table to determine who among them were her enemies. The helmets prevented her from entering their minds, but she was feeling danger. Where was it coming from?

"Anastasia, these gentlemen are from NASA. They want to ask you a few questions," Dr. Tyson said.

"How do you do, Anastasia?" one of the men said. "I hope you are well."

"Okay . . . thanks," she responded in an atypical halting voice.

"We're sorry Bryan is unable to join us. I understand he is not well."

"No, he's not. He's in a coma," she explained as she began rubbing her head. She could feel the sudden onset of a headache.

"I wonder if you could tell us about your telepathic abilities—when they started, how you acquired them, and any other information related to that."

She was becoming so distracted by random thoughts racing through her mind that she began looking at Carol and not hearing much of what the NASA staff member had asked. Her mind seemed on fire, jumping from one strange disconnected thought to another. She began hearing voices, as if everyone in the complex were talking at the same time. The voices were becoming louder and louder as if the volume were slowly being turned up to ten. She watched the lips of the NASA visitors moving, but she could no longer hear what they were saying.

"What's happening, Anna?" Carol asked as she noticed Anna's hands shaking.

"I'm not sure. I'm trying to concentrate, but . . ."

She tried to focus her mind on the meeting. Her head began to throb as the headache got much worse. She concentrated harder and the pain eased off but didn't go away as she put her elbows on the table and her head in her hands. She began thinking of Bryan in the infirmary, but that was one more distraction to her concentration as the pain in her head increased.

Her feelings of uneasiness were escalating. She felt a creeping helplessness enter her mind as she looked around at what seemed to be an ever-darkening room. It was as if the sun were setting, but there weren't any windows here. Fear took over her mind as her eyes flitted back and forth looking for the evil about to consume her. She leaned closer to Carol at the table, taking hold and squeezing her hand trying not to shake, searching for some relief.

As she glanced at the others in the room, they seemed to be acting as if nothing were happening. She began hyperventilating and spoke in a trembling voice.

"Dr. Tyson . . . I'm not feeling well. I need to leave."

First one and then the second NASA visitor reached up, unsnapped their helmets and lifted them off their heads as they began to focus all their attention on her. There was a sudden surge of enormous pain in Anna's head as she cried out. Dr. Tyson frowned and yelled.

"Put your helmets back on."

The NASA visitors ignored his instructions and almost immediately Anna began reacting.

"Where is this coming from? What's causing this pain?" she yelled as she grimaced and squeezed her head between her hands.

"Anna. What's happening?" Carol turned toward her.

She screamed from the pain and leapt from her chair, struggling unsuccessfully to cover her ears, now hearing a shrieking noise creating excruciating pain in her head. She looked over, squinting at the two NASA visitors standing facing her. She grabbed her chair and threw it as hard as she could at one of them. For a moment her pain lessened, but as soon as the man standing there recovered, the pain was back with a vengeance. She was trying unsuccessfully to concentrate on Bryan. She grabbed another chair and threw it at the two men, then grabbed a notebook in front of another staff member, then coffee cups and the coffee urn—anything she could get her hands on to throw at them. She struggled to remember her experience with the distant dream and the voice in her head that had attempted to get her to jump out the window of her room. She stopped, bent over from the pain and tried to focus her mind to resist the intrusion.

Carol raced over to her and put her arms around her, attempting to help. "Help her. She needs help," Carol yelled.

Just hearing Carol's voice destroyed Anna's concentration and the pain surged.

She finally collapsed to the floor, fighting to survive.

"Anna? *Anna!* What's happening? Dr. Tyson. Help her." These were the last words Anna heard Carol say.

"Bryan . . . Bryan . . . come to me," she yelled out as she fell unconscious.

Dr. Tyson stood and moved around the table toward Anastasia as Carol reached up, unstrapped her helmet, and threw it across the room in frustration. Immediately she fell to the floor, grabbing her head and appearing to be in excruciating pain. Dr. Tyson looked at the two visitors standing in a trance and staring down at Anastasia. He ran to the wall and pressed the emergency button near the door. Sirens began to sound and a bright red strobe light in the corner of the room began flashing. One of the staff reached over and attempted to put the visitors' helmets back on their heads. One of the visitors struck him, knocking him to the floor. A moment later Carol slumped in silence and was unconscious. Three security personnel entered the room and Dr. Tyson called to the guards, "Arrest these two men. Put their helmets on them and make certain they are not removed. I want them in confinement." The men resisted for a moment but were soon overpowered and handcuffed by the security staff.

"Get Dr. Anderson." Dr. Tyson yelled to one of the guards.

What the hell did those men do to Anastasia and Carol, Dr. Tyson wondered, as he clenched his fists before bending down to turn

Anastasia's head and look at her face as she lay unconscious on the floor. He could still hear her screams in the dead silence of the conference room.

A minute later, Dr. Anderson arrived with his nurse at his side.

"What's happened here?"

"The visitors from NASA did something to Anastasia and Carol. Anastasia was screaming in severe pain and grabbing her head," Dr. Tyson said.

Gurneys were brought in while Dr. Anderson checked Anna's and Carol's vital signs.

"Anna's breathing is shallow, and her heartbeat is weak. Get her on the gurney," he said as he moved to Carol.

"Carol is in cardiac arrest and she is not breathing. Help me get her on the gurney. We'll start CPR while we move them to the infirmary."

Another medical attendant arrived and relieved Dr. Anderson of his CPR on Carol.

/////////////////////

Dr. Tyson entered the infirmary ten minutes later after checking on the NASA staff members who he now believed were imposters. How had they injured Anastasia and Carol? The two pale and unconscious patients lay on beds parallel to each other with IVs connected to their forearms and wires running from their chest areas and heads to equipment on carts at the head of each bed. Heart monitors could be heard beeping rapidly out of sync as the trail of their heartbeats were displayed on separate electrocardiogram strip charts. Carol had a breathing tube taped to her mouth and the soft rhythmic action of air being pumped into her lungs could be heard from the ventilator.

"What's their condition, Karl?"

"Not good," Dr. Anderson said as he stood over Anna, listening with his stethoscope. "Carol is in critical condition. I'm not sure she will survive. She is showing symptoms of a serious neurological event. Her heart rate is unstable. We are monitoring her closely. I'll know more as soon as we can stabilize her enough to obtain an MRI. Anastasia appears somewhat better. She is stable but still in critical condition. What happened in there?"

"The two NASA visitors appeared to do something to them. They removed their helmets and then Anastasia seemed to experience severe pain. She grabbed her head and then collapsed to the floor screaming and writhing. Carol removed her helmet to assist and the same thing happened to her. Shortly after that they fell unconscious."

"What could they have done?" he asked, frowning as he listened to Carol's heart.

"Our visitors aren't saying much." Dr. Tyson shook his head. "Keep me informed of any change in their condition, and as soon as you obtain the MRI results, call me. I don't need to tell you how important Anastasia is, Doctor. If we lose her, there will be hell to pay."

Dr. Tyson returned to his office. He sat down. Something on the table to the right of his desk caught his attention. He turned to look at the small children's toys placed on the surface of the table under a glass dome, the ones that had been brought back from the Blackman residence in the Village of Oak Creek. One of the balls he believed belonged to Athena had begun to revolve in a circle on the table.

"Fascinating," he said as he got out of his chair slowly and walked over to the table. He bent over and squinted closely at the ball through the glass dome covering the toys. It had never moved as it did now, at least not since he took it from the drawer in The Village. "How is it doing this? Why has it begun moving?" he murmured to himself.

He reached over, lifting the dome, and stopped the ball with his right forefinger then let it go. The ball began moving in the same circle again.

A buzzer rang on Dr. Tyson's desk phone.

"Yes."

"It's Doctor Anderson, sir."

Dr. Tyson received a brief update from Dr. Anderson on the status of his two patients.

"Any change in Bryan's status?"

"No, Harry. He's still in a coma, but his vital signs are remaining stable."

"Keep me informed of any changes in any of them." Three almost brain-dead victims in my facility. Why would the Visitors want to kill Anastasia? She's captive here, unable to do anything. What is it that she knows that would have necessitated her death? He returned his view to the ball circling on its own on the adjacent table. I have to find and bring Athena here, he thought. He picked up the phone and placed a call to Colonel Blake Charles at the Special Operations Command.

Athena was communicating with Segam on Xynthanthium in a room protected from capturing thoughts and memories from its occupants. They had just finished discussing the challenge of retrieving Bryan's memories from the Library.

"Until our investigation is complete, there can be no access to the Library, Athena. His memories will be safe there, however. No need to concern yourself about them."

Segam took Athena to introduce her to Fliona. As soon as their minds had left the protected room, Athena heard Aphrodite screaming for her return to the SOC.

Her subconscious mind quickly left Xynthanthium and returned to the SOC. Aphrodite was leaning over her, shaking her.

"What is it, Aphrodite?"

"Our mom. Something terrible has happened to Mom."

Athena could hear Dr. Tyson's thoughts. He was thinking about her toys moving on the table in his office. All of them were now in motion. Athena couldn't reach her mother's mind. Her mind was racing as she and Aphrodite left her mother's bedroom headed toward the infirmary.

"We must hurry, Aphrodite."

Athena and Aphrodite ran down the hall toward the door marked "Infirmary & Doctor's Office." There was a sign above all the doors "WARNING You are Within a Restricted Area — Wear Electromagnetic Head Protection at All Times." Athena reached up and touched the card reader and keypad. The door opened. They walked down to the end of the corridor to a door labeled "Infirmary." She touched the keypad and walked in with Aphrodite.

Her mother was lying on a bed in a room with dim lighting attached to medical monitoring equipment. She was unconscious. Bryan and Carol were in an adjacent room behind a glass window.

Athena approached her mother's bed. The heart monitor beeped softly. There was the smell of a hospital. Her mother was breathing normally on her own and had a blood pressure cuff on one arm and an IV drip inserted in the other. Electrical sensors were taped to her chest. Her vital signs, displayed on the monitor at the head of her bed, appeared normal. Athena pressed the bed control switch to lower the bed so she could see her mother better. She stepped close to her side, ever so slowly, almost reluctantly, like a child coming to apologize for something she had done wrong. She lowered the bed rail and held her mother's hand. She looked pale and as if she were sleeping. She had a small amount of white discharge in the corners of her eyes. Some of the hair on her head had been shaved and electrodes attached to monitor her brain wave activity.

"Forgive me, Mom. I wasn't here to protect you. I should have anticipated this by the Visitors. This is my fault for leaving you here by yourself," Athena said in a quiet voice.

"I heard her fighting the Visitor avatars, but it was over before I could reach her to help," Aphrodite said as she began to cry.

"It's not your fault, Aphrodite. There wasn't anything you could have done, and you probably would have been seriously injured if you had been there," Athena said as she reached to put her arm around Aphrodite.

"Her brain injuries do not appear to be permanent," Athena said as she stood with her hand on her mother's head. "There is some internal hemorrhaging from a cerebral aneurism triggered by induced accelerated hypertension."

"Mom. Can you hear me?"

"Yes. I can hear you, Athena. Are you safe? They attacked me. You must get away, Athena. It's the Visitors. They will kill you. You must get away—"

The beeping from the heart rate monitor increased and her blood pressure began to rise.

"It's okay, Mom. It's okay. We are safe. Don't try and do anything with your mind. Your brain has been damaged. I'm going to start repairing it. It may take some time, so I would like you to relax and don't try and use telepathy. You need to sleep. Okay?"

"Okay, but Bryan . . . is he safe? Were you able to retrieve his memories? Is he—"

"He's resting in the next room, Mom. Now sleep—I need you to sleep."

"But the Visitors. They're here. You must get away . . ."

"I'm safe. Just sleep, Mom. You need to let your mind rest."

Athena held her mother's hand and explored her mind, while she and Aphrodite initiated molecular and cellular processes to repair the damaged areas of her brain. After thirty minutes, as they finished, she held her mother's hand. The familiar smell of her mother drifted around her, creating beautiful memories of their time in the Village, laughing, listening to music, her mother telling her stories. A teardrop formed in the corner of Athena's eye. It dripped down her cheek; she took her finger and caught it, reached over to her mother's cheek and let it drop into the corner of one of her eyes.

"I'm sharing my tears, Mom. This is my first," she said, speaking in a whisper as she bent over and kissed her mother's cheek.

"She will be okay," Aphrodite said as Athena came out of a daze and lifted her eyes from her mother.

"It will take some time. We should check on Bryan and Carol, Aphrodite."

They moved to the connecting door and walked into the second intensive care treatment unit at the SOC. There was a nurse seated at a desk making notes in the dimly lit room. Athena planted a thought in the nurse's mind that she and Aphrodite were nurses doing routine checks of Bryan and Carol's functioning organs and to ignore them.

Electronic monitors displaying their vital signs were connected to Bryan and Carol. They both had IV tubes, blood pressure cuffs, and heart rate monitors attached to their arms. Carol was attached to a respirator to keep her breathing. Her heart rate was erratic, beating normally for several seconds and then skipping a beat or two. A crash cart was positioned closest to her. Catheter tubes snaked from under the sheets to collection bags hanging from the sides of their beds. Electrical sensors were attached at several points on Bryan's scalp where it had been shaved. An electroencephalograph was on a cart at the head of Bryan's bed.

Aphrodite, I need your help," Athena said. "Hold my hand. I will enter Bryan's mind and I would like you to—"

"Enter Carol's mind and examine her injuries."

"Yes."

Athena entered the mind of her mother's best friend and the person she most closely thought of as her human father. While he had little physical damage from the taking of his memories, his neurological structure was deteriorating with the lack of stimulation and inability to dream. Too long a period without his memories and portions of his brain would atrophy and die, losing all the remaining dendritic patterns formed during his early life. Major portions of this labyrinth of brain tissue had been disconnected at key points during the taking of his memories. It was too complex to properly correct. Only the Library knew how to repair these and return Bryan's memories. Athena tried seeing his memories beyond the time he had entered the Library, but there were too few, other than the very limited ones of his presence in the Library with her and her mother. Even these memories had atrophied, becoming sparse and disconnected. She initiated repair processes in Bryan's brain to stop the cascade of deteriorating neurotransmitters and the associated neurological functions they triggered. She needed to find a way to stimulate his mind without the presence of his memories.

Aphrodite began corrective and repair measures to Carol, whose brain suffered even greater damage to the neurons of the hypothalamus, the region that regulated her involuntary nervous system—control of her heart and respiration. A massive number of her neurons were dead, and many others were dying—tens of millions of them each hour. Aphrodite initiated a process of regeneration. This was Carol's only hope of survival.

The two of them stood motionless working in the cerebral cortex and other regions of their patients' brains for over an hour.

"Do you think this will succeed in returning their brains to normal function?" Aphrodite asked.

"I hope so. You found so much more damage in Carol's brain. I'm not as certain of her potential for recovery. Bryan has lost any ability to sustain normal neurological functioning without his memories. It will take a significant amount of time for the regenerative process to work. Even then, I'm not certain we can keep his brain from deteriorating. His neuro-dendritic structures built by his long-term memories are deteriorating. Without his ability to recall them or be stimulated by new, related thoughts and memories, I'm concerned he won't recover."

Athena thought for a moment. "I have an idea." She turned to Aphrodite. "If we can take his mind to a place where it can be stimulated by new memories and can dream and rest, that may trigger the synapses of his brain and release neurotransmitters that will integrate all his feelings, emotions and sensations that his senses normally stimulate. Then the dendritic structures and synaptic connections that previously carried his memories that were taken may survive long enough for us to get them back and restore them. If we can immerse his mind in this very stimulating environment, he may recover and live in more than the vegetative state he now is drifting toward. I'm going to take his mind to Xynthanthium."

"Athena, is that possible?"

"Yes, the stimulation may just work. It's my fault Bryan is suffering. He sacrificed himself in order to save me in the Library." She looked at Bryan lying unconscious as she reached out to his mind.

"Bryan, can you hear me?"

"Yes. Who are you? Where are—?"

"It's Athena. I need you to do something for me, Bryan."

"I seem to remember . . . was in pain . . . who are you? Where am I?"

"You are in a safe place, Bryan. But I need you to concentrate for a moment."

"Where is . . .? I can't seem to remember."

"Anna, her name is Anna. She is resting in another room. You can't reach her with your mind right now, Bryan, so relax and sleep. I want you to dream in a special place. I'm going to take you there."

"Okay. I . . ."

Athena took Bryan's mind to Xynthanthium but for a very different purpose this time.

A universe of stars appeared in front of them as they traveled thirty-five million light years into deep space, leaving the Earth, their solar system, traveling through the Milky Way galaxy and beyond. A faint star cluster could be seen at a great distance. They entered a region of space devoid of stars in the dark, cold abyss of empty space. As they approached the star cluster, passing several galaxies within this region, a spiral galaxy emerged, eventually filling their entire field of view. Among the billions of stars, a bright yellow sun began to grow larger and larger near the outer edge of one of the spiral arms. The disc grew to over twice the size of their own sun.

"Is this where . . . going, Athe . . . ?"

"Yes, Bryan, but relax and dream of what you see. I need you to calm your mind and take in the beauty of this place. It is important that you don't think of anything else."

They continued their journey to one of the planets circling this sun and descended through the atmosphere and clouds. Athena stimulated Bryan's mind with her memories of the many senses of this wondrous place. The environment of Xynthanthium was filled with telepathic thoughts of its inhabitants and in the region of the city where she was taking Bryan, the artistic imagery of the many creative mental artists who lived there flowed into his brain like giant waves from an ocean of thought.

"Athe . . . I can smell beaut . . . odors and fragr . . . cs; feeling of sea breeze against . . . ; and mus . . . , such soothing mus . . . I can taste something, a fla . . . I've never . . . , something . . . good, something . . ."

Ahead of them they saw the most massive and exquisite display from an enormous fountain with complex patterns, vibrant colors and textures of three-dimensional artistic expressions. It was centered in a large open plaza with a glass railing encircling a beautifully tiled concave oval, perhaps one hundred meters long and sixty meters wide. The glass railing hung with no physical supports and from it streamed the fountain of vibrant colors, appearing much like solar prominences from their sun. They curved upward in an arch that eventually returned to the railing on the distant side of the plaza. They streamed from the entire edge of the oval glass railing in a constant state of movement, continually morphing into images of new and different geometries, shapes and abstract designs, all equally beautiful, intricate, and filled with complexity. It was captivating.

"This is a fountain of electrical and magnetic fields, Bryan. The words won't mean anything to you, but the patterns, colors and structures — think of their beauty and the feelings they create. They are being designed by the minds of many artists collaborating and engaging with each other's ideas and creations as we watch. It is one of the dominant forms of recreation and artistic expression. But this isn't the best part, Bryan. Can you sense them, Bryan?"

"Yes. I smell flow . . . , herb, and things I've never smel . . . . My skin . . . it's tingling all over, Ath . . . . The tastes, my feelings . . . every . . . ing toge . . . oh . . . it's so sooth . . . ."

"Good, Bryan, just let them flow through you, feel them, sense them, enjoy them, let them take your mind to wonderful places it has never been before."

"What is th . . . place?"

"Think of it as a wonderful vacation, Bryan. I want you to relax your mind. Don't think of anything other than what you see and feel and sense here."

"Now tell me what you feel, Bryan?"

"It . . . feels like huge wave . . . emoti . . . and feelings are surg . . . thr . . . ugh me — moments of . . . euphor . . . , of love, of . . . , of delight and hope; then content . . . , relaxa . . . , serenity. Like they are part of me. Not quite . . . min . . . , but they are here."

"Yes, Bryan, in time they will become your own. Don't think about how they have come to be; just experience these emotions, sensations, and feelings; live in them as they enter your mind, and as they do, I will teach you the words that go with them."

"Live . . . in them, Ath . . . ?"

"Yes, Bryan . . . you must live in them; absorb them in your mind; let them carry your thoughts to things you remember, things that relate; you will live as you have never lived before," she said, hoping more than believing he would improve and get well. His brain was so devoid of thought, so deprived of sensory stimulation and his memories of the past. She had tried to ask the Library what else she could do to help him survive, but when the four members of the Golden Cube locked the Library from entry, it closed all communications as well.

Bryan's mind stared into the multitude of patterns created in this tapestry of artistic beauty. "Never exp . . . enced anything . . . so bea . . . iful . . . so captiva . . . so sof . . . Where am I?"

"A long way from home, Bryan. Just take your time and let your mind explore. It will make you better. Don't look for me, I will find you. Don't look for Anna, she will find you. Now dream, my dear friend, dream."

Bryan's mind was trapped in the wonderment of his surroundings and he began floating down the walkway absorbing the senses, feelings, and emotions of this extraordinary place as his brain slowly began its collection of new memories and sensory stimulation.

Athena shed a second tear and deposited it in the corner of Bryan's eye, just as she had with her mother, as she watched her friend fade from her mind on the Visitors planet and the city of Xynthanthium. She returned to the present setting as she looked at him lying in bed under the dim lighting of the intensive care unit. She caught her tear with her finger and placed it on his cheek. "Get well, my good friend and godfather, live and get well." She stood next to his bed listening to the heart monitor as it seemed to settle into a slumbering singular beat, strong, with a will to survive.

Athena and her sister, Aphrodite, turned toward each other.

"I could not reach Carol's mind yet, Athena," Aphrodite said.

"She is too seriously injured. We will see if your efforts will allow enough regeneration of her neurological memory to allow us to bring her together with Bryan on Xynthanthium in a week or so."

They turned and left through the door leading back into Anna's room. Athena glanced at her mother as she and Aphrodite walked passed her bed. Life, she thought, as she listened to the sound of the monitors communicating the melody of the beating heart and a brain that was fighting to survive; soon her mother would return to live and experience the wonderment of feelings and emotions, something the Visitors had lost.

If only they could be here to experience them, to understand their value in the evolving nature of the existence of intelligent life. Soon, she thought, but first these emotions must serve Segam's purpose.

"Segam's purpose?" Aphrodite asked.

"We need to be so much better than the Visitors, Aphrodite. Don't ever let me forget that," as Athena changed the subject.

CHAPTER 50

THE NEW SOC

//

Athena and Aphrodite proceeded back into the hall, appearing as two young sisters holding hands on their way to a park to play, turning left at the corridor to a room being guarded by a uniformed service member. With the encouragement of Athena's thoughts, he turned his back to them and stepped away from the door, acting as if they were not there. Athena opened the door and they walked into a room where the two intruders handcuffed to chairs wearing their electromagnetic protective helmets were being watched by another guard with his helmet on. She looked at the guard and mentally instructed him to sit down. These protective helmets seemed to mean nothing to Athena. Athena and Aphrodite walked toward the two intruders and removed their helmets. The intruders stared back at them, seeing no threat from two small gaunt children, their limbs frail and thin, their skin, wrapped around their bones as if covered by a delicate veil of cloth. Their faces were plain and simple — the kind that emanate great beauty — surrounded by fine blond hair that moved with the breath of the wind, and their eyes, deep, black, and mesmerizing, eyes that captivated the eyes of their viewers, holding their attention.

Athena and Aphrodite entered the minds of the two men as they sat staring into their beautiful eyes. They altered their mental instructions from finding and killing Anna and Bryan to killing each other. Athena instructed the guard to remove their handcuffs. The two men jumped at each other in a frenzy of anger as each mind created enormous pain in the other. Within seconds the two men collapsed to the floor, clutching each other's throats as they fought to their death.

Athena and Aphrodite walked to Dr. Tyson's office. Athena touched the keypad and card reader.

"Aphrodite. Find the Orb. Determine what information he conveyed to Dr. Tyson. I will meet you here when you have finished."

Athena turned the knob and entered. Dr. Tyson stood hunched over a small table to the left of his desk, looking at Athena's toys that were now flying around, energized by some unknown power beneath the glass dome. He appeared tense, gripping the sides of the table. His suit coat appeared crumpled, as if he had slept in it the night before. It was still buttoned in the front, ready for a formal meeting. Floor-to-ceiling bookshelves surrounded the room. His desk was covered with stacks of papers, and a small conference table in front of it occupied the center of the remaining space.

"Dr. Tyson."

He glanced up abruptly from the moving toys and stood, straightening his jacket as he looked toward the door.

"Who are you? How did you get in here?" Dr. Tyson walked back toward his desk, frowning.

Athena walked to the right of the conference table. Her long blond hair swept across the corner of the table as she walked around it to face him. She was wearing a dark purple robe and black tennis shoes.

"I am Athena."

Dr. Tyson stopped in midstride and stood staring at his visitor. "Impossible." He mumbled under his breath.

"Obviously not impossible, Dr. Tyson, as I'm standing right here in front of you."

"How did you get into this facility?"

"I walked in, just like your intruders did. You know, the ones that seriously injured my mother and Carol."

"Your mother—"

"Yes, I know my mother's condition, and Carol's. You haven't protected them."

"I had no idea that those two intruders meant them harm—"

"They controlled your mind, Dr. Tyson. Don't you realize the power of the Visitors, even when using avatars like the two that were here?" Athena was glaring at him and waving her gaunt arms. "They are millions of years ahead of you. They are to you as you are to an *ant*. Don't you see?"

"How did you get here? I thought you were in the Village of Oak Creek."

"The question at hand is not how I got here but whether you can protect my mother. Can you do that?"

"It appears not without her help."

"That is a sign of some intelligence. At least you aren't ignorant enough to think you can stop the Visitors on your own." She took another step toward him. "This terrible outcome should serve as an awakening of your mind to its enormous *weakness* in the presence of the Visitors. While they resist interference, provoked, they will destroy any of you in the blink of an eye. And, *yes*, you did notice correctly that I said any of *you*. Remember that, Dr. Tyson. Don't ever forget it."

"You said 'terrible outcome.' Has something happened that I'm not —?"

"There is much you are not aware of Dr. Tyson," Athena said as she moved closer to his desk, never moving her eyes from him.

"How will you keep Dr. Shilling, your NASA supervisor, from removing you from your position and losing control of the SOC? How will you keep the events of today from happening again? How will your *puny* mind ever comprehend the enormous power of the Visitors and the danger they pose to our world?"

Athena laughed loudly as she listened to his thoughts. "You didn't believe my mother either when she told you the end of your world as you knew it was coming. Well, believe me when I tell you, if it had happened, *you would not have survived*.

"I will provide you with a communication strategy that you will use with Dr. Shilling. You will follow it *exactly* as I tell you."

"I would welcome your mother's help —"

"My mother is very sick. She will not be conscious for five to ten days, perhaps longer. Her brain was severely damaged as a result of your *inept* decisions and of you trusting those you should never have trusted. I can't let anything like that happen again, nor can *you*. And as for your thoughts, as you stand there *gawking*, about 'your inability to attribute any intelligence to this young frail child standing in your office,' I will demonstrate to you how wrong you are before I leave here."

"*Oh*, now you are thinking about how to deal with me? That's easy. You will do *exactly* as I tell you." She looked over at the table with the glass dome. "Or . . . something terrible will happen."

Athena's toys began circling in the air at enormous speed under the glass dome. A moment later they all burst through the glass with an explosive force that shattered the globe into a thousand pieces that flew in all directions around the room. Dr. Tyson cowered behind his desk until the debris fell to the floor, grimacing from the cuts on his face where the glass had struck him. The toys commenced to whip around the perimeter of the room at tremendous speed, creating a vortex of wind that began to disturb the papers on his desk. Athena's voice rose louder over the sound of the wind and flying papers that were now circling the room so fast they were difficult to see. She concentrated on Dr. Tyson, causing him to grab his head and wince in pain as he bent over.

"This is only a fraction of the pain my mother felt. Can you feel it, Dr. Tyson?" He yelled out as it became excruciating and he fell to the floor. His pain eased, and he grabbed the back of his chair and stood, breathing rapidly, staring back at Athena as one of her toys grazed his head and he ducked. She was now three feet from him.

"I would like you to provide sleeping quarters for me near the infirmary and inform your staff that I and my sister, Aphrodite, are your guests and should be afforded *every* assistance during our stay. *Yes, my sister Aphrodite,*" Athena yelled in his mind. He winced from the pain and groaned; her voice sounded like God had vented His anger at him. He bent over the back of his chair taking a deep breath as the pain eased again.

"Also, Room 17A is off limits. *No one* is to enter that room without my permission. You will also have the Orb moved there. Understood?"

Dr. Tyson was holding his chair with one hand and his head with the other while looking at Athena. Perspiration dripped from his brow. He didn't speak as her toys and his papers continued to fly around the room, occasionally striking him.

"Do you understand me, Dr. Tyson?" Athena asked as heavy objects from his bookshelves began to leap into the vortex.

He fell back against the wall behind him to avoid being struck by his books as he watched all of Athena's toys coalesce back on the table next to his desk. The rest of the objects fell to the floor. Thousands of glass shards flew from the floor and tabletops, re-forming the dome in the air above his desk. It hung there in front of him, rotated, then slammed down on the table covering her toys. There was one subtle change. A statement was now etched in large letters on the surface of the glass dome near the handle. "Property of Athena. Do Not Touch!"

"I understand," he finally said as he drew a deep breath.

"Sit in your chair before you fall over," Athena instructed, as she pulled one of the extra chairs up to his desk, climbed up, and sat on the edge of the desk looking down at him. She spoke in a quiet, almost friendly voice.

"From now on, I will be in charge of this facility. Oh, you will appear to be the leader as far as NASA and any other outsiders are concerned." She swung her arm in the air and everything on his desk flew across the room. "But you will do as I instruct, and my instructions will be followed exactly as they are intended. I, along with my mother, Aphrodite, and Bryan, if he recovers from his injuries, will operate from this facility. As far as Dr. Shilling and NASA are concerned, you are continuing to study and learn about what may have happened to Bryan and my mother and to examine the artifact they discovered. You will not allow *any* visitors into the facility without my permission. Do you understand?"

Pain began to return to his body. "Yes, yes, I understand," he shrieked as he eased back in his chair and the pain subsided.

"I want to give you one more thing before I leave your office, one that you will never forget, Dr. Tyson. You will feel no physical pain, but physical pain, as you will soon see, is not the only form of punishment a being like yourself can experience."

Athena began to smile as she stared down at Dr. Tyson slumped in his leather chair. His face developed a blank, emotionless appearance. He winced and scratched his head above his left temple.

"There, that wasn't so bad, was it?" she asked.

He seemed to recover as he frowned at Athena sitting on his desk above him.

"I would like you to think about doing something I might disapprove of, Dr. Tyson."

"I . . . don't understand."

She looked at him in disbelief and shook her head. "Anything. Think of doing anything you know I would not approve of."

He thought of calling security and having Athena detained.

Fear gripped him as he leapt out of his chair and ran to the corner of his office, cowering behind the table as he glanced back toward his desk. He was shaking and looking around for an escape.

"Help me. Stop that hideous thing," he yelled.

Athena entered his mind as the image of a giant bullet ant, perhaps eight feet long, crawled over his desk in his direction with its mandibles clicking and its claws dripping with a horrid oozing substance that smelled like rotting flesh.

"Dr. Tyson, I want you to think about the importance of only doing what I approve of," Athena said very quickly.

"What?" he asked as he cowered in the corner trying to hide.

"You heard me — concentrate. *Now!*" she demanded as the insect moved faster and closed in on him, now only four feet away and rising up to strike him with its deadly stinger.

A few seconds later, as his eyes remained fixed, he stood slowly, breathing rapidly and perspiring profusely. He was looking around the room for the giant insect as he took a deep breath.

"Only you can bring that creature back, Dr. Tyson. And believe me, if it reaches you, you will experience the most excruciating pain ever endured by any human on Earth. You are not likely to survive its sting. Do you understand?"

"Yes," he said without hesitation as he stood leaning on the table in front of him. He could not stop his hands from shaking.

"It will be important to protect me, my mother, Bryan, and my sister, Aphrodite. If anything happens to us . . . well." A brief image of the bullet ant reappeared on the far side of the room and snapped its head toward him before it faded away.

She walked over to him and took his hand. "You need to understand that what you saw here was not a nightmare. It was real, as real as I am. I will leave you one more thing to remind you of that." He was looking at her as he listened. Her lips never moved. She pressed her thumb on the back of his right hand and as she removed it, a small image of the black bullet ant was tattooed where her thumb had been. He reached over and rubbed the back of his hand. It was permanently there for him to see.

"The Visitors may be looking for us. We will need to prepare. There is much to be done," she said as she climbed down and walked over to the conference table in front of his desk and sat down. "Would you ask your key staff to join us? We will begin making plans."

Dr. Tyson moved to his desk and pushed the intercom button, his hands still shaking.

The meeting with Dr. Tyson's staff had gone smoothly. Dr. Tyson informed his staff that Athena and her sister, Aphrodite, who had returned from a visit to the Orb within the facility, were to be treated as VIPs. During their stay they should be afforded every convenience and free access to all aspects of the facility operations. To add credibility to his message, Athena spoke of the enormous importance of their mission at the SOC, to study extraterrestrial artifacts and their role in better understanding Earth's place in the cosmos. She spoke of the exciting potential of discovering life on another planet, understanding its origin and evolution. By the time she finished, she had the entire room captivated with a story about the hypothetical discovery of alien life and the extraordinary opportunity it would provide to mankind. They almost had the feeling that it had already happened and there wasn't a single person who didn't believe that these young girls, who couldn't be more than three and six years of age, were very special visitors. Athena finished with a statement that startled Dr. Tyson.

"In closing, you should know that my mother discovered an extraordinary artifact of great importance to your planet. Our scientists are currently studying this object here at the SOC. Each of you has a role to play on the effect this object will have on Earth and mankind. Each of you will impact the future of your world by ensuring this object and all that is related to it will be protected, understood, and used to better mankind. Do your absolute best. Nothing less is acceptable. Discuss this with *no one*."

There was silence when she finished, leaving the group spellbound, most wondering where this object came from and what exactly it was.

The remainder of the meeting was devoted to facility security and access procedures for all visitors and the need to construct an antenna, that would be connected to the facility in Room 17A, on the top of Mount Tipton. Dr. Tyson had the feeling that none of his staff were listening, as they constantly turned to look at Athena and Aphrodite.

Major Charles Walters, Dr. Tyson's current head of security remained behind after the meeting adjourned and Athena and Aphrodite returned to the infirmary.

"Sir, your memo gives these young girls the broadest access to security protocols in the facility. They don't have a security clearance for any of this. I'm afraid—"

"Follow my instructions to the letter, Major. Look . . ."

As Dr. Tyson began to speak in a quieter voice to explain why he was giving them such broad access, the back of his hand began to itch and then pain began to develop as he unconsciously began rubbing the black spot on his hand. He began to feel nervous and his hands began to shake as his attention drifted from the Major, and his eyes flitted around the room.

"Is something wrong, sir?"

"No . . . Do exactly as I have instructed. You are to provide them whatever access is requested. If there are *any* classification issues, inform me immediately, but do not disobey any request they make of you or your staff. Is that clear?"

"Yes, sir. Clear. Are they allowed to come and go from the facility?"

"Of course, you idiot. Do you not understand the meaning of 'full and complete access to operational aspects of the facility'? But you raise a good point. As long as they do not object, I would like an armed security staff member to be with them at all times while they are outside the facility. Anyone attempting to harm them should be prevented . . . with deadly force if necessary. Understood?"

"Yes, sir. Thank you, sir."

Dr. Tyson took a deep breath and sat back in his chair as Major Walters left his office and closed the door. He felt relaxed and at ease — strange feelings, considering all that had transpired in the past few hours. As the sound of Athena's voice returned and he replayed the actions she had taken in his office, he began to think of her origin; perhaps she wasn't Bryan's child, but, if not, whose? Her abilities certainly demonstrated that she had more power than her mother; he had never seen Anastasia demonstrate anything like what Athena could do. And what about Aphrodite? Did she have similar skills, and where had she come from? He felt awed by Athena's abilities. With her at his side, he could do almost anything. His hand began to itch as he quickly thought of how his support for her would assist her actions at the SOC.

Anna's mind awakened even though her body lay unconscious in the infirmary. Slowly, as if walking from a dense fog, the memories of the

Visitors' attack crept back. The pain, the mind-bending pain, as they removed their protective helmets. She saw their faces as they morphed from the NASA intruders to those of Kelong and another, and then back to their human avatars; straining, concentrating, staring, as hatred surged. They caught her off guard, distracted her. How could she have been so unprepared, so not ready? She should have seen it coming.

She listened with her mind. There was something different. When you listen to the sounds of humanities thoughts, it is like hearing the voices of a large city all at once. It has a certain hum, a comfort of familiarity, and when it changes, you notice, like searching in the living room for that piece of furniture that has been moved. This change in the sound of human thought wasn't there yesterday, but she could feel it now. There was a soothing calmness about it, the loss of harshness within the horde of thoughts in the world. Then it came to her. It was the virus that Athena and Aphrodite had spread. It was beginning to dominate the thinking of mankind. It hadn't struck her how vast an effect that would have, but she could sense it now, like the scent of a meal cooking as ingredients were added to the stew. It felt more comforting than she had remembered. The more she listened, the more she liked it.

The sound in her head made her think of Bryan. Was he among the thoughts she now heard? "Bryan," she called out telepathically as the last vision of him lying unconscious in a hospital bed leapt into her mind. Other visions of him catapulted into her memory — the vivid images of holding him on the hiking trail as their minds intertwined in that beautiful rush of love; then Bryan's hologram in the Library, his memories stripped from him, partly there and partly not. Had she lost him forever? Had they taken him from her?

She listened for his voice, the one that caused her heart to beat a bit faster, her breathing to be a little deeper, and her emotions to bring her the rush that so often consumed her. She knew he wouldn't hear her, wouldn't come to her. Would this last forever or would she ever be with him again? She wouldn't allow her mind to go there.

Her love for him transcended her feelings about saving the Earth or helping some rebel group on Xynthanthium. Strange how a single individual meant so much; how she would give almost anything to be with him, to save him. This was perhaps what separated humanity from the Visitors, what distinguished her species from theirs — a willingness to sacrifice it all for the life of someone you love.

Her memories took her back to the trail where their minds had loved, then to the Rock House that had given birth to that love, holding each other, running her fingers through his hair, sensing the unique smell of his clothing and skin, feeling the warmth of that skin; feeling that strange emotion that jolted humans from logic and rational thought to acts of sacrificial kindness and a willingness to forfeit the desires of self for the needs of others — love.

There . . . she could feel a slight sense of his presence, like fingers touching; a taste of his thoughts; a subtle familiarity drifting by, like a distant voice barely heard; like her dad's cologne — she might not see him, but she knew he was nearby. It had to be; it must be Bryan, but where? He seemed . . . distant, out of reach, his thoughts not quite him; jumbled and confused, images out of focus, indecipherable, almost there but not quite. Where was he? She couldn't hear his thoughts or decipher his words or enter his dreams or see what he was seeing. Something wasn't right. She concentrated and focused on her best friend, the man she loved, recalling their last walk together, holding each other's hands, their kiss.

She thought again of their time in Oak Creek. As she cried for his presence, her mind seemed pulled and began to drift with imagery of the Visitors' home planet Xynthanthium flickering in and out of her memory.

"No, no. I'm not concentrating enough," she thought, grinding her teeth to focus while bringing her most cherished memories of Bryan into view — his motley hair, his warm and inviting eyes, his soft and tender embrace.

The scene from a street on this world of the Visitors, slammed irresistibly into her mind, as a lone figure appeared in the distance on a walkway that lay in front of her. He walked toward her. She squinted as she stepped backward, wanting Bryan's memories, not this distant alien. She began to recede from the planet, rising toward the billowing clouds. The alien began to run toward her, faster and faster. She was leaving the surface of the planet faster than this Visitor was approaching. This now unfamiliar figure was running toward her alone on a deserted cityscape, running as if to try and reach her with his outstretched arm before she could escape. Who was this? He was just an outline now. But what alien knew her?

Finally, as she was so distant she could barely make out this strange being from the planet's surface, he slowed to a walk and came to a stop. He waved. It was a lonely wave. How strange it seemed. But there was something familiar about that wave. She could sense an emotional surge, so very familiar, like what she always felt when around Bryan. She waved back and heard the faint, distant sound of a voice in her head.

"I dream, and it is real,

For what is real and what is dream,

If we hold and touch and sense and feel.

Now a distant view I see,

As darkness envelopes thee.

I yearn to hold and love and clutch,

That which lingers long, alone, and beyond my touch.

But you, I hold, you I touch, you I sense and feel.

Not for dream, are you, but mine, for me, for real."

"Bryan," she yelled. "It's Bryan . . ." The image in her mind faded, ever so slowly, and she smiled, and wept, and smiled again.

THE END

. . . of the middle, Part II of *The Orb, the Link and the Library*.

THE ORB, THE LINK & THE LIBRARY
PART 3 REVELATIONS OF THE LIBRARY

///

D.M. Rosewood

www.ingramcontent.com/pod-product-compliance
Lightning Source LLC
Chambersburg PA
CBHW061614100726
47898CB00002B/650